Short Stories

1882 – 1885

Anton Chekhov

Copyright © this edition Will Jonson

First Edition, 2013

ISBN: 978-1484183342

The author has asserted their moral right under the Copyright, Designs and Patents Act, 1988, to be identified as the author of this work.

All Rights reserved. No part of this publication may be reproduced, copied, stored in a retrieval system, or transmitted, in any form or by any means, without the prior written consent of the copyright holder, nor be otherwise circulated in any form of binding or cover other than that in which it is published and without a similar condition being imposed on the subsequent purchaser. This is a work of fiction: any resemblance to persons living or dead is purely coincidental.

CONTENTS

A Living Chattel   7

Joy   46

At the Barber's   49

An Enigmatic Nature   53

A Classical Student   56

The Death of a Government Clerk   59

The Trousseau   62

A Daughter of Albion   68

An Inquiry   73

Fat and Thin   76

A Tragic Actor   79

The Bird Market	83
A Slander	87
The Swedish Match	92
Choristers	116
The Album	122
Minds in Ferment	125
A Chameleon	130
In the Graveyard	134
Oysters	137
The Marshal's Widow	142
Small Fry	146
In a Hotel	150

Boots	153
Nerves	158
A Country Cottage	163
Malingerers	165
The Fish	169
Gone Astray	175
The Huntsman	180
A Malefactor	185
The Head of the Family	190
A Dead Body	195
The Cook's Wedding	201
In a Strange Land	207

Overdoing It	212
Old Age	217
Sorrow	223
Oh! The Public!	229
Mari d'Elle	234
The Looking Glass	240

A LIVING CHATTEL

Groholsky embraced Liza, kept kissing one after another all her little fingers with their bitten pink nails, and laid her on the couch covered with cheap velvet. Liza crossed one foot over the other, clasped her hands behind her head, and lay down.

Groholsky sat down in a chair beside her and bent over. He was entirely absorbed in contemplation of her.

How pretty she seemed to him, lighted up by the rays of the setting sun!

There was a complete view from the window of the setting sun, golden, lightly flecked with purple.

The whole drawing-room, including Liza, was bathed by it with brilliant light that did not hurt the eyes, and for a little while covered with gold.

Groholsky was lost in admiration. Liza was so incredibly beautiful. It is true her little kittenish face with its brown eyes, and turn up nose was fresh, and even piquant, his scanty hair was black as soot and curly, her little figure was graceful, well proportioned and mobile as the body of an electric eel, but on the whole. . . . However my taste has nothing to do with it. Groholsky who was spoilt by women, and who had been in love and out of love hundreds of times in his life, saw her as a beauty. He loved her, and blind love finds ideal beauty everywhere.

"I say," he said, looking straight into her eyes, "I have come to talk to you, my precious. Love cannot bear anything vague or indefinite. . . . Indefinite relations, you know, I told you yesterday, Liza . . . we will try to-day to settle the question we raised yesterday. Come, let us decide together. . . ."

What are we to do?"

Liza gave a yawn and scowling, drew her right arm from under her head.

"What are we to do?" she repeated hardly audibly after Groholsky.

"Well, yes, what are we to do? Come, decide, wise little head . . . I love you, and a man in love is not fond of sharing. He is more than an egoist. It is too much for me to go shares with your husband. I mentally tear him to pieces, when I remember that he loves you too. In the second place you love me. . . . Perfect freedom is an essential condition for love. . . . And are you free? Are you not tortured by the thought that that man towers for ever over your soul? A man whom you do not love, whom very likely and quite naturally, you hate. . . . That's the second thing. . . . And thirdly. . . . What is the third thing? Oh yes. . . . We are deceiving him and that . . . is dishonourable. Truth before everything, Liza. Let us have done with lying!"

"Well, then, what are we to do?"

"You can guess. . . . I think it necessary, obligatory, to inform him of our relations and to leave him, to begin to live in freedom. Both must be done as quickly as possible. . . . This very evening, for instance. . . . It's time to make an end of it. Surely you must be sick of loving like a thief?"

"Tell! tell Vanya?"

"Why, yes!"

"That's impossible! I told you yesterday, Michel, that it is impossible."

"Why?"

"He will be upset. He'll make a row, do all sorts of unpleasant things. . . . Don't you know what he is like? God forbid! There's no need to tell him. What an idea!"

Groholsky passed his hand over his brow, and heaved a sigh.

"Yes," he said, "he will be more than upset. I am robbing him of his happiness. Does he love you?"

"He does love me. Very much."

"There's another complication! One does not know where to begin. To conceal it from him is base, telling him would kill him. . . . Goodness knows what's one to do. Well, how is it to be?"

Groholsky pondered. His pale face wore a frown.

"Let us go on always as we are now," said Liza. "Let him find out for himself, if he wants to."

"But you know that . . . is sinful, and besides the fact is you are mine, and no one has the right to think that you do not belong to me but to someone else! You are mine! I will not give way to anyone! . . . I am sorry for him - God knows how sorry I am for him, Liza! It hurts me to see him! But . . . it can't be helped after all. You don't love him, do you? What's the good of your going on being miserable with him? We must have it out! We will have it out with him, and you will come to me. You are my wife, and not his. Let him do what he likes. He'll get over his troubles somehow. . . . He is not the first, and he won't be the last. . . . Will you run away? Eh? Make haste and tell me! Will you run away?"

Liza got up and looked inquiringly at Groholsky.

"Run away?"

"Yes. . . . To my estate. . . . Then to the Crimea. . . . We will tell him by letter. . . . We can go at night. There is a train at half past one. Well? Is that all right?"

Liza scratched the bridge of her nose, and hesitated.

"Very well," she said, and burst into tears.

Patches of red came out of her cheeks, her eyes swelled, and tears flowed down her kittenish face. . . .

"What is it?" cried Groholsky in a flutter. "Liza! what's the matter? Come! what are you crying for? What a girl! Come, what is it? Darling! Little woman!"

Liza held out her hands to Groholsky, and hung on his neck. There was a sound of sobbing.

"I am sorry for him . . ." muttered Liza. "Oh, I am so sorry for him!"

"Sorry for whom?"

"Va-Vanya...."

"And do you suppose I'm not? But what's to be done? We are causing him suffering.... He will be unhappy, will curse us ... but is it our fault that we love one another?"

As he uttered the last word, Groholsky darted away from Liza as though he had been stung and sat down in an easy chair. Liza sprang away from his neck and rapidly - in one instant - dropped on the lounge.

They both turned fearfully red, dropped their eyes, and coughed.

A tall, broad-shouldered man of thirty, in the uniform of a government clerk, had walked into the drawing-room. He had walked in unnoticed. Only the bang of a chair which he knocked in the doorway had warned the lovers of his presence, and made them look round. It was the husband.

They had looked round too late.

He had seen Groholsky's arm round Liza's waist, and had seen Liza hanging on Groholsky's white and aristocratic neck.

"He saw us!" Liza and Groholsky thought at the same moment, while they did not know what to do with their heavy hands and embarrassed eyes....

The petrified husband, rosy-faced, turned white.

An agonising, strange, soul-revolting silence lasted for three minutes. Oh, those three minutes! Groholsky remembers them to this day.

The first to move and break the silence was the husband. He stepped up to Groholsky and, screwing his face into a senseless grimace like a smile, gave him his hand. Groholsky shook the soft perspiring hand and shuddered all over as though he had crushed a cold frog in his fist.

"Good evening," he muttered.

"How are you?" the husband brought out in a faint husky, almost inaudible voice, and he sat down opposite Groholsky, straightening his collar at the back of his neck.

Again, an agonising silence followed . . . but that silence was no longer so stupid. . . . The first step, most difficult and colourless, was over.

All that was left now was for one of the two to depart in search of matches or on some such trifling errand. Both longed intensely to get away. They sat still, not looking at one another, and pulled at their beards while they ransacked their troubled brains for some means of escape from their horribly awkward position. Both were perspiring. Both were unbearably miserable and both were devoured by hatred. They longed to begin the tussle but how were they to begin and which was to begin first? If only she would have gone out!

"I saw you yesterday at the Assembly Hall," muttered Bugrov (that was the husband's name).

"Yes, I was there . . . the ball . . . did you dance?"

"M'm . . . yes . . . with that . . . with the younger Lyukovtsky. . . . She dances heavily. . . . She dances impossibly. She is a great chatterbox." (Pause.) "She is never tired of talking."

"Yes. . . . It was slow. I saw you too. . ."

Groholsky accidentally glanced at Bugrov. . . . He caught the shifting eyes of the deceived husband and could not bear it. He got up quickly, quickly seized Bugrov's hand, shook it, picked up his hat, and walked towards the door, conscious of his own back. He felt as though thousands of eyes were looking at his back. It is a feeling known to the actor who has been hissed and is making his exit from the stage, and to the young dandy who has received a blow on the back of the head and is being led away in charge of a policeman.

As soon as the sound of Groholsky's steps had died away and the door in the hall creaked, Bugrov leapt up, and after making two or three rounds of the drawing-room, strolled up to his wife. The kittenish face puckered up and began blinking its eyes as though expecting a slap. Her husband went up to her, and with a pale, distorted face, with arms, head, and shoulders shaking, stepped on her dress and knocked her knees with his.

"If, you wretched creature," he began in a hollow, wailing voice, "you let him come here once again, I'll. . . . Don't let him dare to set his foot. . . . I'll kill you. Do you understand? A-a-ah . . . worthless creature, you shudder! Fil-thy woman!"

Bugrov seized her by the elbow, shook her, and flung her like an India rubber ball towards the window. . . .

"Wretched, vulgar woman! you have no shame!"

She flew towards the window, hardly touching the floor with her feet, and caught at the curtains with her hands.

"Hold your tongue," shouted her husband, going up to her with flashing eyes and stamping his foot.

She did hold her tongue, she looked at the ceiling, and whimpered while her face wore the expression of a little girl in disgrace expecting to be punished.

"So that's what you are like! Eh? Carrying on with a fop! Good! And your promise before the altar? What are you? A nice wife and mother. Hold your tongue!"

And he struck her on her pretty supple shoulder. "Hold your tongue, you wretched creature. I'll give you worse than that! If that scoundrel dares to show himself here ever again, if I see you - listen! - with that blackguard ever again, don't ask for mercy! I'll kill you, if I go to Siberia for it! And him too. I shouldn't think twice about it! You can go, I don't want to see you!"

Bugrov wiped his eyes and his brow with his sleeve and strode about the drawing-room, Liza sobbing more and more loudly, twitching her shoulders and her little turned up nose, became absorbed in examining the lace on the curtain.

"You are crazy," her husband shouted. "Your silly head is full of nonsense! Nothing but whims! I won't allow it, Elizaveta, my girl! You had better be careful with me! I don't like it! If you want to behave like a pig, then . . . then out you go, there is no place in my house for you! Out you pack if. . . . You are a wife, so you must forget these dandies, put them out of your silly head! It's all foolishness! Don't let it happen again! You try defending yourself! Love your husband! You have been given to your husband, so you must love him. Yes, indeed! Is one not enough? Go away till. . . . Torturers!"

Bugrov paused; then shouted:

"Go away I tell you, go to the nursery! Why are you blubbering, it is your own fault, and you blubber! What a woman! Last year you were after Petka Totchkov, now you are after this devil. Lord forgive us! . . . Tfoo, it's time you understood what you are! A wife! A mother! Last year there were unpleasantnesses, and now there will be unpleasantnesses. . . . Tfoo!"

Bugrov heaved a loud sigh, and the air was filled with the smell of sherry. He had come back from dining and was slightly drunk. . . .

"Don't you know your duty? No! . . . you must be taught, you've not been taught so far! Your mamma was a gad-about, and you . . . you can blubber. Yes! blubber away. . . ."

Bugrov went up to his wife and drew the curtain out of her hands.

"Don't stand by the window, people will see you blubbering. . . . Don't let it happen again. You'll go from embracing to worse trouble. You'll come to grief. Do you suppose I like to be made a fool of? And you will make a fool of me if you carry on with them, the low brutes. . . . Come, that's enough. . . . Don't you. . . . Another time. . . . Of course I . . Liza . . . stay. . . ."

Bugrov heaved a sigh and enveloped Liza in the fumes of sherry.

"You are young and silly, you don't understand anything. . . . I am never at home. . . . And they take advantage of it. You must be sensible, prudent. They will deceive you. And then I won't endure it. . . . Then I may do anything. . . . Of course! Then you can just lie down, and die. I . . . I am capable of doing anything if you deceive me, my good girl. I might beat you to death. . . . And . . . I shall turn you out of the house, and then you can go to your rascals."

And Bugrov (horribile dictu) wiped the wet, tearful face of the traitress Liza with his big soft hand. He treated his twenty-year-old wife as though she were a child.

"Come, that's enough. . . . I forgive you. Only God forbid it should happen again! I forgive you for the fifth time, but I shall not forgive you for the sixth, as God is holy. God does not forgive such as you for such things."

Bugrov bent down and put out his shining lips towards Liza's little head. But the kiss did not follow. The doors of the hall, of the dining-room, of the parlour, and of the drawing-room all slammed, and Groholsky flew into the drawing-room like a whirlwind. He was pale and trembling. He was flourishing his arms and crushing his expensive hat in his hands. His coat fluttered upon him as though it were on a peg. He was the incarnation of acute fever. When Bugrov saw him he moved away from his wife and began looking out of the other window. Groholsky flew up to him, and waving his arms and breathing heavily and looking at no one, he began in a shaking voice:

"Ivan Petrovitch! Let us leave off keeping up this farce with one another! We have deceived each other long enough! It's too much! I cannot stand it. You must do as you like, but I cannot! It's hateful and mean, it's revolting! Do you understand that it is revolting?"

Groholsky spluttered and gasped for breath.

"It's against my principles. And you are an honest man. I love her! I love her more than anything on earth! You have noticed it and . . . it's my duty to say this!"

"What am I to say to him?" Ivan Petrovitch wondered.

"We must make an end of it. This farce cannot drag on much longer! It must be settled somehow."

Groholsky drew a breath and went on:

"I cannot live without her; she feels the same. You are an educated man, you will understand that in such circumstances your family life is impossible. This woman is not yours, so . . . in short, I beg you to look at the matter from an indulgent humane point of view. . . . Ivan Petrovitch, you must understand at last that I love her - love her more than myself, more than anything in the world, and to struggle against that love is beyond my power!"

"And she?" Bugrov asked in a sullen, somewhat ironical tone.

"Ask her; come now, ask her! For her to live with a man she does not love, to live with you is . . . is a misery!"

"And she?" Bugrov repeated, this time not in an ironical tone.

"She . . . she loves me! We love each other, Ivan Petrovitch! Kill us, despise us, pursue us, do as you will, but we can no longer conceal it from you. We are standing face to face - you may judge us with all the severity of a man whom we . . . whom fate has robbed of happiness!"

Bugrov turned as red as a boiled crab, and looked out of one eye at Liza. He began blinking. His fingers, his lips, and his eyelids twitched. Poor fellow! The eyes of his weeping wife told him that Groholsky was right, that it was a serious matter.

"Well!" he muttered. "If you. . . . In these days. . . . You are always. . . ."

"As God is above," Groholsky shrilled in his high tenor, "we understand you. Do you suppose we have no sense, no feeling? I know what agonies I am causing you, as God's above! But be indulgent, I beseech you! We are not to blame. Love is not a crime. No will can struggle against it. . . . Give her up to me, Ivan Petrovitch! Let her go with me! Take from me what you will for your sufferings. Take my life, but give me Liza. I am ready to do anything. . . . Come, tell me how I can do something to make up in part at least! To make up for that lost happiness, I can give you other happiness. I can, Ivan Petrovitch; I am ready to do anything! It would be base on my part to leave you without satisfaction. . . . I understand you at this moment."

Bugrov waved his hand as though to say, 'For God's sake, go away.' His eyes began to be dimmed by a treacherous moisture - in a moment they would see him crying like a child.

"I understand you, Ivan Petrovitch. I will give you another happiness, such as hitherto you have not known. What would you like? I have money, my father is an influential man. . . . Will you? Come, how much do you want?"

Bugrov's heart suddenly began throbbing. . . . He clutched at the window curtains with both hands. . . .

"Will you have fifty thousand? Ivan Petrovitch, I entreat you. . . . It's not a bribe, not a bargain. . I only want by a sacrifice on my part to atone a little for your inevitable loss. Would you like a hundred thousand? I am willing. A hundred thousand?"

My God! Two immense hammers began beating on the perspiring temples of the unhappy Ivan Petrovitch. Russian sledges with tinkling bells began racing in his ears. . . .

"Accept this sacrifice from me," Groholsky went on, "I entreat you! You will take a load off my conscience. . . . I implore you!"

My God! A smart carriage rolled along the road wet from a May shower, passed the window through which Bugrov's wet eyes were looking. The horses were fine, spirited, well-trained beasts. People in straw hats, with contented faces, were sitting in the carriage with long fishing-rods and bags. . . . A schoolboy in a white cap was holding a gun. They were driving out into the country to catch fish, to shoot, to walk about and have tea in the open air. They were driving to that region of bliss in which Bugrov as a boy- the barefoot, sunburnt, but infinitely happy son of a village deacon - had once raced about the meadows, the woods, and the river banks. Oh, how fiendishly seductive was that May! How happy those who can take off their heavy uniforms, get into a carriage and fly off to the country where the quails are calling and there is the scent of fresh hay. Bugrov's heart ached with a sweet thrill that made him shiver. A hundred thousand! With the carriage there floated before him all the secret dreams over which he had gloated, through the long years of his life as a government clerk as he sat in the office of his department or in his wretched little study. . . . A river, deep, with fish, a wide garden with narrow avenues, little fountains, shade, flowers, arbours, a luxurious villa with terraces and turrets with an Aeolian harp and little silver bells (he had heard of the existence of an Aeolian harp from German romances); a cloudless blue sky; pure limpid air fragrant with the scents that recall his hungry, barefoot, crushed childhood. . . . To get up at five, to go to bed at nine; to spend the day catching fish, talking with the peasants. . . . What happiness!

"Ivan Petrovitch, do not torture me! Will you take a hundred thousand?"

"H'm . . . a hundred and fifty thousand!" muttered Bugrov in a hollow voice, the voice of a husky bull. He muttered it, and bowed his head, ashamed of his words, and awaiting the answer.

"Good," said Groholsky, "I agree. I thank you, Ivan Petrovitch . . . . In a minute. . . . I will not keep you waiting. . . ."

Groholsky jumped up, put on his hat, and staggering backwards, ran out of the drawing-room.

Bugrov clutched the window curtains more tightly than ever. . . . He was ashamed . . . . There was a nasty, stupid feeling in his soul, but, on the other hand, what fair shining hopes swarmed between his throbbing temples! He was rich!

Liza, who had grasped nothing of what was happening, darted through the half-opened door trembling all over and afraid that he would come to her window and fling her away from it. She went into the nursery, laid herself down on the nurse's bed, and curled herself up. She was shivering with fever.

Bugrov was left alone. He felt stifled, and he opened the window. What glorious air breathed fragrance on his face and neck! It would be good to breathe such air lolling on the cushions of a carriage. . . . Out there, far beyond the town, among the villages and the summer villas, the air was sweeter still. . . . Bugrov actually smiled as he dreamed of the air that would be about him when he would go out on the verandah of his villa and admire the view. A long while he dreamed. . . . The sun had set, and still he stood and dreamed, trying his utmost to cast out of his mind the image of Liza which obstinately pursued him in all his dreams.

"I have brought it, Ivan Petrovitch!" Groholsky, re-entering, whispered above his ear. "I have brought it - take it. . . . Here in this roll there are forty thousand. . . . With this cheque will you kindly get twenty the day after to-morrow from Valentinov? . . . Here is a bill of exchange . . . a cheque. . . . The remaining thirty thousand in a day or two. . . . My steward will bring it to you."

Groholsky, pink and excited, with all his limbs in motion, laid before Bugrov a heap of rolls of notes and bundles of papers. The heap was big, and of all sorts of hues and tints. Never in the course of his life had Bugrov seen such a heap. He spread out his fat fingers and, not looking at Groholsky, fell to going through the bundles of notes and bonds. . . .

Groholsky spread out all the money, and moved restlessly about the room, looking for the Dulcinea who had been bought and sold.

Filling his pockets and his pocket-book, Bugrov thrust the securities into the table drawer, and, drinking off half a decanter full of water, dashed out into the street.

"Cab!" he shouted in a frantic voice.

At half-past eleven that night he drove up to the entrance of the Paris Hotel. He went noisily upstairs and knocked at the door of Groholsky's apartments. He was admitted. Groholsky was packing his things in a portmanteau, Liza was sitting at the table trying on bracelets. They were both frightened when Bugrov went in to them. They fancied that he had come for Liza and had brought back the money which he had taken in haste without reflection. But Bugrov had not come for Liza. Ashamed of his new get-up and feeling frightfully awkward in it, he bowed and stood at the door in the attitude of a flunkey. The get-up was superb. Bugrov was unrecognisable. His huge person, which had never hitherto worn anything but a uniform, was clothed in a fresh, brand-new suit of fine French cloth and of the most fashionable cut. On his feet spats shone with sparkling buckles. He stood ashamed of his new get-up, and with his right hand covered the watch-chain for which he had, an hour before, paid three hundred roubles.

"I have come about something," he began. "A business agreement is beyond price. I am not going to give up Mishutka. . . ."

"What Mishutka?" asked Groholsky.

"My son."

Groholsky and Liza looked at each other. Liza's eyes bulged, her cheeks flushed, and her lips twitched. . . .

"Very well," she said.

She thought of Mishutka's warm little cot. It would be cruel to exchange that warm little cot for a chilly sofa in the hotel, and she consented.

"I shall see him," she said.

Bugrov bowed, walked out, and flew down the stairs in his splendour, cleaving the air with his expensive cane. . . .

"Home," he said to the cabman. "I am starting at five o'clock to-morrow morning. . . . You will come; if I am asleep, you will wake me. We are driving out of town."

II

It was a lovely August evening. The sun, set in a golden background lightly flecked with purple, stood above the western horizon on the point of sinking behind the far-away tumuli. In the garden, shadows and half-shadows had vanished, and the air had grown damp, but the golden light was still playing on the tree-tops. . . . It was warm. . . . Rain had just fallen, and made the fresh, transparent fragrant air still fresher.

I am not describing the August of Petersburg or Moscow, foggy, tearful, and dark, with its cold, incredibly damp sunsets. God forbid! I am not describing our cruel northern August. I ask the reader to move with me to the Crimea, to one of its shores, not far from Feodosia, the spot where stands the villa of one of our heroes. It is a pretty, neat villa surrounded by flower-beds and clipped bushes. A hundred paces behind it is an orchard in which its inmates walk. . . . Groholsky pays a high rent for that villa, a thousand roubles a year, I believe. . . . The villa is not worth that rent, but it is pretty. . . . Tall, with delicate walls and very delicate parapets, fragile, slender, painted a pale blue colour, hung with curtains, portières, draperies, it suggests a charming, fragile Chinese lady. . . .

On the evening described above, Groholsky and Liza were sitting on the verandah of this villa. Groholsky was reading Novoye Vremya and drinking milk out of a green mug. A syphon of Seltzer water was standing on the table before him. Groholsky imagined that he was suffering from catarrh of the lungs, and by the advice of Dr. Dmitriev consumed an immense quantity of grapes, milk, and Seltzer water. Liza was sitting in a soft easy chair some distance from the table. With her elbows on the parapet, and her little face propped on her little fists, she was gazing at the villa opposite. . . . The sun was playing upon the windows of the villa opposite, the glittering panes reflected the dazzling light. . . . Beyond the little garden and the few trees that surrounded the villa there was a glimpse of the sea with its waves, its dark blue colour, its immensity, its white masts. . . . It was so delightful! Groholsky was reading an article by Anonymous, and after every dozen lines he raised his blue eyes to Liza's back. . . . The same passionate, fervent love was shining in those eyes still. . . . He was infinitely happy in spite of his imaginary catarrh of the lungs. . . . Liza was conscious of his eyes upon her back, and was thinking of Mishutka's brilliant future, and she felt so comfortable, so serene. . . .

She was not so much interested by the sea, and the glittering reflection on the windows of the villa opposite as by the waggons which were trailing up to that villa one after another.

The waggons were full of furniture and all sorts of domestic articles. Liza watched the trellis gates and big glass doors of the villa being opened and the men bustling about the furniture and wrangling incessantly. Big armchairs and a sofa covered with dark raspberry coloured velvet, tables for the hall, the drawing-room and the dining-room, a big double bed and a child's cot were carried in by the glass doors; something big, wrapped up in sacking, was carried in too. A grand piano, thought Liza, and her heart throbbed.

It was long since she had heard the piano, and she was so fond of it. They had not a single musical instrument in their villa. Groholsky and she were musicians only in soul, no more. There were a great many boxes and packages with the words: "with care" upon them carried in after the piano.

They were boxes of looking-glasses and crockery. A gorgeous and luxurious carriage was dragged in, at the gate, and two white horses were led in looking like swans.

"My goodness, what riches!" thought Liza, remembering her old pony which Groholsky, who did not care for riding, had bought her for a hundred roubles. Compared with those swan-like steeds, her pony seemed to her no better than a bug. Groholsky, who was afraid of riding fast, had purposely bought Liza a poor horse.

"What wealth!" Liza thought and murmured as she gazed at the noisy carriers.

The sun hid behind the tumuli, the air began to lose its dryness and limpidity, and still the furniture was being driven up and hauled into the house. At last it was so dark that Groholsky left off reading the newspaper while Liza still gazed and gazed.

"Shouldn't we light the lamp?" said Groholsky, afraid that a fly might drop into his milk and be swallowed in the darkness.

"Liza! shouldn't we light the lamp? Shall we sit in darkness, my angel?"

Liza did not answer. She was interested in a chaise which had driven up to the villa opposite. . . . What a charming little mare was in that chaise. Of medium size, not large, but graceful. . . . A gentleman in a top hat was sitting in the chaise, a child about three, apparently a boy, was sitting on his knees waving his little hands. . . . He was waving his little hands and shouting with delight.

Liza suddenly uttered a shriek, rose from her seat and lurched forward.

"What is the matter?" asked Groholsky.

"Nothing. . . I only . . . I fancied. . . ."

The tall, broad-shouldered gentleman in the top hat jumped out of the chaise, lifted the boy down, and with a skip and a hop ran gaily in at the glass door. The door opened noisily and he vanished into the darkness of the villa apartments.

Two smart footmen ran up to the horse in the chaise, and most respectfully led it to the gate. Soon the villa opposite was lighted up, and the clatter of plates, knives, and forks was audible. The gentleman in the top hat was having his supper, and judging by the duration of the clatter of crockery, his supper lasted long. Liza fancied she could smell chicken soup and roast duck. After supper discordant sounds of the piano floated across from the villa. In all probability the gentleman in the top hat was trying to amuse the child in some way, and allowing it to strum on it.

Groholsky went up to Liza and put his arm round her waist.

"What wonderful weather!" he said. "What air! Do you feel it? I am very happy, Liza, very happy indeed. My happiness is so great that I am really afraid of its destruction. The greatest things are usually destroyed, and do you know, Liza, in spite of all my happiness, I am not absolutely . . . at peace. . . . One haunting thought torments me . . . it torments me horribly. It gives me no peace by day or by night. . . ."

"What thought?"

"An awful thought, my love. I am tortured by the thought of your husband. I have been silent hitherto. I have feared to trouble your inner peace, but I cannot go on being silent. Where is he? What has happened to him? What has become of him with his money? It is awful! Every night I see his face, exhausted, suffering, imploring. . . . Why, only think, my angel - can the money he so generously accepted make up to him for you? He loved you very much, didn't he?"

"Very much!"

"There you see! He has either taken to drink now, or . . . I am anxious about him! Ah, how anxious I am! Should we write to him, do you think? We ought to comfort him . . . a kind word, you know."

Groholsky heaved a deep sigh, shook his head, and sank into an easy chair exhausted by painful reflection. Leaning his head on his fists he fell to musing. Judging from his face, his musings were painful.

"I am going to bed," said Liza; "it's time."

Liza went to her own room, undressed, and dived under the bedclothes. She used to go to bed at ten o'clock and get up at ten. She was fond of her comfort.

She was soon in the arms of Morpheus. Throughout the whole night she had the most fascinating dreams. . . . She dreamed whole romances, novels, Arabian Nights. . . . The hero of all these dreams was the gentleman in the top hat, who had caused her to utter a shriek that evening.

The gentleman in the top hat was carrying her off from Groholsky, was singing, was beating Groholsky and her, was flogging the boy under the window, was declaring his love, and driving her off in the chaise. . . . Oh, dreams! In one night, lying with one's eyes shut, one may sometimes live through more than ten years of happiness. . . . That night Liza lived through a great variety of experiences, and very happy ones, even in spite of the beating.

Waking up between six and seven, she flung on her clothes, hurriedly did her hair, and without even putting on her Tatar slippers with pointed toes, ran impulsively on to the verandah. Shading her eyes from the sun with one hand, and with the other holding up her slipping clothes, she gazed at the villa opposite. Her face beamed. . . . There could be no further doubt it was he.

On the verandah in the villa opposite there was a table in front of the glass door. A tea service was shining and glistening on the table with a silver samovar at the head. Ivan Petrovitch was sitting at the table. He had in his hand a glass in a silver holder, and was drinking tea. He was drinking it with great relish. That fact could be deduced from the smacking of his lips, the sound of which reached Liza's ears. He was wearing a brown dressing-gown with black flowers on it. Massive tassels fell down to the ground. It was the first time in her life Liza had seen her husband in a dressing-gown, and such an expensive-looking one.

Mishutka was sitting on one of his knees, and hindering him from drinking his tea. The child jumped up and down and tried to clutch his papa's shining lip. After every three or four sips the father bent down to his son and kissed him on the head. A grey cat with its tail in the air was rubbing itself against one of the table legs, and with a plaintive mew proclaiming its desire for food. Liza hid behind the verandah curtain, and fastened her eyes upon the members of her former family; her face was radiant with joy.

"Misha!" she murmured, "Misha! Are you really here, Misha? The darling! And how he loves Vanya! Heavens!"

And Liza went off into a giggle when Mishutka stirred his father's tea with a spoon. "And how Vanya loves Misha! My darlings!"

Liza's heart throbbed, and her head went round with joy and happiness. She sank into an armchair and went on observing them, sitting down.

"How did they come here?" she wondered as she sent airy kisses to Mishutka. "Who gave them the idea of coming here? Heavens! Can all that wealth belong to them? Can those swan-like horses that were led in at the gate belong to Ivan Petrovitch? Ah!"

When he had finished his tea, Ivan Petrovitch went into the house. Ten minutes later, he appeared on the steps and Liza was astounded. . . . He, who in his youth only seven years ago had been called Vanushka and Vanka and had been ready to punch a man in the face and turn the house upside down over twenty kopecks, was dressed devilishly well. He had on a broad-brimmed straw hat, exquisite brilliant boots, a piqué waistcoat. . . . Thousands of suns, big and little, glistened on his watch-chain. With much chic he held in his right hand his gloves and cane.

And what swagger, what style there was in his heavy figure when, with a graceful motion of his hand, he bade the footman bring the horse round.

He got into the chaise with dignity, and told the footmen standing round the chaise to give him Mishutka and the fishing tackle they had brought. Setting Mishutka beside him, and putting his left arm round him, he held the reins and drove off.

"Ge-ee up!" shouted Mishutka.

Liza, unaware of what she was doing, waved her handkerchief after them. If she had looked in the glass she would have been surprised at her flushed, laughing, and, at the same time, tear-stained face. She was vexed that she was not beside her gleeful boy, and that she could not for some reason shower kisses on him at once.

For some reason! . . . Away with all your petty delicacies!

"Grisha! Grisha!" Liza ran into Groholsky's bedroom and set to work to wake him. "Get up, they have come! The darling!"

"Who has come?" asked Groholsky, waking up.

"Our people . . . Vanya and Misha, they have come, they are in the villa opposite. . . . I looked out, and there they were drinking tea. . . . And Misha too. . . . What a little angel our Misha has grown! If only you had seen him! Mother of God!"

"Seen whom? Why, you are. . . . Who has come? Come where?"

"Vanya and Misha. . . . I have been looking at the villa opposite, while they were sitting drinking tea. Misha can drink his tea by himself now. . . . Didn't you see them moving in yesterday, it was they who arrived!"

Groholsky rubbed his forehead and turned pale.

"Arrived? Your husband?" he asked.

"Why, yes."

"What for?"

"Most likely he is going to live here. They don't know we are here. If they did, they would have looked at our villa, but they drank their tea and took no notice."

"Where is he now? But for God's sake do talk sense! Oh, where is he?"

"He has gone fishing with Misha in the chaise. Did you see the horses yesterday? Those are their horses . . . Vanya's . . . Vanya drives with them. Do you know what, Grisha? We will have Misha to stay with us. . . . We will, won't we? He is such a pretty boy. Such an exquisite boy!"

Groholsky pondered, while Liza went on talking and talking.

"This is an unexpected meeting," said Groholsky, after prolonged and, as usual, harrassing reflection. "Well, who could have expected that we should meet here? Well. . . There it is. . . . So be it. It seems that it is fated. I can imagine the awkwardness of his position when he meets us."

"Shall we have Misha to stay with us?"

"Yes, we will. . . . It will be awkward meeting him. . . . Why, what can I say to him? What can I talk of? It will be awkward for him and awkward for me. . . . We ought not to meet. We will carry on communications, if necessary, through the servants. . . . My head does ache so, Lizotchka. My arms and legs too, I ache all over. Is my head feverish?"

Liza put her hand on his forehead and found that his head was hot.

"I had dreadful dreams all night . . . I shan't get up to-day. I shall stay in bed . . . I must take some quinine. Send me my breakfast here, little woman."

Groholsky took quinine and lay in bed the whole day. He drank warm water, moaned, had the sheets and pillowcase changed, whimpered, and induced an agonising boredom in all surrounding him.

He was insupportable when he imagined he had caught a chill. Liza had continually to interrupt her inquisitive observations and run from the verandah to his room. At dinner-time she had to put on mustard plasters. How boring all this would have been, O reader, if the villa opposite had not been at the service of my heroine! Liza watched that villa all day long and was gasping with happiness.

At ten o'clock Ivan Petrovitch and Mishutka came back from fishing and had breakfast. At two o'clock they had dinner, and at four o'clock they drove off somewhere in a carriage. The white horses bore them away with the swiftness of lightning. At seven o'clock visitors came to see them - all of them men. They were playing cards on two tables in the verandah till midnight. One of the men played superbly on the piano. The visitors played, ate, drank, and laughed. Ivan Petrovitch guffawing loudly, told them an anecdote of Armenian life at the top of his voice, so that all the villas round could hear. It was very gay and Mishutka sat up with them till midnight.

"Misha is merry, he is not crying," thought Liza, "so he does not remember his mamma. So he has forgotten me!"

And there was a horrible bitter feeling in Liza' s soul. She spent the whole night crying. She was fretted by her little conscience, and by vexation and misery, and the desire to talk to Mishutka and kiss him. . . . In the morning she got up with a headache and tear-stained eyes. Her tears Groholsky put down to his own account.

"Do not weep, darling," he said to her, "I am all right to-day, my chest is a little painful, but that is nothing."

While they were having tea, lunch was being served at the villa opposite. Ivan Petrovitch was looking at his plate, and seeing nothing but a morsel of goose dripping with fat.

"I am very glad," said Groholsky, looking askance at Bugrov, "very glad that his life is so tolerable! I hope that decent surroundings anyway may help to stifle his grief. Keep out of sight, Liza! They will see you . . . I am not disposed to talk to him just now . . . God be with him! Why trouble his peace?"

But the dinner did not pass off so quietly. During dinner precisely that "awkward position" which Groholsky so dreaded occurred. Just when the partridges, Groholsky's favorite dish, had been put on the table, Liza was suddenly overcome with confusion, and Groholsky began wiping his face with his dinner napkin. On the verandah of the villa opposite they saw Bugrov. He was standing with his arms leaning on the parapet, and staring straight at them, with his eyes starting out of his head.

"Go in, Liza, go in," Groholsky whispered. "I said we must have dinner indoors! What a girl you are, really. . . ."

Bugrov stared and stared, and suddenly began shouting. Groholsky looked at him and saw a face full of astonishment. . . .

"Is that you?" bawled Ivan Petrovitch, "you! Are you here too?"

Groholsky passed his fingers from one shoulder to another, as though to say, "My chest is weak, and so I can't shout across such a distance." Liza's heart began throbbing, and everything turned round before her eyes. Bugrov ran from his verandah, ran across the road, and a few seconds later was standing under the verandah on which Groholsky and Liza were dining. Alas for the partridges!

"How are you?" he began, flushing crimson, and stuffing his big hands in his pockets. "Are you here? Are you here too?"

"Yes, we are here too. . . ."

"How did you get here?"

"Why, how did you?"

"I? It's a long story, a regular romance, my good friend! But don't put yourselves out - eat your dinner! I've been living, you know, ever since then . . . in the Oryol province. I rented an estate. A splendid estate! But do eat your dinner! I stayed there from the end of May, but now I have given it up. . . . It was cold there, and - well, the doctor advised me to go to the Crimea. . . ."

"Are you ill, then?" inquired Groholsky.

"Oh, well. . . . There always seems, as it were. . . something gurgling here. . . ."

And at the word "here" Ivan Petrovitch passed his open hand from his neck down to the middle of his stomach.

"So you are here too. . . . Yes . . . that's very pleasant. Have you been here long?"

"Since July."

"Oh, and you, Liza, how are you? Quite well?"

"Quite well," answered Liza, and was embarrassed.

"You miss Mishutka, I'll be bound. Eh? Well, he's here with me. . . . I'll send him over to you directly with Nikifor. This is very nice. Well, good-bye! I have to go off directly. . . . I made the acquaintance of Prince Ter-Haimazov yesterday; delightful man, though he is an Armenian. So he has a croquet party to-day; we are going to play croquet. . . . Good-bye! The carriage is waiting. . . ."

Ivan Petrovitch whirled round, tossed his head, and, waving adieu to them, ran home.

"Unhappy man," said Groholsky, heaving a deep sigh as he watched him go off.

"In what way is he unhappy?" asked Liza.

"To see you and not have the right to call you his!"

"Fool!" Liza was so bold to think. "Idiot!"

Before evening Liza was hugging and kissing Mishutka. At first the boy howled, but when he was offered jam, he was all friendly smiles.

For three days Groholsky and Liza did not see Bugrov. He had disappeared somewhere, and was only at home at night. On the fourth day he visited them again at dinner-time. He came in, shook hands with both of them, and sat down to the table. His face was serious.

"I have come to you on business," he said. "Read this." And he handed Groholsky a letter. "Read it! Read it aloud!"

Groholsky read as follows:

"My beloved and consoling, never-forgotten son Ioann! I have received the respectful and loving letter in which you invite your aged father to the mild and salubrious Crimea, to breathe the fragrant air, and behold strange lands. To that letter I reply that on taking my holiday, I will come to you, but not for long. My colleague, Father Gerasim, is a frail and delicate man, and cannot be left alone for long. I am very sensible of your not forgetting your parents, your father and your mother. . . . You rejoice your father with your affection, and you remember your mother in your prayers, and so it is fitting to do. Meet me at Feodosia. What sort of town is Feodosia - what is it like? It will be very agreeable to see it. Your godmother, who took you from the font, is called Feodosia. You write that God has been graciously pleased that you should win two hundred thousand roubles. That is gratifying to me. But I cannot approve of your having left the service while still of a grade of little importance; even a rich man ought to be in the service. I bless you always, now and hereafter. Ilya and Seryozhka Andronov send you their greetings. You might send them ten roubles each - they are badly off!

"Your loving Father, Pyotr Bugrov, Priest."

Groholsky read this letter aloud, and he and Liza both looked inquiringly at Bugrov.

"You see what it is," Ivan Petrovitch began hesitatingly. "I should like to ask you, Liza, not to let him see you, to keep out of his sight while he is here. I have written to him that you are ill and gone to the Caucasus for a cure. If you meet him... You see yourself.... It's awkward... H'm...."

"Very well," said Liza.

"We can do that," thought Groholsky, "since he makes sacrifices, why shouldn't we?"

"Please do.... If he sees you there will be trouble.... My father is a man of strict principles. He would curse me in seven churches. Don't go out of doors, Liza, that is all. He won't be here long. Don't be afraid."

Father Pyotr did not long keep them waiting. One fine morning Ivan Petrovitch ran in and hissed in a mysterious tone:

"He has come! He is asleep now, so please be careful."

And Liza was shut up within four walls. She did not venture to go out into the yard or on to the verandah. She could only see the sky from behind the window curtain. Unluckily for her, Ivan Petrovitch's papa spent his whole time in the open air, and even slept on the verandah. Usually Father Pyotr, a little parish priest, in a brown cassock and a top hat with a curly brim, walked slowly round the villas and gazed with curiosity at the "strange lands" through his grandfatherly spectacles. Ivan Petrovitch with the Stanislav on a little ribbon accompanied him. He did not wear a decoration as a rule, but before his own people he liked to show off. In their society he always wore the Stanislav.

Liza was bored to death. Groholsky suffered too. He had to go for his walks alone without a companion. He almost shed tears, but . . . had to submit to his fate. And to make things worse, Bugrov would run across every morning and in a hissing whisper would give some quite unnecessary bulletin concerning the health of Father Pyotr. He bored them with those bulletins.

"He slept well," he informed them. "Yesterday he was put out because I had no salted cucumbers. . . He has taken to Mishutka; he keeps patting him on the head."

At last, a fortnight later, little Father Pyotr walked for the last time round the villas and, to Groholsky's immense relief, departed. He had enjoyed himself, and went off very well satisfied. Liza and Groholsky fell back into their old manner of life. Groholsky once more blessed his fate. But his happiness did not last for long. A new trouble worse than Father Pyotr followed. Ivan Petrovitch took to coming to see them every day. Ivan Petrovitch, to be frank, though a capital fellow, was a very tedious person. He came at dinner-time, dined with them and stayed a very long time. That would not have mattered. But they had to buy vodka, which Groholsky could not endure, for his dinner. He would drink five glasses and talk the whole dinner-time. That, too, would not have mattered. . . . But he would sit on till two o'clock in the morning, and not let them get to bed, and, worse still, he permitted himself to talk of things about which he should have been silent. When towards two o'clock in the morning he had drunk too much vodka and champagne, he would take Mishutka in his arms, and weeping, say to him, before Groholsky and Liza:

"Mihail, my son, what am I? I . . . am a scoundrel. I have sold your mother! Sold her for thirty pieces of silver, may the Lord punish me! Mihail Ivanitch, little sucking pig, where is your mother? Lost! Gone! Sold into slavery! Well, I am a scoundrel."

These tears and these words turned Groholsky's soul inside out. He would look timidly at Liza's pale face and wring his hands.

"Go to bed, Ivan Petrovitch," he would say timidly.

"I am going. . . . Come along, Mishutka. . . . The Lord be our judge! I cannot think of sleep while I know that my wife is a slave. . . . But it is not Groholsky's fault. . . . The goods were mine, the money his. . . . Freedom for the free and Heaven for the saved."

By day Ivan Petrovitch was no less insufferable to Groholsky. To Groholsky's intense horror, he was always at Liza's side. He went fishing with her, told her stories, walked with her, and even on one occasion, taking advantage of Groholsky's having a cold, carried her off in his carriage, goodness knows where, and did not bring her back till night!

"It's outrageous, inhuman," thought Groholsky, biting his lips.

Groholsky liked to be continually kissing Liza. He could not exist without those honeyed kisses, and it was awkward to kiss her before Ivan Petrovitch. It was agony. The poor fellow felt forlorn, but fate soon had compassion on him. Ivan Petrovitch suddenly went off somewhere for a whole week. Visitors had come and carried him off with them . . . And Mishutka was taken too.

One fine morning Groholsky came home from a walk good-humoured and beaming.

"He has come," he said to Liza, rubbing his hands. "I am very glad he has come. Ha-ha-ha!"

"What are you laughing at?"

"There are women with him."

"What women?"

"I don't know. . . . It's a good thing he has got women. . . . A capital thing, in fact. . . . He is still young and fresh. Come here! Look!"

Groholsky led Liza on to the verandah, and pointed to the villa opposite. They both held their sides, and roared with laughter. It was funny. Ivan Petrovitch was standing on the verandah of the villa opposite, smiling. Two dark-haired ladies and Mishutka were standing below, under the verandah. The ladies were laughing, and loudly talking French.

"French women," observed Groholsky. "The one nearest us isn't at all bad-looking. Lively damsels, but that's no matter. There are good women to be found even among such. . . . But they really do go too far."

What was funny was that Ivan Petrovitch bent across the verandah, and stretching with his long arms, put them round the shoulders of one of the French girls, lifted her in the air, and set her giggling on the verandah. After lifting up both ladies on to the verandah, he lifted up Mishutka too. The ladies ran down and the proceedings were repeated.

"Powerful muscles, I must say," muttered Groholsky looking at this scene. The operation was repeated some six times, the ladies were so amiable as to show no embarrassment whatever when the boisterous wind disposed of their inflated skirts as it willed while they were being lifted. Groholsky dropped his eyes in a shamefaced way when the ladies flung their legs over the parapet as they reached the verandah. But Liza watched and laughed! What did she care? It was not a case of men misbehaving themselves, which would have put her, as a woman, to shame, but of ladies.

In the evening, Ivan Petrovitch flew over, and with some embarrassment announced that he was now a man with a household to look after. . . .

"You mustn't imagine they are just anybody," he said. "It is true they are French. They shout at the top of their voices, and drink . . . but we all know! The French are brought up to be like that! It can't be helped. . . . The prince," Ivan Petrovitch added, "let me have them almost for nothing. . . . He said: 'take them, take them. . . .' I must introduce you to the prince sometime. A man of culture! He's for ever writing, writing. . . . And do you know what their names are? One is Fanny, the other Isabella. . . . There's Europe, ha-ha-ha! . . . The west! Good-bye!"

Ivan Petrovitch left Liza and Groholsky in peace, and devoted himself to his ladies. All day long sound of talk, laughter, and the clatter of crockery came from his villa. . . . The lights were not put out till far into the night. . . . Groholsky was in bliss. . . . At last, after a prolonged interval of agony, he felt happy and at peace again. Ivan Petrovitch with his two ladies had no such happiness as he had with one. But alas, destiny has no heart. She plays with the Groholskys, the Lizas, the Ivans, and the Mishutkas as with pawns. . . . Groholsky lost his peace again. . . .

One morning, about ten days afterwards, on waking up late, he went out on to the verandah and saw a spectacle which shocked him, revolted him, and moved him to intense indignation. Under the verandah of the villa opposite stood the French women, and between them Liza. She was talking and looking askance at her own villa as though to see whether that tyrant, that despot were awake (so Groholsky interpreted those looks). Ivan Petrovitch standing on the verandah with his sleeves tucked up, lifted Isabella into the air, then Fanny, and then Liza. When he was lifting Liza it seemed to Groholsky that he pressed her to himself. . . . Liza too flung one leg over the parapet. . . . Oh these women! All sphinxes, every one of them!

When Liza returned home from her husband's villa and went into the bedroom on tip-toe, as though nothing had happened, Groholsky, pale, with hectic flushes on his cheeks, was lying in the attitude of a man at his last gasp and moaning.

On seeing Liza, he sprang out of bed, and began pacing about the bedroom.

"So that's what you are like, is it?" he shrieked in a high tenor. "So that's it! Very much obliged to you! It's revolting, madam! Immoral, in fact! Let me tell you that!"

Liza turned pale, and of course burst into tears. When women feel that they are in the right, they scold and shed tears; when they are conscious of being in fault, they shed tears only.

"On a level with those depraved creatures! It's . . . it's . . . it's . . . lower than any impropriety! Why, do you know what they are? They are kept women! Cocottes! And you a respectable woman go rushing off where they are. . . And he . . . He! What does he want? What more does he want of me? I don't understand it! I have given him half of my property - I have given him more! You know it yourself! I have given him what I have not myself. . . . I have given him almost all. . . . And he! I've put up with your calling him Vanya, though he has no right whatever to such intimacy. I have put up with your walks, kisses after dinner. . . . I have put up with everything, but this I will not put up with. . . . Either he or I! Let him go away, or I go away! I'm not equal to living like this any longer, no! You can see that for yourself! . . . Either he or I. . . . Enough! The cup is brimming over. . . . I have suffered a great deal as it is. . . . I am going to talk to him at once - this minute! What is he, after all? What has he to be proud of? No, indeed. . . . He has no reason to think so much of himself. . . . "

Groholsky said a great many more valiant and stinging things, but did not "go at once"; he felt timid and abashed. . . . He went to Ivan Petrovitch three days later.

When he went into his apartment, he gaped with astonishment. He was amazed at the wealth and luxury with which Bugrov had surrounded himself. Velvet hangings, fearfully expensive chairs. . . . One was positively ashamed to step on the carpet. Groholsky had seen many rich men in his day, but he had never seen such frenzied luxury. . . . And the higgledy-piggledy muddle he saw when, with an inexplicable tremor, he walked into the drawing-room - plates with bits of bread on them were lying about on the grand piano, a glass was standing on a chair, under the table there was a basket with a filthy rag in it. . . . Nut shells were strewn about in the windows. Bugrov himself was not quite in his usual trim when Groholsky walked in. . . . With a red face and uncombed locks he was pacing about the room in deshabille, talking to himself, apparently much agitated. Mishutka was sitting on the sofa there in the drawing-room, and was making the air vibrate with a piercing scream.

"It's awful, Grigory Vassilyevitch!" Bugrov began on seeing Groholsky, "such disorder. . . such disorder. . . Please sit down. You must excuse my being in the costume of Adam and Eve. . . . It's of no consequence. . . . Horrible disorderliness! I don't understand how people can exist here, I don't understand it! The servants won't do what they are told, the climate is horrible, everything is expensive. . . . Stop your noise,"

Bugrov shouted, suddenly coming to a halt before Mishutka; "stop it, I tell you! Little beast, won't you stop it?"

And Bugrov pulled Mishutka's ear.

"That's revolting, Ivan Petrovitch," said Groholsky in a tearful voice. "How can you treat a tiny child like that? You really are. . ."

"Let him stop yelling then. . . . Be quiet - I'll whip you!"

"Don't cry, Misha darling. . . . Papa won't touch you again. Don't beat him, Ivan Petrovitch; why, he is hardly more than a baby. . . . There, there. . . . Would you like a little horse? I'll send you a little horse. . . . You really are hard-hearted. . . ."

Groholsky paused, and then asked:

"And how are your ladies getting on, Ivan Petrovitch?"

"Not at all. I've turned them out without ceremony. I might have gone on keeping them, but it's awkward. . . . The boy will grow up. . . . A father's example. . . . If I were alone, then it would be a different thing. . . . Besides, what's the use of my keeping them? Poof . . . it's a regular farce! I talk to them in Russian, and they answer me in French. They don't understand a thing - you can't knock anything into their heads."

"I've come to you about something, Ivan Petrovitch, to talk things over. . . . H'm. . . . It's nothing very particular. But just . . . two or three words. . . . In reality, I have a favour to ask of you."

"What's that?"

"Would you think it possible, Ivan Petrovitch, to go away? We are delighted that you are here; it's very agreeable for us, but it's inconvenient, don't you know. . . . You will understand me. It's awkward in a way. . . . Such indefinite relations, such continual awkwardness in regard to one another. . . . We must part. . . . It's essential in fact. Excuse my saying so, but . . . you must see for yourself, of course, that in such circumstances to be living side by side leads to . . . reflections. . . that is . . . not to reflections, but there is a certain awkward feeling. . . ."

"Yes.... That is so, I have thought of it myself. Very good, I will go away."

"We shall be very grateful to you.... Believe me, Ivan Petrovitch, we shall preserve the most flattering memory of you. The sacrifice which you..."

"Very good.... Only what am I to do with all this? I say, you buy this furniture of mine! What do you say? It's not expensive, eight thousand ... ten.... The furniture, the carriage, the grand piano...."

"Very good.... I will give you ten thousand...."

"Well, that is capital! I will set off to-morrow. I shall go to Moscow. It's impossible to live here. Everything is so dear! Awfully dear! The money fairly flies.... You can't take a step without spending a thousand! I can't go on like that. I have a child to bring up.... Well, thank God that you will buy my furniture.... That will be a little more in hand, or I should have been regularly bankrupt...."

Groholsky got up, took leave of Bugrov, and went home rejoicing. In the evening he sent him ten thousand roubles.

Early next morning Bugrov and Mishutka were already at Feodosia.

III

Several months had passed; spring had come. With spring, fine bright days had come too. Life was not so dull and hateful, and the earth was more fair to look upon.... There was a warm breeze from the sea and the open country.... The earth was covered with fresh grass, fresh leaves were green upon the trees. Nature had sprung into new life, and had put on new array.

It might be thought that new hopes and new desires would surge up in man when everything in nature is renewed, and young and fresh ... but it is hard for man to renew life....

Groholsky was still living in the same villa. His hopes and desires, small and unexacting, were still concentrated on the same Liza, on her alone, and on nothing else! As before, he could not take his eyes off her, and gloated over the thought: how happy I am! The poor fellow really did feel awfully happy. Liza sat as before on the verandah, and unaccountably stared with bored eyes at the villa opposite and the trees near it through which there was a peep at the dark blue sea. . . . As before, she spent her days for the most part in silence, often in tears and from time to time in putting mustard plasters on Groholsky. She might be congratulated on one new sensation, however. There was a worm gnawing at her vitals. . . . That worm was misery. . . . She was fearfully miserable, pining for her son, for her old, her cheerful manner of life. Her life in the past had not been particularly cheerful, but still it was livelier than her present existence. When she lived with her husband she used from time to time to go to a theatre, to an entertainment, to visit acquaintances. But here with Groholsky it was all quietness and emptiness. . . . Besides, here there was one man, and he with his ailments and his continual mawkish kisses, was like an old grandfather for ever shedding tears of joy.

It was boring! Here she had not Mihey Sergeyitch who used to be fond of dancing the mazurka with her. She had not Spiridon Nikolaitch, the son of the editor of the Provincial News. Spiridon Nikolaitch sang well and recited poetry. Here she had not a table set with lunch for visitors. She had not Gerasimovna, the old nurse who used to be continually grumbling at her for eating too much jam. . . . She had no one! There was simply nothing for her but to lie down and die of depression. Groholsky rejoiced in his solitude, but . . . he was wrong to rejoice in it. All too soon he paid for his egoism. At the beginning of May when the very air seemed to be in love and faint with happiness, Groholsky lost everything; the woman he loved and....

That year Bugrov, too, visited the Crimea. He did not take the villa opposite, but pottered about, going from one town to another with Mishutka. He spent his time eating, drinking, sleeping, and playing cards. He had lost all relish for fishing, shooting and the French women, who, between ourselves, had robbed him a bit. He had grown thin, lost his broad and beaming smiles, and had taken to dressing in canvas. Ivan Petrovitch from time to time visited Groholsky's villa. He brought Liza jam, sweets, and fruit, and seemed trying to dispel her ennui. Groholsky was not troubled by these visits, especially as they were brief and infrequent, and were apparently paid on account of Mishutka, who could not under any circumstances have been altogether deprived of the privilege of seeing his mother. Bugrov came, unpacked his presents, and after saying a few words, departed. And those few words he said not to Liza but to Groholsky. . . . With Liza he was silent and Groholsky's mind was at rest; but there is a Russian proverb which he would have done well to remember: "Don't fear the dog that barks, but fear the dog that's quiet. . . ." A fiendish proverb, but in practical life sometimes indispensable.

As he was walking in the garden one day, Groholsky heard two voices in conversation. One voice was a man's, the other was a woman's. One belonged to Bugrov, the other to Liza. Groholsky listened, and turning white as death, turned softly towards the speakers. He halted behind a lilac bush, and proceeded to watch and listen. His arms and legs turned cold. A cold sweat came out upon his brow. He clutched several branches of the lilac that he might not stagger and fall down. All was over!

Bugrov had his arm round Liza' s waist, and was saying to her:

"My darling! what are we to do? It seems it was God's will. . . . I am a scoundrel. . . . I sold you. I was seduced by that Herod's money, plague take him, and what good have I had from the money? Nothing but anxiety and display! No peace, no happiness, no position. . . . One sits like a fat invalid at the same spot, and never a step forwarder. . . . Have you heard that Andrushka Markuzin has been made a head clerk? Andrushka, that fool! While I stagnate. . . . Good heavens! I have lost you, I have lost my happiness. I am a scoundrel, a blackguard, how do you think I shall feel at the dread day of judgment?"

"Let us go away, Vanya," wailed Liza. "I am dull. . . . I am dying of depression."

"We cannot, the money has been taken. . . ."

"Well, give it back again."

"I should be glad to, but . . . wait a minute. I have spent it all. We must submit, my girl. God is chastising us. Me for my covetousness and you for your frivolity. Well, let us be tortured. . . . It will be the better for us in the next world."

And in an access of religious feeling, Bugrov turned up his eyes to heaven.

"But I cannot go on living here; I am miserable."

"Well, there is no help for it. I'm miserable too. Do you suppose I am happy without you? I am pining and wasting away! And my chest has begun to be bad! . . . You are my lawful wife, flesh of my flesh . . . one flesh. . . . You must live and bear it! While I . . . will drive over . . . visit you."

And bending down to Liza, Bugrov whispered, loudly enough, however, to be heard several yards away:

"I will come to you at night, Lizanka. . . . Don't worry. . . . I am staying at Feodosia close by. . . . I will live here near you till I have run through everything . . . and I soon shall be at my last farthing! A-a-ah, what a life it is! Dreariness, ill . . . my chest is bad, and my stomach is bad."

Bugrov ceased speaking, and then it was Liza's turn. . . . My God, the cruelty of that woman! She began weeping, complaining, enumerating all the defects of her lover and her own sufferings. Groholsky as he listened to her, felt that he was a villain, a miscreant, a murderer.

"He makes me miserable. . . ." Liza said in conclusion.

After kissing Liza at parting, and going out at the garden gate, Bugrov came upon Groholsky, who was standing at the gate waiting for him.

"Ivan Petrovitch," said Groholsky in the tone of a dying man, "I have seen and heard it all. . . It's not honourable on your part, but I do not blame you. . . . You love her too, but you must understand that she is mine. Mine! I cannot live without her! How is it you don't understand that? Granted that you love her, that you are miserable. . . . Have I not paid you, in part at least, for your sufferings? For God's sake, go away! For God's sake, go away! Go away from here for ever, I implore you, or you will kill me. . . ."

"I have nowhere to go," Bugrov said thickly.

"H'm, you have squandered everything. . . . You are an impulsive man. Very well. . . . Go to my estate in the province of Tchernigov. If you like I will make you a present of the property. It's a small estate, but a good one.... On my honour, it's a good one!"

Bugrov gave a broad grin. He suddenly felt himself in the seventh heaven.

"I will give it you.... This very day I will write to my steward and send him an authorisation for completing the purchase. You must tell everyone you have bought it.... Go away, I entreat you."

"Very good, I will go. I understand."

"Let us go to a notary ... at once," said Groholsky, greatly cheered, and he went to order the carriage.

On the following evening, when Liza was sitting on the garden seat where her rendezvous with Ivan Petrovitch usually took place, Groholsky went quietly to her. He sat down beside her, and took her hand.

"Are you dull, Lizotchka?" he said, after a brief silence. "Are you depressed? Why shouldn't we go away somewhere? Why is it we always stay at home? We want to go about, to enjoy ourselves, to make acquaintances.... Don't we?"

"I want nothing," said Liza, and turned her pale, thin face towards the path by which Bugrov used to come to her.

Groholsky pondered. He knew who it was she expected, who it was she wanted.

"Let us go home, Liza," he said, "it is damp here...."

"You go; I'll come directly."

Groholsky pondered again.

"You are expecting him?" he asked, and made a wry face as though his heart had been gripped with red-hot pincers.

"Yes.... I want to give him the socks for Misha...."

"He will not come."

"How do you know?"

"He has gone away...."

Liza opened her eyes wide....

"He has gone away, gone to the Tchernigov province. I have given him my estate...."

Liza turned fearfully pale, and caught at Groholsky's shoulder to save herself from falling.

"I saw him off at the steamer at three o'clock."

Liza suddenly clutched at her head, made a movement, and falling on the seat, began shaking all over.

"Vanya," she wailed, "Vanya! I will go to Vanya.... Darling!"

She had a fit of hysterics....

And from that evening, right up to July, two shadows could be seen in the park in which the summer visitors took their walks. The shadows wandered about from morning till evening, and made the summer visitors feel dismal.... After Liza's shadow invariably walked the shadow of Groholsky.... I call them shadows because they had both lost their natural appearance. They had grown thin and pale and shrunken, and looked more like shadows than living people.... Both were pining away like fleas in the classic anecdote of the Jew who sold insect powder.

At the beginning of July, Liza ran away from Groholsky, leaving a note in which she wrote that she was going for a time to "her son" ... For a time! She ran away by night when Groholsky was asleep.... After reading her letter Groholsky spent a whole week wandering round about the villa as though he were mad, and neither ate nor slept. In August, he had an attack of recurrent fever, and in September he went abroad. There he took to drink.... He hoped in drink and dissipation to find comfort.... He squandered all his fortune, but did not succeed, poor fellow, in driving out of his brain the image of the beloved woman with the kittenish face.... Men do not die of happiness, nor do they die of misery. Groholsky's hair went grey, but he did not die:

he is alive to this day. . . . He came back from abroad to have "just a peep" at Liza. . . . Bugrov met him with open arms, and made him stay for an indefinite period. He is staying with Bugrov to this day.

This year I happened to be passing through Groholyovka, Bugrov's estate. I found the master and the mistress of the house having supper. . . . Ivan Petrovitch was highly delighted to see me, and fell to pressing good things upon me. . . . He had grown rather stout, and his face was a trifle puffy, though it was still rosy and looked sleek and well-nourished. . . . He was not bald. Liza, too, had grown fatter. Plumpness did not suit her. Her face was beginning to lose the kittenish look, and was, alas! more suggestive of the seal. Her cheeks were spreading upwards, outwards, and to both sides. The Bugrovs were living in first-rate style. They had plenty of everything. The house was overflowing with servants and edibles. . . .

When we had finished supper we got into conversation. Forgetting that Liza did not play, I asked her to play us something on the piano.

"She does not play," said Bugrov; "she is no musician. . . . Hey, you there! Ivan! call Grigory Vassilyevitch here! What's he doing there?" And turning to me, Bugrov added, "Our musician will come directly; he plays the guitar. We keep the piano for Mishutka - we are having him taught. . . ."

Five minutes later, Groholsky walked into the room - sleepy, unkempt, and unshaven. . . . He walked in, bowed to me, and sat down on one side.

"Why, whoever goes to bed so early?" said Bugrov, addressing him. "What a fellow you are really! He's always asleep, always asleep. . . . The sleepy head! Come, play us something lively...."

Groholsky turned the guitar, touched the strings, and began singing:

"Yesterday I waited for my dear one. . . ."

I listened to the singing, looked at Bugrov's well-fed countenance, and thought: "Nasty brute!" I felt like crying. . . . When he had finished singing, Groholsky bowed to us, and went out.

"And what am I to do with him?" Bugrov said when he had gone away. "I do have trouble with him! In the day he is always brooding and brooding. . . . And at night he moans. . . . He sleeps, but he sighs and moans in his sleep. . . . It is a sort of illness. . . . What am I to do with him, I can't think! He won't let us sleep. . . . I am afraid that he will go out of his mind. People think he is badly treated here. . . . In what way is he badly treated? He eats with us, and he drinks with us. . . . Only we won't give him money. If we were to give him any he would spend it on drink or waste it. . . . That's another trouble for me! Lord forgive me, a sinner!"

They made me stay the night. When I woke next morning, Bugrov was giving someone a lecture in the adjoining room. . . .

"Set a fool to say his prayers, and he will crack his skull on the floor! Why, who paints oars green! Do think, blockhead! Use your sense! Why don't you speak?"

"I . . . I . . . made a mistake," said a husky tenor apologetically.

The tenor belonged to Groholsky.

Groholsky saw me to the station.

"He is a despot, a tyrant," he kept whispering to me all the way. "He is a generous man, but a tyrant! Neither heart nor brain are developed in him. . . . He tortures me! If it were not for that noble woman, I should have gone away long ago. I am sorry to leave her. It's somehow easier to endure together."

Groholsky heaved a sigh, and went on:

"She is with child. . . . You notice it? It is really my child. . . . Mine. . . . She soon saw her mistake, and gave herself to me again. She cannot endure him. . . ."

"You are a rag," I could not refrain from saying to Groholsky.

"Yes, I am a man of weak character. . . . That is quite true. I was born so. Do you know how I came into the world? My late papa cruelly oppressed a certain little clerk - it was awful how he treated him! He poisoned his life. Well . . . and my late mama was tender-hearted. She came from the people, she was of the working class. . . . She took that little clerk to her heart from pity. . . . Well . . . and so I came into the world. . . . The son of the ill-treated clerk. How could I have a strong will? Where was I to get it from? But that's the second bell. . . . Good-bye. Come and see us again, but don't tell Ivan Petrovitch what I have said about him."

I pressed Groholsky's hand, and got into the train. He bowed towards the carriage, and went to the water-barrel - I suppose he was thirsty!

JOY

It was twelve o'clock at night.

Mitya Kuldarov, with excited face and ruffled hair, flew into his parents' flat, and hurriedly ran through all the rooms. His parents had already gone to bed. His sister was in bed, finishing the last page of a novel. His schoolboy brothers were asleep.

"Where have you come from?" cried his parents in amazement. "What is the matter with you?"

"Oh, don't ask! I never expected it; no, I never expected it! It's . . . it's positively incredible!"

Mitya laughed and sank into an armchair, so overcome by happiness that he could not stand on his legs.

"It's incredible! You can't imagine! Look!"

His sister jumped out of bed and, throwing a quilt round her, went in to her brother. The schoolboys woke up.

"What's the matter? You don't look like yourself!"

"It's because I am so delighted, Mamma! Do you know, now all Russia knows of me! All Russia! Till now only you knew that there was a registration clerk called Dmitry Kuldarov, and now all Russia knows it! Mamma! Oh, Lord!"

Mitya jumped up, ran up and down all the rooms, and then sat down again.

"Why, what has happened? Tell us sensibly!"

"You live like wild beasts, you don't read the newspapers and take no notice of what's published, and there's so much that is interesting in the papers. If anything happens it's all known at once, nothing is hidden! How happy I am! Oh, Lord! You know it's only celebrated people whose names are published in the papers, and now they have gone and published mine!"

"What do you mean? Where?"

The papa turned pale. The mamma glanced at the holy image and crossed herself. The schoolboys jumped out of bed and, just as they were, in short nightshirts, went up to their brother.

"Yes! My name has been published! Now all Russia knows of me! Keep the paper, mamma, in memory of it! We will read it sometimes! Look!"

Mitya pulled out of his pocket a copy of the paper, gave it to his father, and pointed with his finger to a passage marked with blue pencil.

"Read it!"

The father put on his spectacles.

"Do read it!"

The mamma glanced at the holy image and crossed herself. The papa cleared his throat and began to read: "At eleven o'clock on the evening of the 29th of December, a registration clerk of the name of Dmitry Kuldarov . . ."

"You see, you see! Go on!"

". . . a registration clerk of the name of Dmitry Kuldarov, coming from the beershop in Kozihin's buildings in Little Bronnaia in an intoxicated condition. . ."

"That's me and Semyon Petrovitch. . . . It's all described exactly! Go on! Listen!"

". . . intoxicated condition, slipped and fell under a horse belonging to a sledge-driver, a peasant of the village of Durikino in the Yuhnovsky district, called Ivan Drotov. The frightened horse, stepping over Kuldarov and drawing the sledge over him, together with a Moscow merchant of the second guild called Stepan Lukov, who was in it, dashed along the street and was caught by some house-porters. Kuldarov, at first in an unconscious condition, was taken to the police station and there examined by the doctor. The blow he had received on the back of his head. . ."

"It was from the shaft, papa. Go on! Read the rest!"

". . . he had received on the back of his head turned out not to be serious. The incident was duly reported. Medical aid was given to the injured man. . . ."

"They told me to foment the back of my head with cold water. You have read it now? Ah! So you see. Now it's all over Russia! Give it here!"

Mitya seized the paper, folded it up and put it into his pocket.

"I'll run round to the Makarovs and show it to them. . . . I must show it to the Ivanitskys too, Natasya Ivanovna, and Anisim Vassilyitch. . . . I'll run! Good-bye!"

Mitya put on his cap with its cockade and, joyful and triumphant, ran into the street.

AT THE BARBER'S

Morning. It is not yet seven o'clock, but Makar Kuzmitch Blyostken's shop is already open. The barber himself, an unwashed, greasy, but foppishly dressed youth of three and twenty, is busy clearing up; there is really nothing to be cleared away, but he is perspiring with his exertions. In one place he polishes with a rag, in another he scrapes with his finger or catches a bug and brushes it off the wall.

The barber's shop is small, narrow, and unclean. The log walls are hung with paper suggestive of a cabman's faded shirt. Between the two dingy, perspiring windows there is a thin, creaking, rickety door, above it, green from the damp, a bell which trembles and gives a sickly ring of itself without provocation. Glance into the looking-glass which hangs on one of the walls, and it distorts your countenance in all directions in the most merciless way! The shaving and haircutting is done before this looking-glass. On the little table, as greasy and unwashed as Makar Kuzmitch himself, there is everything: combs, scissors, razors, a ha'porth of wax for the moustache, a ha'porth of powder, a ha'porth of much watered eau de Cologne, and indeed the whole barber's shop is not worth more than fifteen kopecks.

There is a squeaking sound from the invalid bell and an elderly man in a tanned sheepskin and high felt over-boots walks into the shop. His head and neck are wrapped in a woman's shawl.

This is Erast Ivanitch Yagodov, Makar Kuzmitch's godfather. At one time he served as a watchman in the Consistory, now he lives near the Red Pond and works as a locksmith.

"Makarushka, good-day, dear boy!" he says to Makar Kuzmitch, who is absorbed in tidying up.

They kiss each other. Yagodov drags his shawl off his head, crosses himself, and sits down.

"What a long way it is!" he says, sighing and clearing his throat. "It's no joke! From the Red Pond to the Kaluga gate."

"How are you?"

"In a poor way, my boy. I've had a fever."

"You don't say so! Fever!"

"Yes, I have been in bed a month; I thought I should die. I had extreme unction. Now my hair's coming out. The doctor says I must be shaved. He says the hair will grow again strong. And so, I thought, I'll go to Makar. Better to a relation than to anyone else. He will do it better and he won't take anything for it. It's rather far, that's true, but what of it? It's a walk."

"I'll do it with pleasure. Please sit down."

With a scrape of his foot Makar Kuzmitch indicates a chair. Yagodov sits down and looks at himself in the glass and is apparently pleased with his reflection: the looking-glass displays a face awry, with Kalmuck lips, a broad, blunt nose, and eyes in the forehead. Makar Kuzmitch puts round his client's shoulders a white sheet with yellow spots on it, and begins snipping with the scissors.

"I'll shave you clean to the skin!" he says.

"To be sure. So that I may look like a Tartar, like a bomb. The hair will grow all the thicker."

"How's auntie?"

"Pretty middling. The other day she went as midwife to the major's lady. They gave her a rouble."

"Oh, indeed, a rouble. Hold your ear."

"I am holding it. . . . Mind you don't cut me. Oy, you hurt! You are pulling my hair."

"That doesn't matter. We can't help that in our work. And how is Anna Erastovna?"

"My daughter? She is all right, she's skipping about. Last week on the Wednesday we betrothed her to Sheikin. Why didn't you come?"

The scissors cease snipping. Makar Kuzmitch drops his hands and asks in a fright:

"Who is betrothed?"

"Anna."

"How's that? To whom?"

"To Sheikin. Prokofy Petrovitch. His aunt's a housekeeper in Zlatoustensky Lane. She is a nice woman. Naturally we are all delighted, thank God. The wedding will be in a week. Mind you come; we will have a good time."

"But how's this, Erast Ivanitch?" says Makar Kuzmitch, pale, astonished, and shrugging his shoulders. "It's . . . it's utterly impossible. Why, Anna Erastovna . . . why I . . . why, I cherished sentiments for her, I had intentions. How could it happen?"

"Why, we just went and betrothed her. He's a good fellow."

Cold drops of perspiration come on the face of Makar Kuzmitch. He puts the scissors down on the table and begins rubbing his nose with his fist.

"I had intentions," he says. "It's impossible, Erast Ivanitch. I . . . I am in love with her and have made her the offer of my heart. . . . And auntie promised. I have always respected you as though you were my father. . . . I always cut your hair for nothing. . . . I have always obliged you, and when my papa died you took the sofa and ten roubles in cash and have never given them back. Do you remember?"

"Remember! of course I do. Only, what sort of a match would you be, Makar? You are nothing of a match. You've neither money nor position, your trade's a paltry one."

"And is Sheikin rich?"

"Sheikin is a member of a union. He has a thousand and a half lent on mortgage. So my boy . . . . It's no good talking about it, the thing's done. There is no altering it, Makarushka. You must look out for another bride. . . . The world is not so small. Come, cut away. Why are you stopping?"

Makar Kuzmitch is silent and remains motionless, then he takes a handkerchief out of his pocket and begins to cry.

"Come, what is it?" Erast Ivanitch comforts him. "Give over. Fie, he is blubbering like a woman! You finish my head and then cry. Take up the scissors!"

Makar Kuzmitch takes up the scissors, stares vacantly at them for a minute, then drops them again on the table. His hands are shaking.

"I can't," he says. "I can't do it just now. I haven't the strength! I am a miserable man! And she is miserable! We loved each other, we had given each other our promise and we have been separated by unkind people without any pity. Go away, Erast Ivanitch! I can't bear the sight of you."

"So I'll come to-morrow, Makarushka. You will finish me to-morrow."

"Right."

"You calm yourself and I will come to you early in the morning."

Erast Ivanitch has half his head shaven to the skin and looks like a convict. It is awkward to be left with a head like that, but there is no help for it. He wraps his head in the shawl and walks out of the barber's shop. Left alone, Makar Kuzmitch sits down and goes on quietly weeping.

Early next morning Erast Ivanitch comes again.

"What do you want?" Makar Kuzmitch asks him coldly.

"Finish cutting my hair, Makarushka. There is half the head left to do."

"Kindly give me the money in advance. I won't cut it for nothing."

Without saying a word Erast Ivanitch goes out, and to this day his hair is long on one side of the head and short on the other. He regards it as extravagance to pay for having his hair cut and is waiting for the hair to grow of itself on the shaven side.

He danced at the wedding in that condition.

AN ENIGMATIC NATURE

On the red velvet seat of a first-class railway carriage a pretty lady sits half reclining. An expensive fluffy fan trembles in her tightly closed fingers, a pince-nez keeps dropping off her pretty little nose, the brooch heaves and falls on her bosom, like a boat on the ocean. She is greatly agitated.

On the seat opposite sits the Provincial Secretary of Special Commissions, a budding young author, who from time to time publishes long stories of high life, or "Novelli" as he calls them, in the leading paper of the province. He is gazing into her face, gazing intently, with the eyes of a connoisseur. He is watching, studying, catching every shade of this exceptional, enigmatic nature. He understands it, he fathoms it. Her soul, her whole psychology lies open before him.

"Oh, I understand, I understand you to your inmost depths!" says the Secretary of Special Commissions, kissing her hand near the bracelet. "Your sensitive, responsive soul is seeking to escape from the maze of- Yes, the struggle is terrific, titanic. But do not lose heart, you will be triumphant! Yes!"

"Write about me, Voldemar!" says the pretty lady, with a mournful smile. "My life has been so full, so varied, so chequered. Above all, I am unhappy. I am a suffering soul in some page of Dostoevsky. Reveal my soul to the world, Voldemar. Reveal that hapless soul. You are a psychologist. We have not been in the train an hour together, and you have already fathomed my heart."

"Tell me! I beseech you, tell me!"

"Listen. My father was a poor clerk in the Service. He had a good heart and was not without intelligence; but the spirit of the age - of his environment - vous comprenez? - I do not blame my poor father. He drank, gambled, took bribes. My mother - but why say more? Poverty, the struggle for daily bread, the consciousness of insignificance - ah, do not force me to recall it! I had to make my own way. You know the monstrous education at a boarding-school, foolish novel-reading, the errors of early youth, the first timid flutter of love. It was awful! The vacillation! And the agonies of losing faith in life, in oneself! Ah, you are an author. You know us women. You will understand. Unhappily I have an intense nature. I looked for happiness - and what happiness! I longed to set my soul free. Yes. In that I saw my happiness!"

"Exquisite creature!" murmured the author, kissing her hand close to the bracelet. "It's not you I am kissing, but the suffering of humanity. Do you remember Raskolnikov and his kiss?"

"Oh, Voldemar, I longed for glory, renown, success, like every - why affect modesty? - every nature above the commonplace. I yearned for something extraordinary, above the common lot of woman! And then - and then - there crossed my path - an old general - very well off. Understand me, Voldemar! It was self-sacrifice, renunciation! You must see that! I could do nothing else. I restored the family fortunes, was able to travel, to do good. Yet how I suffered, how revolting, how loathsome to me were his embraces - though I will be fair to him - he had fought nobly in his day. There were moments - terrible moments - but I was kept up by the thought that from day to day the old man might die, that then I would begin to live as I liked, to give myself to the man I adore - be happy. There is such a man, Voldemar, indeed there is!"

The pretty lady flutters her fan more violently. Her face takes a lachrymose expression. She goes on:

"But at last the old man died. He left me something. I was free as a bird of the air. Now is the moment for me to be happy, isn't it, Voldemar? Happiness comes tapping at my window, I had only to let it in - but - Voldemar, listen, I implore you! Now is the time for me to give myself to the man I love, to become the partner of his life, to help, to uphold his ideals, to be happy - to find rest - but - how ignoble, repulsive, and senseless all our life is! How mean it all is, Voldemar. I am wretched, wretched, wretched! Again there is an obstacle in my path! Again I feel that my happiness is far, far away! Ah, what anguish! - if only you knew what anguish!"

"But what - what stands in your way? I implore you tell me! What is it?"

"Another old general, very well off-"

The broken fan conceals the pretty little face. The author props on his fist his thought - heavy brow and ponders with the air of a master in psychology. The engine is whistling and hissing while the window curtains flush red with the glow of the setting sun.

A CLASSICAL STUDENT

Before setting off for his examination in Greek, Vanya kissed all the holy images. His stomach felt as though it were upside down; there was a chill at his heart, while the heart itself throbbed and stood still with terror before the unknown. What would he get that day? A three or a two? Six times he went to his mother for her blessing, and, as he went out, asked his aunt to pray for him. On the way to school he gave a beggar two kopecks, in the hope that those two kopecks would atone for his ignorance, and that, please God, he would not get the numerals with those awful forties and eighties.

He came back from the high school late, between four and five. He came in, and noiselessly lay down on his bed. His thin face was pale. There were dark rings round his red eyes.

"Well, how did you get on? How were you marked?" asked his mother, going to his bedside.

Vanya blinked, twisted his mouth, and burst into tears. His mother turned pale, let her mouth fall open, and clasped her hands. The breeches she was mending dropped out of her hands.

"What are you crying for? You've failed, then?" she asked.

"I am plucked. . . . I got a two."

"I knew it would be so! I had a presentiment of it," said his mother. "Merciful God! How is it you have not passed? What is the reason of it? What subject have you failed in?"

"In Greek. . . . Mother, I . . . They asked me the future of phero, and I . . . instead of saying oisomai said opsomai. Then . . . then there isn't an accent, if the last syllable is long, and I . . . I got flustered. . . . I forgot that the alpha was long in it. . . . I went and put in the accent. Then Artaxerxov told me to give the list of the enclitic particles. . . . I did, and I accidentally mixed in a pronoun . . . and made a mistake . . . and so he gave me a two. . . . I am a miserable person. . . . I was working all night. . . I've been getting up at four o'clock all this week . . . ."

"No, it's not you but I who am miserable, you wretched boy! It's I that am miserable! You've worn me to a threadpaper, you Herod, you torment, you bane of my life! I pay for you, you good-for-nothing rubbish; I've bent my back toiling for you, I'm worried to death, and, I may say, I am unhappy, and what do you care? How do you work?"

"I . . . I do work. All night. . . . You've seen it yourself."

"I prayed to God to take me, but He won't take me, a sinful woman. . . . You torment! Other people have children like everyone else, and I've one only and no sense, no comfort out of him. Beat you? I'd beat you, but where am I to find the strength? Mother of God, where am I to find the strength?"

The mamma hid her face in the folds of her blouse and broke into sobs. Vanya wriggled with anguish and pressed his forehead against the wall. The aunt came in.

"So that's how it is. . . . Just what I expected," she said, at once guessing what was wrong, turning pale and clasping her hands. "I've been depressed all the morning. . . . There's trouble coming, I thought . . . and here it's come. . . ."

"The villain, the torment!"

"Why are you swearing at him?" cried the aunt, nervously pulling her coffee-coloured kerchief off her head and turning upon the mother. "It's not his fault! It's your fault! You are to blame! Why did you send him to that high school? You are a fine lady! You want to be a lady? A-a-ah! I dare say, as though you'll turn into gentry! But if you had sent him, as I told you, into business . . . to an office, like my Kuzya . . . here is Kuzya getting five hundred a year. . . . Five hundred roubles is worth having, isn't it? And you are wearing yourself out, and wearing the boy out with this studying, plague take it! He is thin, he coughs. . . just look at him! He's thirteen, and he looks no more than ten."

"No, Nastenka, no, my dear! I haven't thrashed him enough, the torment! He ought to have been thrashed, that's what it is! Ugh . . . Jesuit, Mahomet, torment!" she shook her fist at her son. "You want a flogging, but I haven't the strength. They told me years ago when he was little, 'Whip him, whip him!' I didn't heed them, sinful woman as I am. And now I am suffering for it. You wait a bit! I'll flay you! Wait a bit...."

The mamma shook her wet fist, and went weeping into her lodger's room. The lodger, Yevtihy Kuzmitch Kuporossov, was sitting at his table, reading "Dancing Self-taught." Yevtihy Kuzmitch was a man of intelligence and education. He spoke through his nose, washed with a soap the smell of which made everyone in the house sneeze, ate meat on fast days, and was on the look-out for a bride of refined education, and so was considered the cleverest of the lodgers. He sang tenor.

"My good friend," began the mamma, dissolving into tears. "If you would have the generosity - thrash my boy for me.... Do me the favour! He's failed in his examination, the nuisance of a boy! Would you believe it, he's failed! I can't punish him, through the weakness of my ill-health.... Thrash him for me, if you would be so obliging and considerate, Yevtihy Kuzmitch! Have regard for a sick woman!"

Kuporossov frowned and heaved a deep sigh through his nose. He thought a little, drummed on the table with his fingers, and sighing once more, went to Vanya.

"You are being taught, so to say," he began, "being educated, being given a chance, you revolting young person! Why have you done it?"

He talked for a long time, made a regular speech. He alluded to science, to light, and to darkness.

"Yes, young person."

When he had finished his speech, he took off his belt and took Vanya by the hand.

"It's the only way to deal with you," he said. Vanya knelt down submissively and thrust his head between the lodger's knees. His prominent pink ears moved up and down against the lodger's new serge trousers, with brown stripes on the outer seams.

Vanya did not utter a single sound. At the family council in the evening, it was decided to send him into business.

THE DEATH OF A GOVERNMENT CLERK

One fine evening, a no less fine government clerk called Ivan Dmitritch Tchervyakov was sitting in the second row of the stalls, gazing through an opera glass at the Cloches de Corneville. He gazed and felt at the acme of bliss. But suddenly. . . . In stories one so often meets with this "But suddenly." The authors are right: life is so full of surprises! But suddenly his face puckered up, his eyes disappeared, his breathing was arrested . . . he took the opera glass from his eyes, bent over and . . . "Aptchee!!" he sneezed as you perceive. It is not reprehensible for anyone to sneeze anywhere. Peasants sneeze and so do police superintendents, and sometimes even privy councillors. All men sneeze. Tchervyakov was not in the least confused, he wiped his face with his handkerchief, and like a polite man, looked round to see whether he had disturbed anyone by his sneezing. But then he was overcome with confusion. He saw that an old gentleman sitting in front of him in the first row of the stalls was carefully wiping his bald head and his neck with his glove and muttering something to himself. In the old gentleman, Tchervyakov recognised Brizzhalov, a civilian general serving in the Department of Transport.

"I have spattered him," thought Tchervyakov, "he is not the head of my department, but still it is awkward. I must apologise."

Tchervyakov gave a cough, bent his whole person forward, and whispered in the general's ear.

"Pardon, your Excellency, I spattered you accidentally. . . ."

"Never mind, never mind."

"For goodness sake excuse me, I . . . I did not mean to."

"Oh, please, sit down! let me listen!"

Tchervyakov was embarrassed, he smiled stupidly and fell to gazing at the stage. He gazed at it but was no longer feeling bliss. He began to be troubled by uneasiness. In the interval, he went up to Brizzhalov, walked beside him, and overcoming his shyness, muttered:

"I spattered you, your Excellency, forgive me . . . you see . . . I didn't do it to . . . ."

"Oh, that's enough . . . I'd forgotten it, and you keep on about it!" said the general, moving his lower lip impatiently.

"He has forgotten, but there is a fiendish light in his eye," thought Tchervyakov, looking suspiciously at the general. "And he doesn't want to talk. I ought to explain to him . . . that I really didn't intend . . . that it is the law of nature or else he will think I meant to spit on him. He doesn't think so now, but he will think so later!"

On getting home, Tchervyakov told his wife of his breach of good manners. It struck him that his wife took too frivolous a view of the incident; she was a little frightened, but when she learned that Brizzhalov was in a different department, she was reassured.

"Still, you had better go and apologise," she said, "or he will think you don't know how to behave in public."

"That's just it! I did apologise, but he took it somehow queerly . . . he didn't say a word of sense. There wasn't time to talk properly."

Next day Tchervyakov put on a new uniform, had his hair cut and went to Brizzhalov's to explain; going into the general's reception room he saw there a number of petitioners and among them the general himself, who was beginning to interview them. After questioning several petitioners the general raised his eyes and looked at Tchervyakov.

"Yesterday at the Arcadia, if you recollect, your Excellency," the latter began, "I sneezed and . . . accidentally spattered . . . Exc. . . ."

"What nonsense. . . . It's beyond anything! What can I do for you," said the general addressing the next petitioner.

"He won't speak," thought Tchervyakov, turning pale; "that means that he is angry. . . . No, it can't be left like this. . . . I will explain to him."

When the general had finished his conversation with the last of the petitioners and was turning towards his inner apartments, Tchervyakov took a step towards him and muttered:

"Your Excellency! If I venture to trouble your Excellency, it is simply from a feeling I may say of regret! . . . It was not intentional if you will graciously believe me."

The general made a lachrymose face, and waved his hand.

"Why, you are simply making fun of me, sir," he said as he closed the door behind him.

"Where's the making fun in it?" thought Tchervyakov, "there is nothing of the sort! He is a general, but he can't understand. If that is how it is I am not going to apologise to that fanfaron any more! The devil take him. I'll write a letter to him, but I won't go. By Jove, I won't."

So thought Tchervyakov as he walked home; he did not write a letter to the general, he pondered and pondered and could not make up that letter. He had to go next day to explain in person.

"I ventured to disturb your Excellency yesterday," he muttered, when the general lifted enquiring eyes upon him, "not to make fun as you were pleased to say. I was apologising for having spattered you in sneezing. . . . And I did not dream of making fun of you. Should I dare to make fun of you, if we should take to making fun, then there would be no respect for persons, there would be. . . ."

"Be off!" yelled the general, turning suddenly purple, and shaking all over.

"What?" asked Tchervyakov, in a whisper turning numb with horror.

"Be off!" repeated the general, stamping.

Something seemed to give way in Tchervyakov's stomach. Seeing nothing and hearing nothing he reeled to the door, went out into the street, and went staggering along. . . . Reaching home mechanically, without taking off his uniform, he lay down on the sofa and died.

THE TROUSSEAU

I have seen a great many houses in my time, little and big, new and old, built of stone and of wood, but of one house I have kept a very vivid memory. It was, properly speaking, rather a cottage than a house - a tiny cottage of one story, with three windows, looking extraordinarily like a little old hunchback woman with a cap on. Its white stucco walls, its tiled roof, and dilapidated chimney, were all drowned in a perfect sea of green. The cottage was lost to sight among the mulberry-trees, acacias, and poplars planted by the grandfathers and great-grandfathers of its present occupants. And yet it is a town house. Its wide courtyard stands in a row with other similar green courtyards, and forms part of a street. Nothing ever drives down that street, and very few persons are ever seen walking through it.

The shutters of the little house are always closed; its occupants do not care for sunlight-the light is no use to them. The windows are never opened, for they are not fond of fresh air. People who spend their lives in the midst of acacias, mulberries, and nettles have no passion for nature. It is only to the summer visitor that God has vouchsafed an eye for the beauties of nature. The rest of mankind remain steeped in profound ignorance of the existence of such beauties. People never prize what they have always had in abundance. "What we have, we do not treasure," and what's more we do not even love it.

The little house stands in an earthly paradise of green trees with happy birds nesting in them. But inside . . . alas . . . ! In summer, it is close and stifling within; in winter, hot as a Turkish bath, not one breath of air, and the dreariness! . . .

The first time I visited the little house was many years ago on business. I brought a message from the Colonel who was the owner of the house to his wife and daughter. That first visit I remember very distinctly. It would be impossible, indeed, to forget it.

Imagine a limp little woman of forty, gazing at you with alarm and astonishment while you walk from the passage into the parlour. You are a stranger, a visitor, "a young man"; that's enough to reduce her to a state of terror and bewilderment. Though you have no dagger, axe, or revolver in your hand, and though you smile affably, you are met with alarm.

"Whom have I the honour and pleasure of addressing?" the little lady asks in a trembling voice.

I introduced myself and explained why I had come. The alarm and amazement were at once succeeded by a shrill, joyful "Ach!" and she turned her eyes upwards to the ceiling. This "Ach!" was caught up like an echo and repeated from the hall to the parlour, from the parlour to the kitchen, and so on down to the cellar. Soon the whole house was resounding with "Ach!" in various voices.

Five minutes later I was sitting on a big, soft, warm lounge in the drawing-room listening to the "Ach!" echoing all down the street. There was a smell of moth powder, and of goatskin shoes, a pair of which lay on a chair beside me wrapped in a handkerchief. In the windows were geraniums, and muslin curtains, and on the curtains were torpid flies. On the wall hung the portrait of some bishop, painted in oils, with the glass broken at one corner, and next to the bishop a row of ancestors with lemon-coloured faces of a gipsy type. On the table lay a thimble, a reel of cotton, and a half-knitted stocking, and paper patterns and a black blouse, tacked together, were lying on the floor. In the next room two alarmed and fluttered old women were hurriedly picking up similar patterns and pieces of tailor's chalk from the floor.

"You must, please, excuse us; we are dreadfully untidy," said the little lady.

While she talked to me, she stole embarrassed glances towards the other room where the patterns were still being picked up. The door, too, seemed embarrassed, opening an inch or two and then shutting again.

"What's the matter?" said the little lady, addressing the door.

"Où est mon cravatte lequel mon père m'avait envoyé de Koursk?" asked a female voice at the door.

"Ah, est-ce que, Marie . . . que. . . Really, it's impossible. . . . Nous avons donc chez nous un homme peu connu de nous. Ask Lukerya."

"How well we speak French, though!" I read in the eyes of the little lady, who was flushing with pleasure.

Soon afterwards the door opened and I saw a tall, thin girl of nineteen, in a long muslin dress with a gilt belt from which, I remember, hung a mother-of-pearl fan. She came in, dropped a curtsy, and flushed crimson. Her long nose, which was slightly pitted with smallpox, turned red first, and then the flush passed up to her eyes and her forehead.

"My daughter," chanted the little lady, "and, Manetchka, this is a young gentleman who has come," etc.

I was introduced, and expressed my surprise at the number of paper patterns. Mother and daughter dropped their eyes.

"We had a fair here at Ascension," said the mother; "we always buy materials at the fair, and then it keeps us busy with sewing till the next year's fair comes around again. We never put things out to be made. My husband's pay is not very ample, and we are not able to permit ourselves luxuries. So we have to make up everything ourselves."

"But who will ever wear such a number of things? There are only two of you?"

"Oh . . . as though we were thinking of wearing them! They are not to be worn; they are for the trousseau!"

"Ah, mamam, what are you saying?" said the daughter, and she crimsoned again. "Our visitor might suppose it was true. I don't intend to be married. Never!"

She said this, but at the very word "married" her eyes glowed.

Tea, biscuits, butter, and jam were brought in, followed by raspberries and cream. At seven o'clock, we had supper, consisting of six courses, and while we were at supper I heard a loud yawn from the next room. I looked with surprise towards the door: it was a yawn that could only come from a man.

"That's my husband's brother, Yegor Semyonitch," the little lady explained, noticing my surprise. "He's been living with us for the last year. Please excuse him; he cannot come in to see you. He is such an unsociable person, he is shy with strangers. He is going into a monastery. He was unfairly treated in the service, and the disappointment has preyed on his mind."

After supper the little lady showed the vestment which Yegor Semyonitch was embroidering with his own hands as an offering for the Church. Manetchka threw off her shyness for a moment and showed me the tobacco-pouch she was embroidering for her father. When I pretended to be greatly struck by her work, she flushed crimson and whispered something in her mother's ear. The latter beamed all over, and invited me to go with her to the store-room. There I was shown five large trunks, and a number of smaller trunks and boxes.

"This is her trousseau," her mother whispered; "we made it all ourselves."

After looking at these forbidding trunks I took leave of my hospitable hostesses. They made me promise to come and see them again someday.

It happened that I was able to keep this promise. Seven years after my first visit, I was sent down to the little town to give expert evidence in a case that was being tried there.

As I entered the little house I heard the same "Ach!" echo through it. They recognised me at once. . . . Well they might! My first visit had been an event in their lives, and when events are few they are long remembered.

I walked into the drawing-room: the mother, who had grown stouter and was already getting grey, was creeping about on the floor, cutting out some blue material. The daughter was sitting on the sofa, embroidering.

There was the same smell of moth powder; there were the same patterns, the same portrait with the broken glass. But yet there was a change. Beside the portrait of the bishop hung a portrait of the

Colonel, and the ladies were in mourning. The Colonel's death had occurred a week after his promotion to be a general.

Reminiscences began. . . . The widow shed tears.

"We have had a terrible loss," she said. "My husband, you know, is dead. We are alone in the world now, and have no one but ourselves to look to. Yegor Semyonitch is alive, but I have no good news to tell of him. They would not have him in the monastery on account of - of intoxicating beverages. And now in his disappointment he drinks more than ever. I am thinking of going to the Marshal of Nobility to lodge a complaint. Would you believe it, he has more than once broken open the trunks and . . . taken Manetchka's trousseau and given it to beggars. He has taken everything out of two of the trunks! If he goes on like this, my Manetchka will be left without a trousseau at all."

"What are you saying, mamam?" said Manetchka, embarrassed. "Our visitor might suppose . . . there's no knowing what he might suppose. . . . I shall never-never marry."

Manetchka cast her eyes up to the ceiling with a look of hope and aspiration, evidently not for a moment believing what she said.

A little bald-headed masculine figure in a brown coat and goloshes instead of boots darted like a mouse across the passage and disappeared. "Yegor Semyonitch, I suppose," I thought.

I looked at the mother and daughter together. They both looked much older and terribly changed. The mother's hair was silvered, but the daughter was so faded and withered that her mother might have been taken for her elder sister, not more than five years her senior.

"I have made up my mind to go to the Marshal," the mother said to me, forgetting she had told me this already. "I mean to make a complaint. Yegor Semyonitch lays his hands on everything we make, and offers it up for the sake of his soul. My Manetchka is left without a trousseau."

Manetchka flushed again, but this time she said nothing.

"We have to make them all over again. And God knows we are not so well off. We are all alone in the world now."

"We are alone in the world," repeated Manetchka.

A year ago fate brought me once more to the little house.

Walking into the drawing-room, I saw the old lady. Dressed all in black with heavy crape pleureuses, she was sitting on the sofa sewing. Beside her sat the little old man in the brown coat and the goloshes instead of boots. On seeing me, he jumped up and ran out of the room.

In response to my greeting, the old lady smiled and said:

"Je suis charmée de vous revoir, monsieur."

"What are you making?" I asked, a little later.

"It's a blouse. When it's finished I shall take it to the priest's to be put away, or else Yegor Semyonitch would carry it off. I store everything at the priest's now," she added in a whisper.

And looking at the portrait of her daughter which stood before her on the table, she sighed and said:

"We are all alone in the world."

And where was the daughter? Where was Manetchka? I did not ask. I did not dare to ask the old mother dressed in her new deep mourning. And while I was in the room, and when I got up to go, no Manetchka came out to greet me. I did not hear her voice, nor her soft, timid footstep...

I understood, and my heart was heavy.

A DAUGHTER OF ALBION

A fine carriage with rubber tyres, a fat coachman, and velvet on the seats, rolled up to the house of a landowner called Gryabov. Fyodor Andreitch Otsov, the district Marshal of Nobility, jumped out of the carriage. A drowsy footman met him in the hall.

"Are the family at home?" asked the Marshal.

"No, sir. The mistress and the children are gone out paying visits, while the master and mademoiselle are catching fish. Fishing all the morning, sir."

Otsov stood a little, thought a little, and then went to the river to look for Gryabov. Going down to the river he found him a mile and a half from the house. Looking down from the steep bank and catching sight of Gryabov, Otsov gushed with laughter. . . . Gryabov, a large stout man, with a very big head, was sitting on the sand, angling, with his legs tucked under him like a Turk. His hat was on the back of his head and his cravat had slipped on one side. Beside him stood a tall thin Englishwoman, with prominent eyes like a crab's, and a big bird-like nose more like a hook than a nose. She was dressed in a white muslin gown through which her scraggy yellow shoulders were very distinctly apparent. On her gold belt hung a little gold watch. She too was angling. The stillness of the grave reigned about them both. Both were motionless, as the river upon which their floats were swimming.

"A desperate passion, but deadly dull!" laughed Otsov. "Good-day, Ivan Kuzmitch."

"Ah . . . is that you?" asked Gryabov, not taking his eyes off the water. "Have you come?"

"As you see . . . . And you are still taken up with your crazy nonsense! Not given it up yet?"

"The devil's in it. . . . I begin in the morning and fish all day. . . . The fishing is not up to much to-day. I've caught nothing and this dummy hasn't either. We sit on and on and not a devil of a fish! I could scream!"

"Well, chuck it up then. Let's go and have some vodka!"

"Wait a little, maybe we shall catch something. Towards evening the fish bite better . . . . I've been sitting here, my boy, ever since the morning! I can't tell you how fearfully boring it is. It was the devil drove me to take to this fishing! I know that it is rotten idiocy for me to sit here. I sit here like some scoundrel, like a convict, and I stare at the water like a fool. I ought to go to the haymaking, but here I sit catching fish. Yesterday His Holiness held a service at Haponyevo, but I didn't go. I spent the day here with this . . . with this she-devil."

"But . . . have you taken leave of your senses?" asked Otsov, glancing in embarrassment at the Englishwoman. "Using such language before a lady and she . . . ."

"Oh, confound her, it doesn't matter, she doesn't understand a syllable of Russian, whether you praise her or blame her, it is all the same to her! Just look at her nose! Her nose alone is enough to make one faint. We sit here for whole days together and not a single word! She stands like a stuffed image and rolls the whites of her eyes at the water."

The Englishwoman gave a yawn, put a new worm on, and dropped the hook into the water.

"I wonder at her not a little," Gryabov went on, "the great stupid has been living in Russia for ten years and not a word of Russian! . . . Any little aristocrat among us goes to them and learns to babble away in their lingo, while they . . . there's no making them out. Just look at her nose, do look at her nose!"

"Come, drop it . . . it's uncomfortable. Why attack a woman?"

"She's not a woman, but a maiden lady. . . . I bet she's dreaming of suitors. The ugly doll. And she smells of something decaying . . . . I've got a loathing for her, my boy! I can't look at her with indifference. When she turns her ugly eyes on me it sends a twinge all through me as though I had knocked my elbow on the parapet. She likes fishing too. Watch her: she fishes as though it were a holy rite! She looks upon everything with disdain . . . . She stands there, the wretch, and is conscious that she is a human being, and that therefore she is the monarch of nature. And do you know what her name is? Wilka Charlesovna Fyce! Tfoo! There is no getting it out!"

The Englishwoman, hearing her name, deliberately turned her nose in Gryabov's direction and scanned him with a disdainful glance; she raised her eyes from Gryabov to Otsov and steeped him in disdain. And all this in silence, with dignity and deliberation.

"Did you see?" said Gryabov chuckling. "As though to say 'take that.' Ah, you monster! It's only for the children's sake that I keep that triton. If it weren't for the children, I wouldn't let her come within ten miles of my estate. . . . She has got a nose like a hawk's . . . and her figure! That doll makes me think of a long nail, so I could take her, and knock her into the ground, you know. Stay, I believe I have got a bite. . . ."

Gryabov jumped up and raised his rod. The line drew taut. . . . Gryabov tugged again, but could not pull out the hook.

"It has caught," he said, frowning, "on a stone I expect . . . damnation take it . . . ."

There was a look of distress on Gryabov's face. Sighing, moving uneasily, and muttering oaths, he began tugging at the line.

"What a pity; I shall have to go into the water."

"Oh, chuck it!"

"I can't. . . . There's always good fishing in the evening. . . . What a nuisance. Lord, forgive us, I shall have to wade into the water, I must! And if only you knew, I have no inclination to undress. I shall have to get rid of the Englishwoman. . . . It's awkward to undress before her. After all, she is a lady, you know!"

Gryabov flung off his hat, and his cravat.

"Meess . . . er, er . . . ." he said, addressing the Englishwoman, "Meess Fyce, je voo pree . . . ? Well, what am I to say to her? How am I to tell you so that you can understand? I say . . . over there! Go away over there! Do you hear?"

Miss Fyce enveloped Gryabov in disdain, and uttered a nasal sound.

"What? Don't you understand? Go away from here, I tell you! I must undress, you devil's doll! Go over there! Over there!"

Gryabov pulled the lady by her sleeve, pointed her towards the bushes, and made as though he would sit down, as much as to say: Go behind the bushes and hide yourself there. . . . The Englishwoman, moving her eyebrows vigorously, uttered rapidly a long sentence in English. The gentlemen gushed with laughter.

"It's the first time in my life I've heard her voice. There's no denying, it is a voice! She does not understand! Well, what am I to do with her?"

"Chuck it, let's go and have a drink of vodka!"

"I can't. Now's the time to fish, the evening. . . . It's evening . . . . Come, what would you have me do? It is a nuisance! I shall have to undress before her. . . ."

Gryabov flung off his coat and his waistcoat and sat on the sand to take off his boots.

"I say, Ivan Kuzmitch," said the marshal, chuckling behind his hand. "It's really outrageous, an insult."

"Nobody asks her not to understand! It's a lesson for these foreigners!"

Gryabov took off his boots and his trousers, flung off his undergarments and remained in the costume of Adam. Otsov held his sides, he turned crimson both from laughter and embarrassment. The Englishwoman twitched her brows and blinked . . . . A haughty, disdainful smile passed over her yellow face.

"I must cool off," said Gryabov, slapping himself on the ribs. "Tell me if you please, Fyodor Andreitch, why I have a rash on my chest every summer."

"Oh, do get into the water quickly or cover yourself with something, you beast."

"And if only she were confused, the nasty thing," said Gryabov, crossing himself as he waded into the water. "Brrrr . . . the water's cold. . . . Look how she moves her eyebrows! She doesn't go away . . . she is far above the crowd! He, he, he . . . . and she doesn't reckon us as human beings."

Wading knee deep in the water and drawing his huge figure up to its full height, he gave a wink and said:

"This isn't England, you see!"

Miss Fyce coolly put on another worm, gave a yawn, and dropped the hook in. Otsov turned away, Gryabov released his hook, ducked into the water and, spluttering, waded out. Two minutes later he was sitting on the sand and angling as before.

AN INQUIRY

It was midday. Voldyrev, a tall, thick-set country gentleman with a cropped head and prominent eyes, took off his overcoat, mopped his brow with his silk handkerchief, and somewhat diffidently went into the government office. There they were scratching away....

"Where can I make an inquiry here?" he said, addressing a porter who was bringing a trayful of glasses from the furthest recesses of the office. "I have to make an inquiry here and to take a copy of a resolution of the Council."

"That way please! To that one sitting near the window!" said the porter, indicating with the tray the furthest window. Voldyrev coughed and went towards the window; there, at a green table spotted like typhus, was sitting a young man with his hair standing up in four tufts on his head, with a long pimply nose, and a long faded uniform. He was writing, thrusting his long nose into the papers. A fly was walking about near his right nostril, and he was continually stretching out his lower lip and blowing under his nose, which gave his face an extremely care-worn expression.

"May I make an inquiry about my case here . . . of you? My name is Voldyrev. and, by the way, I have to take a copy of the resolution of the Council of the second of March."

The clerk dipped his pen in the ink and looked to see if he had got too much on it. Having satisfied himself that the pen would not make a blot, he began scribbling away. His lip was thrust out, but it was no longer necessary to blow: the fly had settled on his ear.

"Can I make an inquiry here?" Voldyrev repeated a minute later, "my name is Voldyrev, I am a landowner...."

"Ivan Alexeitch!" the clerk shouted into the air as though he had not observed Voldyrev, "will you tell the merchant Yalikov when he comes to sign the copy of the complaint lodged with the police! I've told him a thousand times!"

"I have come in reference to my lawsuit with the heirs of Princess Gugulin," muttered Voldyrev. "The case is well known. I earnestly beg you to attend to me."

Still failing to observe Voldyrev, the clerk caught the fly on his lip, looked at it attentively and flung it away. The country gentleman coughed and blew his nose loudly on his checked pocket handkerchief. But this was no use either. He was still unheard. The silence lasted for two minutes. Voldyrev took a rouble note from his pocket and laid it on an open book before the clerk. The clerk wrinkled up his forehead, drew the book towards him with an anxious air and closed it.

"A little inquiry. . . . I want only to find out on what grounds the heirs of Princess Gugulin. . . . May I trouble you?"

The clerk, absorbed in his own thoughts, got up and, scratching his elbow, went to a cupboard for something. Returning a minute later to his table he became absorbed in the book again: another rouble note was lying upon it.

"I will trouble you for one minute only. . . . I have only to make an inquiry.

The clerk did not hear, he had begun copying something.

Voldyrev frowned and looked hopelessly at the whole scribbling brotherhood.

"They write!" he thought, sighing. "They write, the devil take them entirely!"

He walked away from the table and stopped in the middle of the room, his hands hanging hopelessly at his sides. The porter, passing again with glasses, probably noticed the helpless expression of his face, for he went close up to him and asked him in a low voice:

"Well? Have you inquired?"

"I've inquired, but he wouldn't speak to me."

"You give him three roubles," whispered the porter.

"I've given him two already."

"Give him another."

Voldyrev went back to the table and laid a green note on the open book.

The clerk drew the book towards him again and began turning over the leaves, and all at once, as though by chance, lifted his eyes to Voldyrev. His nose began to shine, turned red, and wrinkled up in a grin.

"Ah . . . what do you want?" he asked.

"I want to make an inquiry in reference to my case. . . . My name is Voldyrev."

"With pleasure! The Gugulin case, isn't it? Very good. What is it then exactly?"

Voldyrev explained his business.

The clerk became as lively as though he were whirled round by a hurricane. He gave the necessary information, arranged for a copy to be made, gave the petitioner a chair, and all in one instant. He even spoke about the weather and asked after the harvest. And when Voldyrev went away he accompanied him down the stairs, smiling affably and respectfully, and looking as though he were ready any minute to fall on his face before the gentleman. Voldyrev for some reason felt uncomfortable, and in obedience to some inward impulse he took a rouble out of his pocket and gave it to the clerk. And the latter kept bowing and smiling, and took the rouble like a conjuror, so that it seemed to flash through the air.

"Well, what people!" thought the country gentleman as he went out into the street, and he stopped and mopped his brow with his handkerchief.

FAT AND THIN

Two friends - one a fat man and the other a thin man - met at the Nikolaevsky station. The fat man had just dined in the station and his greasy lips shone like ripe cherries. He smelt of sherry and fleur d'orange. The thin man had just slipped out of the train and was laden with portmanteaus, bundles, and bandboxes. He smelt of ham and coffee grounds. A thin woman with a long chin, his wife, and a tall schoolboy with one eye screwed up came into view behind his back.

"Porfiry," cried the fat man on seeing the thin man. "Is it you? My dear fellow! How many summers, how many winters!"

"Holy saints!" cried the thin man in amazement. "Misha! The friend of my childhood! Where have you dropped from?"

The friends kissed each other three times, and gazed at each other with eyes full of tears. Both were agreeably astounded.

"My dear boy!" began the thin man after the kissing. "This is unexpected! This is a surprise! Come have a good look at me! Just as handsome as I used to be! Just as great a darling and a dandy! Good gracious me! Well, and how are you? Made your fortune? Married? I am married as you see. . . . This is my wife Luise, her maiden name was Vantsenbach . . . of the Lutheran persuasion. . . . And this is my son Nafanail, a schoolboy in the third class. This is the friend of my childhood, Nafanya. We were boys at school together!"

Nafanail thought a little and took off his cap.

"We were boys at school together," the thin man went on. "Do you remember how they used to tease you? You were nicknamed Herostratus because you burned a hole in a schoolbook with a cigarette, and I was nicknamed Ephialtes because I was fond of telling tales. Ho-ho! . . . we were children! . . . Don't be shy, Nafanya. Go nearer to him. And this is my wife, her maiden name was Vantsenbach, of the Lutheran persuasion. . . ."

Nafanail thought a little and took refuge behind his father's back.

"Well, how are you doing my friend?" the fat man asked, looking enthusiastically at his friend. "Are you in the service? What grade have you reached?"

"I am, dear boy! I have been a collegiate assessor for the last two years and I have the Stanislav. The salary is poor, but that's no great matter! The wife gives music lessons, and I go in for carving wooden cigarette cases in a private way. Capital cigarette cases! I sell them for a rouble each. If anyone takes ten or more I make a reduction of course. We get along somehow. I served as a clerk, you know, and now I have been transferred here as a head clerk in the same department. I am going to serve here. And what about you? I bet you are a civil councillor by now? Eh?"

"No dear boy, go higher than that," said the fat man. "I have risen to privy councillor already . . . I have two stars."

The thin man turned pale and rigid all at once, but soon his face twisted in all directions in the broadest smile; it seemed as though sparks were flashing from his face and eyes. He squirmed, he doubled together, crumpled up. . . . His portmanteaus, bundles and cardboard boxes seemed to shrink and crumple up too. . . . His wife's long chin grew longer still; Nafanail drew himself up to attention and fastened all the buttons of his uniform.

"Your Excellency, I . . . delighted! The friend, one may say, of childhood and to have turned into such a great man! He-he!"

"Come, come!" the fat man frowned. "What's this tone for? You and I were friends as boys, and there is no need of this official obsequiousness!"

"Merciful heavens, your Excellency! What are you saying. . . ?" sniggered the thin man, wriggling more than ever. "Your Excellency's gracious attention is like refreshing manna. . . . This, your Excellency, is my son Nafanail, . . . my wife Luise, a Lutheran in a certain sense."

The fat man was about to make some protest, but the face of the thin man wore an expression of such reverence, sugariness, and mawkish respectfulness that the privy councillor was sickened. He turned away from the thin man, giving him his hand at parting.

The thin man pressed three fingers, bowed his whole body and sniggered like a Chinaman: "He-he-he!" His wife smiled. Nafanail scraped with his foot and dropped his cap. All three were agreeably overwhelmed.

A TRAGIC ACTOR

It was the benefit night of Fenogenov, the tragic actor. They were acting "Prince Serebryany." The tragedian himself was playing Vyazemsky; Limonadov, the stage manager, was playing Morozov; Madame Beobahtov, Elena. The performance was a grand success. The tragedian accomplished wonders indeed. When he was carrying off Elena, he held her in one hand above his head as he dashed across the stage. He shouted, hissed, banged with his feet, tore his coat across his chest. When he refused to fight Morozov, he trembled all over as nobody ever trembles in reality, and gasped loudly. The theatre shook with applause. There were endless calls. Fenogenov was presented with a silver cigarette-case and a bouquet tied with long ribbons. The ladies waved their handkerchiefs and urged their men to applaud, many shed tears. . . . But the one who was the most enthusiastic and most excited was Masha, daughter of Sidoretsky the police captain. She was sitting in the first row of the stalls beside her papa; she was ecstatic and could not take her eyes off the stage even between the acts. Her delicate little hands and feet were quivering, her eyes were full of tears, her cheeks turned paler and paler. And no wonder - she was at the theatre for the first time in her life.

"How well they act! how splendidly!" she said to her papa the police captain, every time the curtain fell. How good Fenogenov is!"

And if her papa had been capable of reading faces he would have read on his daughter's pale little countenance a rapture that was almost anguish. She was overcome by the acting, by the play, by the surroundings. When the regimental band began playing between the acts, she closed her eyes, exhausted.

"Papa!" she said to the police captain during the last interval, "go behind the scenes and ask them all to dinner to-morrow!"

The police captain went behind the scenes, praised them for all their fine acting, and complimented Madame Beobahtov.

"Your lovely face demands a canvas, and I only wish I could wield the brush!"

And with a scrape, he thereupon invited the company to dinner.

"All except the fair sex," he whispered. "I don't want the actresses, for I have a daughter."

Next day the actors dined at the police captain's. Only three turned up, the manager Limonadov, the tragedian Fenogenov, and the comic man Vodolazov; the others sent excuses. The dinner was a dull affair. Limonadov kept telling the police captain how much he respected him, and how highly he thought of all persons in authority; Vodolazov mimicked drunken merchants and Armenians; and Fenogenov (on his passport his name was Knish), a tall, stout Little Russian with black eyes and frowning brow, declaimed "At the portals of the great," and "To be or not to be." Limonadov, with tears in his eyes, described his interview with the former Governor, General Kanyutchin. The police captain listened, was bored, and smiled affably. He was well satisfied, although Limonadov smelt strongly of burnt feathers, and Fenogenov was wearing a hired dress coat and boots trodden down at heel. They pleased his daughter and made her lively, and that was enough for him. And Masha never took her eyes off the actors. She had never before seen such clever, exceptional people!

In the evening the police captain and Masha were at the theatre again. A week later the actors dined at the police captain's again, and after that came almost every day either to dinner or supper. Masha became more and more devoted to the theatre, and went there every evening.

She fell in love with the tragedian. One fine morning, when the police captain had gone to meet the bishop, Masha ran away with Limonadov's company and married her hero on the way. After celebrating the wedding, the actors composed a long and touching letter and sent it to the police captain.

It was the work of their combined efforts.

"Bring out the motive, the motive!" Limonadov kept saying as he dictated to the comic man. "Lay on the respect. . . . These official chaps like it. Add something of a sort . . . to draw a tear."

The answer to this letter was most discomforting. The police captain disowned his daughter for marrying, as he said, "a stupid, idle Little Russian with no fixed home or occupation."

And the day after this answer was received Masha was writing to her father.

"Papa, he beats me! Forgive us!"

He had beaten her, beaten her behind the scenes, in the presence of Limonadov, the washerwoman, and two lighting men. He remembered how, four days before the wedding, he was sitting in the London Tavern with the whole company, and all were talking about Masha. The company were advising him to "chance it," and Limonadov, with tears in his eyes urged: "It would be stupid and irrational to let slip such an opportunity! Why, for a sum like that one would go to Siberia, let alone getting married! When you marry and have a theatre of your own, take me into your company. I shan't be master then, you'll be master."

Fenogenov remembered it, and muttered with clenched fists:

"If he doesn't send money I'll smash her! I won't let myself be made a fool of, damn my soul!"

At one provincial town the company tried to give Masha the slip, but Masha found out, ran to the station, and got there when the second bell had rung and the actors had all taken their seats.

"I've been shamefully treated by your father," said the tragedian; "all is over between us!"

And though the carriage was full of people, she went down on her knees and held out her hands, imploring him:

"I love you! Don't drive me away, Kondraty Ivanovitch," she besought him. "I can't live without you!"

They listened to her entreaties, and after consulting together, took her into the company as a "countess" - the name they used for the minor actresses who usually came on to the stage in crowds or in dumb parts. To begin with Masha used to play maid-servants and pages, but when Madame Beobahtov, the flower of Limonadov's company, eloped, they made her ingénue. She acted badly, lisped, and was nervous. She soon grew used to it, however, and began to be liked by the audience. Fenogenov was much displeased.

"To call her an actress!" he used to say. "She has no figure, no deportment, nothing whatever but silliness."

In one provincial town the company acted Schiller's "Robbers." Fenogenov played Franz, Masha, Amalie. The tragedian shouted and quivered. Masha repeated her part like a well-learnt lesson, and the play would have gone off as they generally did had it not been for a trifling mishap. Everything went well up to the point where Franz declares his love for Amalie and she seizes his sword. The tragedian shouted, hissed, quivered, and squeezed Masha in his iron embrace. And Masha, instead of repulsing him and crying "Hence!" trembled in his arms like a bird and did not move, . . . she seemed petrified.

"Have pity on me!" she whispered in his ear. "Oh, have pity on me! I am so miserable!"

"You don't know your part! Listen to the prompter!" hissed the tragedian, and he thrust his sword into her hand.

After the performance, Limonadov and Fenogenov were sitting in the ticket box-office engaged in conversation.

"Your wife does not learn her part, you are right there," the manager was saying. "She doesn't know her line. . . . Every man has his own line, . . . but she doesn't know hers. . . ."

Fenogenov listened, sighed, and scowled and scowled.

Next morning, Masha was sitting in a little general shop writing:

"Papa, he beats me! Forgive us! Send us some money!"

THE BIRD MARKET

There is a small square near the monastery of the Holy Birth which is called Trubnoy, or simply Truboy; there is a market there on Sundays. Hundreds of sheepskins, wadded coats, fur caps, and chimneypot hats swarm there, like crabs in a sieve. There is the sound of the twitter of birds in all sorts of keys, recalling the spring. If the sun is shining, and there are no clouds in the sky, the singing of the birds and the smell of hay make a more vivid impression, and this reminder of spring sets one thinking and carries one's fancy far, far away. Along one side of the square there stands a string of waggons. The waggons are loaded, not with hay, not with cabbages, nor with beans, but with goldfinches, siskins, larks, blackbirds and thrushes, bluetits, bullfinches. All of them are hopping about in rough, home-made cages, twittering and looking with envy at the free sparrows. The goldfinches cost five kopecks, the siskins are rather more expensive, while the value of the other birds is quite indeterminate.

"How much is a lark?"

The seller himself does not know the value of a lark. He scratches his head and asks whatever comes into it, a rouble, or three kopecks, according to the purchaser. There are expensive birds too. A faded old blackbird, with most of its feathers plucked out of its tail, sits on a dirty perch. He is dignified, grave, and motionless as a retired general. He has waved his claw in resignation to his captivity long ago, and looks at the blue sky with indifference. Probably, owing to this indifference, he is considered a sagacious bird. He is not to be bought for less than forty kopecks. Schoolboys, workmen, young men in stylish greatcoats, and bird-fanciers in incredibly shabby caps, in ragged trousers that are turned up at the ankles, and look as though they had been gnawed by mice, crowd round the birds, splashing through the mud. The young people and the workmen are sold hens for cocks, young birds for old ones. . . . They know very little about birds. But there is no deceiving the bird-fancier. He sees and understands his bird from a distance.

"There is no relying on that bird," a fancier will say, looking into a siskin's beak, and counting the feathers on its tail. "He sings now, it's true, but what of that? I sing in company too. No, my boy, shout, sing to me without company; sing in solitude, if you can. . . . You give me that one yonder that sits and holds its tongue! Give me the quiet one! That one says nothing, so he thinks the more. . . ."

Among the waggons of birds there are some full of other live creatures. Here you see hares, rabbits, hedgehogs, guinea-pigs, polecats. A hare sits sorrowfully nibbling the straw. The guinea-pigs shiver with cold, while the hedgehogs look out with curiosity from under their prickles at the public.

"I have read somewhere," says a post-office official in a faded overcoat, looking lovingly at the hare, and addressing no one in particular, "I have read that some learned man had a cat and a mouse and a falcon and a sparrow, who all ate out of one bowl."

"That's very possible, sir. The cat must have been beaten, and the falcon, I dare say, had all its tail pulled out. There's no great cleverness in that, sir. A friend of mine had a cat who, saving your presence, used to eat his cucumbers. He thrashed her with a big whip for a fortnight, till he taught her not to. A hare can learn to light matches if you beat it. Does that surprise you? It's very simple! It takes the match in its mouth and strikes it. An animal is like a man. A man's made wiser by beating, and it's the same with a beast."

Men in long, full-skirted coats move backwards and forwards in the crowd with cocks and ducks under their arms. The fowls are all lean and hungry. Chickens poke their ugly, mangy-looking heads out of their cages and peck at something in the mud. Boys with pigeons stare into your face and try to detect in you a pigeon-fancier.

"Yes, indeed! It's no use talking to you," someone shouts angrily. "You should look before you speak! Do you call this a pigeon? It is an eagle, not a pigeon!"

A tall thin man, with a shaven upper lip and side whiskers, who looks like a sick and drunken footman, is selling a snow-white lap-dog. The old lap-dog whines.

"She told me to sell the nasty thing," says the footman, with a contemptuous snigger. "She is bankrupt in her old age, has nothing to eat, and here now is selling her dogs and cats. She cries, and kisses them on their filthy snouts. And then she is so hard up that she sells them. 'Pon my soul, it is a fact! Buy it, gentlemen! The money is wanted for coffee."

But no one laughs. A boy who is standing by screws up one eye and looks at him gravely with compassion.

The most interesting of all is the fish section. Some dozen peasants are sitting in a row. Before each of them is a pail, and in each pail there is a veritable little hell. There, in the thick, greenish water are swarms of little carp, eels, small fry, water-snails, frogs, and newts. Big water-beetles with broken legs scurry over the small surface, clambering on the carp, and jumping over the frogs. The creatures have a strong hold on life. The frogs climb on the beetles, the newts on the frogs. The dark green tench, as more expensive fish, enjoy an exceptional position; they are kept in a special jar where they can't swim, but still they are not so cramped. . . .

"The carp is a grand fish! The carp's the fish to keep, your honour, plague take him! You can keep him for a year in a pail and he'll live! It's a week since I caught these very fish. I caught them, sir, in Pererva, and have come from there on foot. The carp are two kopecks each, the eels are three, and the minnows are ten kopecks the dozen, plague take them! Five kopecks' worth of minnows, sir? Won't you take some worms?"

The seller thrusts his coarse rough fingers into the pail and pulls out of it a soft minnow, or a little carp, the size of a nail. Fishing lines, hooks, and tackle are laid out near the pails, and pond-worms glow with a crimson light in the sun.

An old fancier in a fur cap, iron-rimmed spectacles, and goloshes that look like two dread-noughts, walks about by the waggons of birds and pails of fish. He is, as they call him here, "a type." He hasn't a farthing to bless himself with, but in spite of that he haggles, gets excited, and pesters purchasers with advice. He has thoroughly examined all the hares, pigeons, and fish; examined them in every detail, fixed the kind, the age, and the price of each one of them a good hour ago. He is as interested as a child in the goldfinches, the carp, and the minnows. Talk to him, for instance, about thrushes, and the queer old fellow will tell you things you could not find in any book. He will tell you them with enthusiasm, with passion, and will scold you too for your ignorance. Of goldfinches and bullfinches he is ready to talk endlessly, opening his eyes wide and gesticulating violently with his hands. He is only to be met here at the market in the cold weather; in the summer he is somewhere in the country, catching quails with a bird-call and angling for fish.

And here is another "type," a very tall, very thin, close-shaven gentleman in dark spectacles, wearing a cap with a cockade, and looking like a scrivener of by-gone days. He is a fancier; he is a man of decent position, a teacher in a high school, and that is well known to the habitués of the market, and they treat him with respect, greet him with bows, and have even invented for him a special title: "Your Scholarship." At Suharev market he rummages among the books, and at Trubnoy looks out for good pigeons.

"Please, sir!" the pigeon-sellers shout to him, "Mr. Schoolmaster, your Scholarship, take notice of my tumblers! your Scholarship!"

"Your Scholarship!" is shouted at him from every side.

"Your Scholarship!" an urchin repeats somewhere on the boulevard.

And his "Scholarship," apparently quite accustomed to his title, grave and severe, takes a pigeon in both hands, and lifting it above his head, begins examining it, and as he does so frowns and looks graver than ever, like a conspirator.

And Trubnoy Square, that little bit of Moscow where animals are so tenderly loved, and where they are so tortured, lives its little life, grows noisy and excited, and the business-like or pious people who pass by along the boulevard cannot make out what has brought this crowd of people, this medley of caps, fur hats, and chimneypots together; what they are talking about there, what they are buying and selling.

A SLANDER

Serge Kapitonich Ahineev, the writing master, was marrying his daughter to the teacher of history and geography. The wedding festivities were going off most successfully. In the drawing room there was singing, playing, and dancing. Waiters hired from the club were flitting distractedly about the rooms, dressed in black swallow-tails and dirty white ties. There was a continual hubbub and din of conversation. Sitting side by side on the sofa, the teacher of mathematics, Tarantulov, the French teacher, Pasdequoi, and the junior assessor of taxes, Mzda, were talking hurriedly and interrupting one another as they described to the guests cases of persons being buried alive, and gave their opinions on spiritualism. None of them believed in spiritualism, but all admitted that there were many things in this world which would always be beyond the mind of man. In the next room the literature master, Dodonsky, was explaining to the visitors the cases in which a sentry has the right to fire on passers-by. The subjects, as you perceive, were alarming, but very agreeable. Persons whose social position precluded them from entering were looking in at the windows from the yard.

Just at midnight the master of the house went into the kitchen to see whether everything was ready for supper. The kitchen from floor to ceiling was filled with fumes composed of goose, duck, and many other odours. On two tables the accessories, the drinks and light refreshments, were set out in artistic disorder. The cook, Marfa, a red-faced woman whose figure was like a barrel with a belt around it, was bustling about the tables.

"Show me the sturgeon, Marfa," said Ahineev, rubbing his hands and licking his lips. "What a perfume! I could eat up the whole kitchen. Come, show me the sturgeon."

Marfa went up to one of the benches and cautiously lifted a piece of greasy newspaper. Under the paper on an immense dish there reposed a huge sturgeon, masked in jelly and decorated with capers, olives, and carrots. Ahineev gazed at the sturgeon and gasped. His face beamed, he turned his eyes up. He bent down and with his lips emitted the sound of an ungreased wheel. After standing a moment he snapped his fingers with delight and once more smacked his lips.

"Ah-ah! the sound of a passionate kiss. . . . Who is it you're kissing out there, little Marfa?" came a voice from the next room, and in the doorway there appeared the cropped head of the assistant usher, Vankin. "Who is it? A-a-h! . . . Delighted to meet you! Sergei Kapitonich! You're a fine grandfather, I must say! *Tête-à-tête* with the fair sex-tette!"

"I'm not kissing," said Ahineev in confusion. "Who told you so, you fool? I was only . . . I smacked my lips . . . in reference to . . . as an indication of. . . pleasure . . . at the sight of the fish."

"Tell that to the marines!" The intrusive face vanished, wearing a broad grin.

Ahineev flushed.

"Hang it!" he thought, "the beast will go now and talk scandal. He'll disgrace me to all the town, the brute."

Ahineev went timidly into the drawing-room and looked stealthily round for Vankin. Vankin was standing by the piano, and, bending down with a jaunty air, was whispering something to the inspector's sister-in-law, who was laughing.

"Talking about me!" thought Ahineev. "About me, blast him! And she believes it . . . believes it! She laughs! Mercy on us! No, I can't let it pass . . . I can't. I must do something to prevent his being believed. . . . I'll speak to them all, and he'll be shown up for a fool and a gossip."

Ahineev scratched his head, and still overcome with embarrassment, went up to Pasdequoi.

"I've just been in the kitchen to see after the supper," he said to the Frenchman. "I know you are fond of fish, and I've a sturgeon, my dear fellow, beyond everything! A yard and a half long! Ha, ha, ha! And, by the way . . . I was just forgetting. . . . In the kitchen just now, with that sturgeon . . . quite a little story! I went into the kitchen just now and wanted to look at the supper dishes. I looked at the sturgeon and I smacked my lips with relish . . . at the piquancy of it. And at the very moment that fool Vankin came in and said: . . . 'Ha, ha, ha! . . . So you're kissing here!' Kissing Marfa, the cook! What a thing to imagine, silly fool! The woman is a perfect fright, like all the beasts put together, and he talks about kissing! Queer fish!"

"Who's a queer fish?" asked Tarantulov, coming up.

"Why he, over there - Vankin! I went into the kitchen . . ."

And he told the story of Vankin. ". . . He amused me, queer fish! I'd rather kiss a dog than Marfa, if you ask me," added Ahineev. He looked round and saw behind him Mzda.

"We were talking of Vankin," he said. "Queer fish, he is! He went into the kitchen, saw me beside Marfa, and began inventing all sorts of silly stories. 'Why are you kissing?' he says. He must have had a drop too much. 'And I'd rather kiss a turkeycock than Marfa,' I said, 'And I've a wife of my own, you fool,' said I. He did amuse me!"

"Who amused you?" asked the priest who taught Scripture in the school, going up to Ahineev.

"Vankin. I was standing in the kitchen, you know, looking at the sturgeon. . . ."

And so on. Within half an hour or so all the guests knew the incident of the sturgeon and Vankin.

"Let him tell away now!" thought Ahineev, rubbing his hands. "Let him! He'll begin telling his story and they'll say to him at once, 'Enough of your improbable nonsense, you fool, we know all about it!' "

And Ahineev was so relieved that in his joy he drank four glasses too many. After escorting the young people to their room, he went to bed and slept like an innocent babe, and next day he thought no more of the incident with the sturgeon. But, alas! man proposes, but God disposes. An evil tongue did its evil work, and Ahineev's strategy was of no avail. Just a week later - to be precise, on Wednesday after the third lesson - when Ahineev was standing in the middle of the teacher's room, holding forth on the vicious propensities of a boy called Visekin, the head master went up to him and drew him aside:

"Look here, Sergei Kapitonich," said the head master, "you must excuse me. . . . It's not my business; but all the same I must make you realize. . . . It's my duty. You see, there are rumors that you are romancing with that . . . cook. . . . It's nothing to do with me, but . . . flirt with her, kiss her . . . as you please, but don't let it be so public, please. I entreat you! Don't forget that you're a schoolmaster."

Ahineev turned cold and faint. He went home like a man stung by a whole swarm of bees, like a man scalded with boiling water. As he walked home, it seemed to him that the whole town was looking at him as though he were smeared with pitch. At home fresh trouble awaited him.

"Why aren't you gobbling up your food as usual?" his wife asked him at dinner. "What are you so pensive about? Brooding over your amours? Pining for your Marfa? I know all about it, Mohammedan! Kind friends have opened my eyes! O-o-o! . . . you savage!"

And she slapped him in the face. He got up from the table, not feeling the earth under his feet, and without his hat or coat, made his way to Vankin. He found him at home.

"You scoundrel!" he addressed him. "Why have you covered me with mud before all the town? Why did you set this slander going about me?"

"What slander? What are you talking about?"

"Who was it gossiped of my kissing Marfa? Wasn't it you? Tell me that. Wasn't it you, you brigand?"

Vankin blinked and twitched in every fibre of his battered countenance, raised his eyes to the icon and articulated, "God blast me! Strike me blind and lay me out, if I said a single word about you! May I be left without house and home, may I be stricken with worse than cholera!"

Vankin's sincerity did not admit of doubt. It was evidently not he who was the author of the slander.

"But who, then, who?" Ahineev wondered, going over all his acquaintances in his mind and beating himself on the breast. "Who, then?"

Who, then? We, too, ask the reader.

THE SWEDISH MATCH

(The Story of a Crime)

I

On the morning of October 6, 1885, a well-dressed young man presented himself at the office of the police superintendent of the 2nd division of the S. district, and announced that his employer, a retired cornet of the guards, called Mark Ivanovitch Klyauzov, had been murdered. The young man was pale and extremely agitated as he made this announcement. His hands trembled and there was a look of horror in his eyes.

"To whom have I the honour of speaking?" the superintendent asked him.

"Psyekov, Klyauzov's steward. Agricultural and engineering expert."

The police superintendent, on reaching the spot with Psyekov and the necessary witnesses, found the position as follows.

Masses of people were crowding about the lodge in which Klyauzov lived. The news of the event had flown round the neighbourhood with the rapidity of lightning, and, thanks to its being a holiday, the people were flocking to the lodge from all the neighbouring villages. There was a regular hubbub of talk. Pale and tearful faces were to be seen here and there. The door into Klyauzov's bedroom was found to be locked. The key was in the lock on the inside.

"Evidently the criminals made their way in by the window" Psyekov observed, as they examined the door.

They went into the garden into which the bedroom window looked. The window had a gloomy, ominous air. It was covered by a faded green curtain. One corner of the curtain was slightly turned back, which made it possible to peep into the bedroom.

"Has anyone of you looked in at the window?" inquired the superintendent.

"No, your honour," said Yefrem, the gardener, a little, grey-haired old man with the face of a veteran non-commissioned officer. "No one feels like looking when they are shaking in every limb!"

"Ech, Mark Ivanitch! Mark Ivanitch!" sighed the superintendent, as he looked at the window. "I told you that you would come to a bad end! I told you, poor dear-you wouldn't listen! Dissipation leads to no good!"

"It's thanks to Yefrem," said Psyekov. "We should never have guessed it but for him. It was he who first thought that something was wrong. He came to me this morning and said: 'Why is it our master hasn't waked up for so long? He hasn't been out of his bedroom for a whole week! When he said that to me I was struck all of a heap. . . . The thought flashed through my mind at once. He hasn't made an appearance since Saturday of last week, and to-day's Sunday. Seven days is no joke!"

"Yes, poor man," the superintendent sighed again. " A clever fellow, well-educated, and so good-hearted. There was no one like him, one may say, in company. But a rake; the kingdom of heaven be his! I'm not surprised at anything with him! Stepan," he said, addressing one of the witnesses, "ride off this minute to my house and send Andryushka to thepolice captain's, let him report to him. Say Mark Ivanitch has been murdered! Yes, and run to the inspector - why should he sit in comfort doing nothing? Let him come here. And you go yourself as fast as you can to the examining magistrate, Nikolay Yermolaitch, and tell him to come here. Wait a bit, I will write him a note."

The police superintendent stationed watchmen round the lodge, and went off to the steward's to have tea. Ten minutes later he was sitting on a stool, carefully nibbling lumps of sugar, and sipping tea as hot as a red-hot coal.

"There it is! . . ." he said to Psyekov, "there it is! . . . a gentleman, and a well-to-do one, too . . . a favourite of the gods, one may say, to use Pushkin's expression, and what has he made of it? Nothing! He gave himself up to drinking and debauchery, and . . . here now . . . he has been murdered!"

Two hours later the examining magistrate drove up. Nikolay Yermolaitch Tchubikov (that was the magistrate's name), a tall, thick-set old man of sixty, had been hard at work for a quarter of a century. He was known to the whole district as an honest, intelligent, energetic man, devoted to his work. His invariable companion, assistant, and secretary, a tall young man of six and twenty, called Dyukovsky, arrived on the scene of action with him.

"Is it possible, gentlemen?" Tchubikov began, going into Psyekov's room and rapidly shaking hands with everyone. "Is it possible? Mark Ivanitch? Murdered? No, it's impossible! Imposs-i-ble!"

"There it is," sighed the superintendent

"Merciful heavens! Why I saw him only last Friday. At the fair at Tarabankovo! Saving your presence, I drank a glass of vodka with him!"

"There it is," the superintendent sighed once more.

They heaved sighs, expressed their horror, drank a glass of tea each, and went to the lodge.

"Make way!" the police inspector shouted to the crowd.

On going into the lodge the examining magistrate first of all set to work to inspect the door into the bedroom. The door turned out to be made of deal, painted yellow, and not to have been tampered with. No special traces that might have served as evidence could be found. They proceeded to break open the door.

"I beg you, gentlemen, who are not concerned, to retire," said the examining magistrate, when, after long banging and cracking, the door yielded to the axe and the chisel. "I ask this in the interests of the investigation. . . . Inspector, admit no one!"

Tchubikov, his assistant, and the police superintendent opened the door and hesitatingly, one after the other, walked into the room. The following spectacle met their eyes. In the solitary window stood a big wooden bedstead with an immense feather bed on it. On the rumpled feather bed lay a creased and crumpled quilt. A pillow, in a cotton pillow case - also much creased, was on the floor. On a little table beside the bed lay a silver watch, and silver coins to the value of twenty kopecks. Some sulphur matches lay there too. Except the bed, the table, and a solitary chair, there was no furniture in the room. Looking under the bed, the superintendent saw two dozen empty bottles, an old straw hat, and a jar of vodka. Under the table lay one boot, covered with dust. Taking a look round the room, Tchubikov frowned and flushed crimson.

"The blackguards!" he muttered, clenching his fists.

"And where is Mark Ivanitch?" Dyukovsky asked quietly.

"I beg you not to put your spoke in," Tchubikov answered roughly. "Kindly examine the floor. This is the second case in my experience, Yevgraf Kuzmitch," he added to the police superintendent, dropping his voice. "In 1870 I had a similar case. But no doubt you remember it. . . . The murder of the merchant Portretov. It was just the same. The blackguards murdered him, and dragged the dead body out of the window."

Tchubikov went to the window, drew the curtain aside, and cautiously pushed the window. The window opened.

"It opens, so it was not fastened. . . . H'm there are traces on the window-sill. Do you see? Here is the trace of a knee. . . . Someone climbed out. . . . We shall have to inspect the window thoroughly."

"There is nothing special to be observed on the floor," said Dyukovsky. "No stains, nor scratches. The only thing I have found is a used Swedish match. Here it is. As far as I remember, Mark Ivanitch didn't smoke; in a general way he used sulphur ones, never Swedish matches. This match may serve as a clue. . . ."

"Oh, hold your tongue, please!" cried Tchubikov, with a wave of his hand. "He keeps on about his match! I can't stand these excitable people! Instead of looking for matches, you had better examine the bed!"

On inspecting the bed, Dyukovsky reported:

"There are no stains of blood or of anything else. . . . Nor are there any fresh rents. On the pillow there are traces of teeth. A liquid, having the smell of beer and also the taste of it, has been spilt on the quilt. . . . The general appearance of the bed gives grounds for supposing there has been a struggle."

"I know there was a struggle without your telling me! No one asked you whether there was a struggle. Instead of looking out for a struggle you had better be . . ."

"One boot is here, the other one is not on the scene."

"Well, what of that?"

"Why, they must have strangled him while he was taking off his boots. He hadn't time to take the second boot off when . . . ."

"He's off again! . . . And how do you know that he was strangled?"

"There are marks of teeth on the pillow. The pillow itself is very much crumpled, and has been flung to a distance of six feet from the bed."

"He argues, the chatterbox! We had better go into the garden. You had better look in the garden instead of rummaging about here. . . . I can do that without your help."

When they went out into the garden their first task was the inspection of the grass. The grass had been trampled down under the windows. The clump of burdock against the wall under the window turned out to have been trodden on too. Dyukovsky succeeded in finding on it some broken shoots, and a little bit of wadding. On the topmost burrs, some fine threads of dark blue wool were found.

"What was the colour of his last suit? Dyukovsky asked Psyekov.

"It was yellow, made of canvas."

"Capital! Then it was they who were in dark blue. . . ."

Some of the burrs were cut off and carefully wrapped up in paper. At that moment Artsybashev-Svistakovsky, the police captain, and Tyutyuev, the doctor, arrived. The police captain greeted the others, and at once proceeded to satisfy his curiosity; the doctor, a tall and extremely lean man with sunken eyes, a long nose, and a sharp chin, greeting no one and asking no questions, sat down on a stump, heaved a sigh and said:

"The Serbians are in a turmoil again! I can't make out what they want! Ah, Austria, Austria! It's your doing!"

The inspection of the window from outside yielded absolutely no result; the inspection of the grass and surrounding bushes furnished many valuable clues. Dyukovsky succeeded, for instance, in detecting a long, dark streak in the grass, consisting of stains, and stretching from the window for a good many yards into the garden. The streak ended under one of the lilac bushes in a big, brownish stain. Under the same bush was found a boot, which turned out to be the fellow to the one found in the bedroom.

"This is an old stain of blood," said Dyukovsky, examining the stain.

At the word "blood," the doctor got up and lazily took a cursory glance at the stain.

"Yes, it's blood," he muttered.

"Then he wasn't strangled since there's blood," said Tchubikov, looking malignantly at Dyukovsky.

"He was strangled in the bedroom, and here, afraid he would come to, they stabbed him with something sharp. The stain under the bush shows that he lay there for a comparatively long time, while they were trying to find some way of carrying him, or something to carry him on out of the garden."

"Well, and the boot?"

"That boot bears out my contention that he was murdered while he was taking off his boots before going to bed. He had taken off one boot, the other, that is, this boot he had only managed to get half off. While he was being dragged and shaken the boot that was only half on came off of itself. . . ."

"What powers of deduction! Just look at him!" Tchubikov jeered. "He brings it all out so pat! And when will you learn not to put your theories forward? You had better take a little of the grass for analysis instead of arguing!"

After making the inspection and taking a plan of the locality they went off to the steward's to write a report and have lunch. At lunch they talked.

"Watch, money, and everything else . . . are untouched," Tchubikov began the conversation. "It is as clear as twice two makes four that the murder was committed not for mercenary motives."

"It was committed by a man of the educated class," Dyukovsky put in.

"From what do you draw that conclusion?"

"I base it on the Swedish match which the peasants about here have not learned to use yet. Such matches are only used by landowners and not by all of them. He was murdered, by the way, not by one but by three, at least: two held him while the third strangled him. Klyauzov was strong and the murderers must have known that."

"What use would his strength be to him, supposing he were asleep?"

"The murderers came upon him as he was taking off his boots. He was taking off his boots, so he was not asleep."

"It's no good making things up! You had better eat your lunch!"

"To my thinking, your honour," said Yefrem, the gardener, as he set the samovar on the table, "this vile deed was the work of no other than Nikolashka."

"Quite possible," said Psyekov.

"Who's this Nikolashka?"

"The master's valet, your honour," answered Yefrem. "Who else should it be if not he? He's a ruffian, your honour! A drunkard, and such a dissipated fellow! May the Queen of Heaven never bring the like again! He always used to fetch vodka for the master, he always used to put the master to bed. . . . Who should it be if not he? And what's more, I venture to bring to your notice, your honour, he boasted once in a tavern, the rascal, that he would murder his master. It's all on account of Akulka, on account of a woman. . . . He had a soldier's wife. . . . The master took a fancy to her and got intimate with her, and he . . . was angered by it, to be sure. He's lolling about in the kitchen now, drunk. He's crying . . . making out he is grieving over the master . . . ."

"And anyone might be angry over Akulka, certainly," said Psyekov. "She is a soldier's wife, a peasant woman, but . . . Mark Ivanitch might well call her Nana. There is something in her that does suggest Nana . . . fascinating . . ."

"I have seen her . . . I know . . ." said the examining magistrate, blowing his nose in a red handkerchief.

Dyukovsky blushed and dropped his eyes. The police superintendent drummed on his saucer with his fingers. The police captain coughed and rummaged in his portfolio for something. On the doctor alone the mention of Akulka and Nana appeared to produce no impression. Tchubikov ordered Nikolashka to be fetched. Nikolashka, a lanky young man with a long pock-marked nose and a hollow chest, wearing a reefer jacket that had been his master's, came into Psyekov's room and bowed down to the ground before Tchubikov. His face looked sleepy and showed traces of tears. He was drunk and could hardly stand up.

"Where is your master?" Tchubikov asked him.

"He's murdered, your honour."

As he said this Nikolashka blinked and began to cry.

"We know that he is murdered. But where is he now? Where is his body?"

"They say it was dragged out of window and buried in the garden."

"H'm . . . the results of the investigation are already known in the kitchen then. . . . That's bad. My good fellow, where were you on the night when your master was killed? On Saturday, that is?"

Nikolashka raised his head, craned his neck, and pondered.

"I can't say, your honour," he said. "I was drunk and I don't remember."

"An alibi!" whispered Dyukovsky, grinning and rubbing his hands.

"Ah! And why is it there's blood under your master's window!"

Nikolashka flung up his head and pondered.

"Think a little quicker," said the police captain.

"In a minute. That blood's from a trifling matter, your honour. I killed a hen; I cut her throat very simply in the usual way, and she fluttered out of my hands and took and ran off. . . .That's what the blood's from."

Yefrem testified that Nikolashka really did kill a hen every evening and killed it in all sorts of places, and no one had seen the half-killed hen running about the garden, though of course it could not be positively denied that it had done so.

"An alibi," laughed Dyukovsky, "and what an idiotic alibi."

"Have you had relations with Akulka?"

"Yes, I have sinned."

"And your master carried her off from you?"

"No, not at all. It was this gentleman here, Mr. Psyekov, Ivan Mihalitch, who enticed her from me, and the master took her from Ivan Mihalitch. That's how it was."

Psyekov looked confused and began rubbing his left eye. Dyukovsky fastened his eyes upon him, detected his confusion, and started. He saw on the steward's legs dark blue trousers which he had not previously noticed. The trousers reminded him of the blue threads found on the burdock. Tchubikov in his turn glanced suspiciously at Psyekov.

"You can go!" he said to Nikolashka. "And now allow me to put one question to you, Mr. Psyekov. You were here, of course, on the Saturday of last week?

"Yes, at ten o'clock I had supper with Mark Ivanitch."

"And afterwards?"

Psyekov was confused, and got up from the table.

"Afterwards . . . afterwards . . . I really don't remember," he muttered. "I had drunk a good deal on that occasion. . . . I can't remember where and when I went to bed. . . . Why do you all look at me like that? As though I had murdered him!"

"Where did you wake up?"

"I woke up in the servants' kitchen on the stove . . . . They can all confirm that. How I got on to the stove I can't say. . . ."

"Don't disturb yourself . . . Do you know Akulina?"

"Oh well, not particularly."

"Did she leave you for Klyauzov?"

"Yes. . . . Yefrem, bring some more mushrooms! Will you have some tea, Yevgraf Kuzmitch?"

There followed an oppressive, painful silence that lasted for some five minutes. Dyukovsky held his tongue, and kept his piercing eyes on Psyekov's face, which gradually turned pale. The silence was broken by Tchubikov.

"We must go to the big house," he said, "and speak to the deceased's sister, Marya Ivanovna. She may give us some evidence."

Tchubikov and his assistant thanked Psyekov for the lunch, then went off to the big house. They found Klyauzov's sister, a maiden lady of five and forty, on her knees before a high family shrine of ikons. When she saw portfolios and caps adorned with cockades in her visitors' hands, she turned pale.

"First of all, I must offer an apology for disturbing your devotions, so to say," the gallant Tchubikov began with a scrape. "We have come to you with a request. You have heard, of course, already. . . . There is a suspicion that your brother has somehow been murdered. God's will, you know. . . . Death no one can escape, neither Tsar nor ploughman. Can you not assist us with some fact, something that will throw light?"

"Oh, do not ask me!" said Marya Ivanovna, turning whiter still, and hiding her face in her hands. "I can tell you nothing! Nothing! I implore you! I can say nothing . . . What can I do? Oh, no, no . . . not a word . . . of my brother! I would rather die than speak!"

Marya Ivanovna burst into tears and went away into another room. The officials looked at each other, shrugged their shoulders, and beat a retreat.

"A devil of a woman!" said Dyukovsky, swearing as they went out of the big house. "Apparently she knows something and is concealing it. And there is something peculiar in the maid-servant's expression too. . . . You wait a bit, you devils! We will get to the bottom of it all!

In the evening, Tchubikov and his assistant were driving home by the light of a pale-faced moon; they sat in their waggonette, summing up in their minds the incidents of the day. Both were exhausted and sat silent. Tchubikov never liked talking on the road. In spite of his talkativeness, Dyukovsky held his tongue in deference to the old man. Towards the end of the journey, however, the young man could endure the silence no longer, and began:

"That Nikolashka has had a hand in the business," he said, "*non dubitandum est*. One can see from his mug too what sort of a chap he is. . . . His alibi gives him away hand and foot. There is no doubt either that he was not the instigator of the crime. He was only the stupid hired tool. Do you agree? The discreet Psyekov plays a not unimportant part in the affair too. His blue trousers, his embarrassment, his lying on the stove from fright after the murder, his alibi, and Akulka."

"Keep it up, you're in your glory! According to you, if a man knows Akulka he is the murderer. Ah, you hot-head! You ought to be sucking your bottle instead of investigating cases! You used to be running after Akulka too, does that mean that you had a hand in this business?"

"Akulka was a cook in your house for a month, too, but . . . I don't say anything. On that Saturday night I was playing cards with you, I saw you, or I should be after you too. The woman is not the point, my good sir. The point is the nasty, disgusting, mean feeling. . . . The discreet young man did not like to be cut out, do you see. Vanity, do you see. . . . He longed to be revenged. Then . . . His thick lips are a strong indication of sensuality. Do you remember how he smacked his lips when he compared Akulka to Nana? That he is burning with passion, the scoundrel, is beyond doubt! And so you have wounded vanity and unsatisfied passion. That's enough to lead to murder. Two of them are in our hands, but who is the third? Nikolashka and Psyekov held him. Who was it smothered him? Psyekov is timid, easily embarrassed, altogether a coward. People like Nikolashka are not equal to smothering with a pillow, they set to work with an axe or a mallet. . . . Some third person must have smothered him, but who?"

Dyukovsky pulled his cap over his eyes, and pondered. He was silent till the waggonette had driven up to the examining magistrate's house.

"Eureka!" he said, as he went into the house, and took off his overcoat. "Eureka, Nikolay Yermolaitch! I can't understand how it is it didn't occur to me before. Do you know who the third is?"

"Do leave off, please! There's supper ready. Sit down to supper!"

Tchubikov and Dyukovsky sat down to supper. Dyukovsky poured himself out a wine-glassful of vodka, got up, stretched, and with sparkling eyes, said:

"Let me tell you then that the third person who collaborated with the scoundrel Psyekov and smothered him was a woman! Yes! I am speaking of the murdered man's sister, Marya Ivanovna!"

Tchubikov coughed over his vodka and fastened his eyes on Dyukovsky.

"Are you . . . not quite right? Is your head . . . not quite right? Does it ache?"

"I am quite well. Very good, suppose I have gone out of my mind, but how do you explain her confusion on our arrival? How do you explain her refusal to give information? Admitting that that is trivial - very good! All right! - but think of the terms they were on! She detested her brother! She is an Old Believer, he was a profligate, a godless fellow . . . that is what has bred hatred between them! They say he succeeded in persuading her that he was an angel of Satan! He used to practise spiritualism in her presence!"

"Well, what then?"

"Don't you understand? She's an Old Believer, she murdered him through fanaticism! She has not merely slain a wicked man, a profligate, she has freed the world from Antichrist - and that she fancies is her merit, her religious achievement! Ah, you don't know these old maids, these Old Believers! You should read Dostoevsky! And what does Lyeskovsay . . . and Petchersky! It's she, it's she, I'll stake my life on it. She smothered him! Oh, the fiendish woman! Wasn't she, perhaps, standing before the ikons when we went in to put us off the scent? 'I'll stand up and say my prayers,' she said to herself, 'they will think I am calm and don't expect them.' That's the method of all novices in crime. Dear Nikolay Yermolaitch! My dear man! Do hand this case over to me! Let me go through with it to the end! My dear fellow! I have begun it, and I will carry it through to the end."

Tchubikov shook his head and frowned.

"I am equal to sifting difficult cases myself," he said. "And it's your place not to put yourself forward. Write what is dictated to you, that is your business!"

Dyukovsky flushed crimson, walked out, and slammed the door.

"A clever fellow, the rogue," Tchubikov muttered, looking after him. "Ve-ery clever! Only inappropriately hasty. I shall have to buy him a cigar-case at the fair for a present."

Next morning a lad with a big head and a hare lip came from Klyauzovka. He gave his name as the shepherd Danilko, and furnished a very interesting piece of information.

"I had had a drop," said he. "I stayed on till midnight at my crony's. As I was going home, being drunk, I got into the river for a bathe. I was bathing and what do I see! Two men coming along the dam carrying something black. 'Tyoo!' I shouted at them. They were scared, and cut along as fast as they could go into the Makarev kitchen-gardens. Strike me dead, if it wasn't the master they were carrying!"

Towards evening of the same day Psyekov and Nikolashka were arrested and taken under guard to the district town. In the town they were put in the prison tower.

II

Twelve days passed.

It was morning. The examining magistrate, Nikolay Yermolaitch, was sitting at a green table at home, looking through the papers, relating to the "Klyauzov case"; Dyukovsky was pacing up and down the room restlessly, like a wolf in a cage.

"You are convinced of the guilt of Nikolashka and Psyekov," he said, nervously pulling at his youthful beard. "Why is it you refuse to be convinced of the guilt of Marya Ivanovna? Haven't you evidence enough?"

"I don't say that I don't believe in it. I am convinced of it, but somehow I can't believe it. . . . There is no real evidence. It's all theoretical, as it were. . . . Fanaticism and one thing and another. . . ."

"And you must have an axe and bloodstained sheets! . . . You lawyers! Well, I will prove it to you then! Do give up your slip-shod attitude to the psychological aspect of the case. Your Marya Ivanovna ought to be in Siberia! I'll prove it. If theoretical proof is not enough for you, I have something material. . . . It will show you how right my theory is! Only let me go about a little!"

"What are you talking about?"

"The Swedish match! Have you forgotten? I haven't forgotten it! I'll find out who struck it in the murdered man's room! It was not struck by Nikolashka, nor by Psyekov, neither of whom turned out to have matches when searched, but a third person, that is Marya Ivanovna. And I will prove it! . . . Only let me drive about the district, make some inquiries. . . ."

"Oh, very well, sit down. . . . Let us proceed to the examination."

Dyukovsky sat down to the table, and thrust his long nose into the papers.

"Bring in Nikolay Tetchov!" cried the examining magistrate.

Nikolashka was brought in. He was pale and thin as a chip. He was trembling.

"Tetchov!" began Tchubikov. "In 1879 you were convicted of theft and condemned to a term of imprisonment. In 1882 you were condemned for theft a second time, and a second time sent to prison . . . We know all about it. . . ."

A look of surprise came up into Nikolashka's face. The examining magistrate's omniscience amazed him, but soon wonder was replaced by an expression of extreme distress. He broke into sobs, and asked leave to go to wash, and calm himself. He was led out.

"Bring in Psyekov!" said the examining magistrate.

Psyekov was led in. The young man's face had greatly changed during those twelve days. He was thin, pale, and wasted. There was a look of apathy in his eyes.

"Sit down, Psyekov," said Tchubikov. "I hope that to-day you will be sensible and not persist in lying as on other occasions. All this time you have denied your participation in the murder of Klyauzov, in spite of the mass of evidence against you. It is senseless. Confession is some mitigation of guilt. To-day I am talking to you for the last time. If you don't confess to-day, to-morrow it will be too late. Come, tell us. . . ."

"I know nothing, and I don't know your evidence," whispered Psyekov.

"That's useless! Well then, allow me to tell you how it happened. On Saturday evening, you were sitting in Klyauzov's bedroom drinking vodka and beer with him." (Dyukovsky riveted his eyes on Psyekov's face, and did not remove them during the whole monologue.) "Nikolay was waiting upon you. Between twelve and one Mark Ivanitch told you he wanted to go to bed. He always did go to bed at that time. While he was taking off his boots and giving you some instructions regarding the estate, Nikolay and you at a given signal seized your intoxicated master and flung him back upon the bed. One of you sat on his feet, the other on his head. At that moment the lady, you know who, in a black dress, who had arranged with you beforehand the part she would take in the crime, came in from the passage. She picked up the pillow, and proceeded to smother him with it. During the struggle, the light went out. The woman took a box of Swedish matches out of her pocket and lighted the candle. Isn't that right? I see from your face that what I say is true. Well, to proceed. . . . Having smothered him, and being convinced that he had ceased to breathe, Nikolay and you dragged him out of window and put him down near the burdocks. Afraid that he might regain consciousness, you struck him with something sharp. Then you carried him, and laid him for some time under a lilac bush. After resting and considering a little, you carried him . . . lifted him over the hurdle. . . . Then went along the road. . . Then comes the dam; near the dam you were frightened by a peasant. But what is the matter with you?"

Psyekov, white as a sheet, got up, staggering.

"I am suffocating!" he said. "Very well. . . . So be it. . . . Only I must go. . . . Please."

Psyekov was led out.

"At last he has admitted it!" said Tchubikov, stretching at his ease. "He has given himself away! How neatly I caught him there."

"And he didn't deny the woman in black!" said Dyukovsky, laughing. "I am awfully worried over that Swedish match, though! I can't endure it any longer. Good-bye! I am going!"

Dyukovsky put on his cap and went off. Tchubikov began interrogating Akulka.

Akulka declared that she knew nothing about it. . . .

"I have lived with you and with nobody else!" she said.

At six o'clock in the evening Dyukovsky returned. He was more excited than ever. His hands trembled so much that he could not unbutton his overcoat. His cheeks were burning. It was evident that he had not come back without news.

"*Veni, vidi, vici!*" he cried, dashing into Tchubikov's room and sinking into an arm-chair. "I vow on my honour, I begin to believe in my own genius. Listen, damnation take us! Listen and wonder, old friend! It's comic and it's sad. You have three in your grasp already . . . haven't you? I have found a fourth murderer, or rather murderess, for it is a woman! And what a woman! I would have given ten years of my life merely to touch her shoulders. But . . . listen. I drove to Klyauzovka and proceeded to describe a spiral round it. On the way I visited all the shopkeepers and innkeepers, asking for Swedish matches. Everywhere I was told 'No.' I have been on my round up to now. Twenty times I lost hope, and as many times regained it. I have been on the go all day long, and only an hour ago came upon what I was looking for. A couple of miles from here they gave me a packet of a dozen boxes of matches. One box was missing . . . I asked at once: 'Who bought that box?' 'So-and-so. She took a fancy to them. . . They crackle.' My dear fellow! Nikolay Yermolaitch! What can sometimes be done by a man who has been expelled from a seminary and studied Gaboriau is beyond all conception! From to-day I shall began to respect myself! . . . Ough. . . . Well, let us go!"

"Go where?"

"To her, to the fourth. . . . We must make haste, or . . . I shall explode with impatience! Do you know who she is? You will never guess. The young wife of our old police superintendent, Yevgraf Kuzmitch, Olga Petrovna; that's who it is! She bought that box of matches!"

"You . . . you. . . . Are you out of your mind?"

"It's very natural! In the first place she smokes, and in the second she was head over ears in love with Klyauzov. He rejected her love for the sake of an Akulka. Revenge. I remember now, I once came upon them behind the screen in the kitchen. She was cursing him, while he was smoking her cigarette and puffing the smoke into her face. But do come along; make haste, for it is getting dark already. . . . Let us go!"

"I have not gone so completely crazy yet as to disturb a respectable, honourable woman at night for the sake of a wretched boy!"

"Honourable, respectable. . . . You are a rag then, not an examining magistrate! I have never ventured to abuse you, but now you force me to it! You rag! you old fogey! Come, dear Nikolay Yermolaitch, I entreat you!"

The examining magistrate waved his hand in refusal and spat in disgust.

"I beg you! I beg you, not for my own sake, but in the interests of justice! I beseech you, indeed! Do me a favour, if only for once in your life!"

Dyukovsky fell on his knees.

"Nikolay Yermolaitch, do be so good! Call me a scoundrel, a worthless wretch if I am in error about that woman! It is such a case, you know! It is a case! More like a novel than a case. The fame of it will be all over Russia. They will make you examining magistrate for particularly important cases! Do understand, you unreasonable old man!"

The examining magistrate frowned and irresolutely put out his hand towards his hat.

"Well, the devil take you!" he said, "let us go."

It was already dark when the examining magistrate's waggonette rolled up to the police superintendent's door.

"What brutes we are!" said Tchubikov, as he reached for the bell. "We are disturbing people."

"Never mind, never mind, don't be frightened. We will say that one of the springs has broken."

Tchubikov and Dyukovsky were met in the doorway by a tall, plump woman of three and twenty, with eyebrows as black as pitch and full red lips. It was Olga Petrovna herself.

"Ah, how very nice," she said, smiling all over her face. "You are just in time for supper. My Yevgraf Kuzmitch is not at home. . . . He is staying at the priest's. But we can get on without him. Sit down. Have you come from an inquiry?"

"Yes.... We have broken one of our springs, you know," began Tchubikov, going into the drawing-room and sitting down in an easy-chair.

"Take her by surprise at once and overwhelm her," Dyukovsky whispered to him.

"A spring ... er ... yes.... We just drove up...."

"Overwhelm her, I tell you! She will guess if you go drawing it out."

"Oh, do as you like, but spare me," muttered Tchubikov, getting up and walking to the window. "I can't! You cooked the mess, you eat it!"

"Yes, the spring," Dyukovsky began, going up to the superintendent's wife and wrinkling his long nose. "We have not come in to ... er-er-er ... supper, nor to see Yevgraf Kuzmitch. We have come to ask you, madam, where is Mark Ivanovitch whom you have murdered?"

"What? What Mark Ivanovitch?" faltered the superintendent's wife, and her full face was suddenly in one instant suffused with crimson. "I ... don't understand."

"I ask you in the name of the law! Where is Klyauzov? We know all about it!"

"Through whom?" the superintendent's wife asked slowly, unable to face Dyukovsky's eyes.

"Kindly inform us where he is!"

"But how did you find out? Who told you?"

"We know all about it. I insist in the name of the law."

The examining magistrate, encouraged by the lady's confusion, went up to her.

"Tell us and we will go away. Otherwise we ..."

"What do you want with him?"

"What is the object of such questions, madam? We ask you for information. You are trembling, confused. . . . Yes, he has been murdered, and if you will have it, murdered by you! Your accomplices have betrayed you!"

The police superintendent's wife turned pale.

"Come along," she said quietly, wringing her hands. "He is hidden in the bath-house. Only for God's sake, don't tell my husband! I implore you! It would be too much for him."

The superintendent's wife took a big key from the wall, and led her visitors through the kitchen and the passage into the yard. It was dark in the yard. There was a drizzle of fine rain. The superintendent's wife went on ahead. Tchubikov and Dyukovsky strode after her through the long grass, breathing in the smell of wild hemp and slops, which made a squelching sound under their feet. It was a big yard. Soon there were no more pools of slops, and their feet felt ploughed land. In the darkness they saw the silhouette of trees, and among the trees a little house with a crooked chimney.

"This is the bath-house," said the superintendent's wife, "but, I implore you, do not tell anyone."

Going up to the bath-house, Tchubikov and Dyukovsky saw a large padlock on the door.

"Get ready your candle-end and matches," Tchubikov whispered to his assistant.

The superintendent's wife unlocked the padlock and let the visitors into the bath-house. Dyukovsky struck a match and lighted up the entry. In the middle of it stood a table. On the table, beside a podgy little samovar, was a soup tureen with some cold cabbage-soup in it, and a dish with traces of some sauce on it.

"Go on!"

They went into the next room, the bath-room. There, too, was a table. On the table there stood a big dish of ham, a bottle of vodka, plates, knives and forks.

"But where is he . . . where's the murdered man?"

He is on the top shelf," whispered the superintendent's wife, turning paler than ever and trembling.

Dyukovsky took the candle-end in his hand and climbed up to the upper shelf. There he saw a long, human body, lying motionless on a big feather bed. The body emitted a faint snore. . . .

"They have made fools of us, damn it all!" Dyukovsky cried. "This is not he! It is some living blockhead lying here. Hi! who are you, damnation take you!"

The body drew in its breath with a whistling sound and moved. Dyukovsky prodded it with his elbow. It lifted up its arms, stretched, and raised its head.

"Who is that poking?" a hoarse, ponderous bass voice inquired. "What do you want?"

Dyukovsky held the candle-end to the face of the unknown and uttered a shriek. In the crimson nose, in the ruffled, uncombed hair, in the pitch-black moustaches of which one was jauntily twisted and pointed insolently towards the ceiling, he recognised Cornet Klyauzov.

"You. . . . Mark . . . Ivanitch! Impossible!"

The examining magistrate looked up and was dumbfounded.

"It is I, yes. . . . And it's you, Dyukovsky! What the devil do you want here? And whose ugly mug is that down there? Holy Saints, it's the examining magistrate! How in the world did you come here?"

Klyauzov hurriedly got down and embraced Tchubikov. Olga Petrovna whisked out of the door.

"However did you come? Let's have a drink! - dash it all! Tra-ta-ti-to-tom. . . . Let's have a drink! Who brought you here, though? How did you get to know I was here? It doesn't matter, though! Have a drink!"

Klyauzov lighted the lamp and poured out three glasses of vodka.

"The fact is, I don't understand you," said the examining magistrate, throwing out his hands. "Is it you, or not you?"

"Stop that. . . . Do you want to give me a sermon? Don't trouble yourself! Dyukovsky boy, drink up your vodka! Friends, let us pass the . . . What are you staring at . . . ? Drink!"

"All the same, I can't understand," said the examining magistrate, mechanically drinking his vodka. "Why are you here?"

"Why shouldn't I be here, if I am comfortable here?"

Klyauzov sipped his vodka and ate some ham.

"I am staying with the superintendent's wife, as you see. In the wilds among the ruins, like some house goblin. Drink! I felt sorry for her, you know, old man! I took pity on her, and, well, I am living here in the deserted bath-house, like a hermit. . . . I am well fed. Next week I am thinking of moving on. . . . I've had enough of it. . . ."

"Inconceivable!" said Dyukovsky.

"What is there inconceivable in it?"

"Inconceivable! For God's sake, how did your boot get into the garden?"

"What boot?"

"We found one of your boots in the bedroom and the other in the garden."

"And what do you want to know that for? It is not your business. But do drink, dash it all. Since you have waked me up, you may as well drink! There's an interesting tale about that boot, my boy. I didn't want to come to Olga's. I didn't feel inclined, you know, I'd had a drop too much. . . . She came under the window and began scolding me. . . . You know how women . . . as a rule. Being drunk, I up and flung my boot at her. Ha-ha! . . . 'Don't scold,' I said. She clambered in at the window, lighted the lamp, and gave me a good drubbing, as I was drunk. I have plenty to eat here. . . . Love, vodka, and good things! But where are you off to? Tchubikov, where are you off to?"

The examining magistrate spat on the floor and walked out of the bathhouse. Dyukovsky followed him with his head hanging. Both got into the waggonette in silence and drove off. Never had the road seemed so long and dreary. Both were silent. Tchubikov was shaking with anger all the way. Dyukovsky hid his face in his collar as though he were afraid the darkness and the drizzling rain might read his shame on his face.

On getting home the examining magistrate found the doctor, Tyutyuev, there. The doctor was sitting at the table and heaving deep sighs as he turned over the pages of the *Neva*.

"The things that are going on in the world," he said, greeting the examining magistrate with a melancholy smile. "Austria is at it again . . . and Gladstone, too, in a way. . . ."

Tchubikov flung his hat under the table and began to tremble.

"You devil of a skeleton! Don't bother me! I've told you a thousand times over, don't bother me with your politics! It's not the time for politics! And as for you," he turned upon Dyukovsky and shook his fist at him, "as for you. . . . I'll never forget it, as long as I live!"

"But the Swedish match, you know! How could I tell. . . ."

"Choke yourself with your match! Go away and don't irritate me, or goodness knows what I shall do to you. Don't let me set eyes on you."

Dyukovsky heaved a sigh, took his hat, and went out.

"I'll go and get drunk!" he decided, as he went out of the gate, and he sauntered dejectedly towards the tavern.

When the superintendent's wife got home from the bath-house she found her husband in the drawing-room.

"What did the examining magistrate come about?" asked her husband.

"He came to say that they had found Klyauzov. Only fancy, they found him staying with another man's wife."

"Ah, Mark Ivanitch, Mark Ivanitch!" sighed the police superintendent, turning up his eyes. "I told you that dissipation would lead to no good! I told you so-you wouldn't heed me!"

CHORISTERS

The Justice of the Peace, who had received a letter from Petersburg, had set the news going that the owner of Yefremovo, Count Vladimir Ivanovitch, would soon be arriving. When he would arrive - there was no saying.

"Like a thief in the night," said Father Kuzma, a grey-headed little priest in a lilac cassock. "And when he does come the place will be crowded with the nobility and other high gentry. All the neighbours will flock here. Mind now, do your best, Alexey Alexeitch. . . . I beg you most earnestly."

"You need not trouble about me," said Alexey Alexeitch, frowning. "I know my business. If only my enemy intones the litany in the right key. He may . . . out of sheer spite. . . ."

"There, there. . . . I'll persuade the deacon. . . I'll persuade him."

Alexey Alexeitch was the sacristan of the Yefremovo church. He also taught the schoolboys church and secular singing, for which he received sixty roubles a year from the revenues of the Count's estate. The schoolboys were bound to sing in church in return for their teaching. Alexey Alexeitch was a tall, thick-set man of dignified deportment, with a fat, clean-shaven face that reminded one of a cow's udder. His imposing figure and double chin made him look like a man occupying an important position in the secular hierarchy rather than a sacristan. It was strange to see him, so dignified and imposing, flop to the ground before the bishop and, on one occasion, after too loud a squabble with the deacon Yevlampy Avdiessov, remain on his knees for two hours by order of the head priest of the district. Grandeur was more in keeping with his figure than humiliation.

On account of the rumours of the Count's approaching visit he had a choir practice every day, morning and evening. The choir practice was held at the school. It did not interfere much with the school work. During the practice the schoolmaster, Sergey Makaritch, set the children writing copies while he joined the tenors as an amateur.

This is how the choir practice was conducted. Alexey Alexeitch would come into the school-room, slamming the door and blowing his nose.

The trebles and altos extricated themselves noisily from the school-tables. The tenors and basses, who had been waiting for some time in the yard, came in, tramping like horses. They all took their places. Alexey Alexeitch drew himself up, made a sign to enforce silence, and struck a note with the tuning fork.

"To-to-li-to-tom . . . Do-mi-sol-do!"

"Adagio, adagio. . . . Once more."

After the "Amen" there followed "Lord have mercy upon us" from the Great Litany. All this had been learned long ago, sung a thousand times and thoroughly digested, and it was gone through simply as a formality. It was sung indolently, unconsciously. Alexey Alexeitch waved his arms calmly and chimed in now in a tenor, now in a bass voice. It was all slow, there was nothing interesting. . . . But before the "Cherubim" hymn the whole choir suddenly began blowing their noses, coughing and zealously turning the pages of their music. The sacristan turned his back on the choir and with a mysterious expression on his face began tuning his violin. The preparations lasted a couple of minutes.

"Take your places. Look at your music carefully. . . . Basses, don't overdo it . . . rather softly."

Bortnyansky's "Cherubim" hymn, No. 7, was selected. At a given signal silence prevailed. All eyes were fastened on the music, the trebles opened their mouths. Alexey Alexeitch softly lowered his arm.

"Piano . . . piano. . . . You see 'piano' is written there. . . . More lightly, more lightly."

When they had to sing "piano" an expression of benevolence and amiability overspread Alexey Alexeitch's face, as though he was dreaming of a dainty morsel.

"Forte . . . forte! Hold it!"

And when they had to sing "forte" the sacristan's fat face expressed alarm and even horror.

The "Cherubim" hymn was sung well, so well that the school-children abandoned their copies and fell to watching the movements of Alexey

Alexeitch. People stood under the windows. The schoolwatchman, Vassily, came in wearing an apron and carrying a dinner-knife in his hand and stood listening. Father Kuzma, with an anxious face appeared suddenly as though he had sprung from out of the earth. . . . After 'Let us lay aside all earthly cares' Alexey Alexeitch wiped the sweat off his brow and went up to Father Kuzma in excitement.

"It puzzles me, Father Kuzma," he said, shrugging his shoulders, "why is it that the Russian people have no understanding? It puzzles me, may the Lord chastise me! Such an uncultured people that you really cannot tell whether they have a windpipe in their throats or some other sort of internal arrangement. Were you choking, or what?" he asked, addressing the bass Gennady Semitchov, the innkeeper's brother.

"Why?"

"What is your voice like? It rattles like a saucepan. I bet you were boozing yesterday! That's what it is! Your breath smells like a tavern. . . . E-ech! You are a clodhopper, brother! You are a lout! How can you be a chorister if you keep company with peasants in the tavern? Ech, you are an ass, brother!"

"It's a sin, it's a sin, brother," muttered Father Kuzma. "God sees everything . . . through and through . . . ."

"That's why you have no idea of singing - because you care more for vodka than for godliness, you fool."

"Don't work yourself up," said Father Kuzma. "Don't be cross. . . . I will persuade him."

Father Kuzma went up to Gennady Semitchov and began "persuading" him: "What do you do it for? Try and put your mind to it. A man who sings ought to restrain himself, because his throat is . . . er . . tender."

Gennady scratched his neck and looked sideways towards the window as though the words did not apply to him.

After the "Cherubim" hymn they sang the Creed, then "It is meet and right"; they sang smoothly and with feeling, and so right on to "Our Father."

"To my mind, Father Kuzma," said the sacristan, "the old 'Our Father' is better than the modern. That's what we ought to sing before the Count."

"No, no. . . . Sing the modern one. For the Count hears nothing but modern music when he goes to Mass in Petersburg or Moscow. . . . In the churches there, I imagine . . . there's very different sort of music there, brother 1"

After "Our Father" there was again a great blowing of noses, coughing and turning over of pages. The most difficult part of the performance came next: the "concert." Alexey Alexeitch was practising two pieces, "Who is the God of glory" and "Universal Praise." Whichever the choir learned best would be sung before the Count. During the "concert" the sacristan rose to a pitch of enthusiasm. The expression of benevolence was continually alternating with one of alarm.

"Forte!" he muttered. "Andante! let yourselves go! Sing, you image! Tenors, you don't bring it off! To-to-ti-to-tom. . . . Sol . . . si . . . sol, I tell you, you blockhead! Glory! Basses, glo . . . o . . . ry.

His bow travelled over the heads and shoulders of the erring trebles and altos. His left hand was continually pulling the ears of the young singers. On one occasion, carried away by his feelings he flipped the bass Gennady under the chin with his bent thumb. But the choristers were not moved to tears or to anger at his blows: they realised the full gravity of their task.

After the "concert" came a minute of silence. Alexey Alexeitch, red, perspiring and exhausted, sat down on the window-sill, and turned upon the company lustreless, wearied, but triumphant eyes. In the listening crowd he observed to his immense annoyance the deacon Avdiessov. The deacon, a tall thick-set man with a red pock-marked face, and straw in his hair, stood leaning against the stove and grinning contemptuously.

"That's right, sing away! Perform your music!" he muttered in a deep bass. "Much the Count will care for your singing! He doesn't care whether you sing with music or without. . . . For he is an atheist."

Father Kuzma looked round in a scared way and twiddled his fingers.

"Come, come," he muttered. "Hush, deacon, I beg."

After the "concert" they sang "May our lips be filled with praise," and the choir practice was over. The choir broke up to reassemble in the evening for another practice. And so it went on every day.

One month passed and then a second. . . . The steward, too, had by then received a notice that the Count would soon be coming. At last the dusty sun-blinds were taken off the windows of the big house, and Yefremovo heard the strains of the broken-down, out-of-tune piano. Father Kuzma was pining, though he could not himself have said why, or whether it was from delight or alarm. . . . The deacon went about grinning.

The following Saturday evening Father Kuzma went to the sacristan's lodgings. His face was pale, his shoulders drooped, the lilac of his cassock looked faded.

"I have just been at his Excellency's," he said to the sacristan, stammering. "He is a cultivated gentleman with refined ideas. But . . . er . . . it's mortifying, brother. . . . 'At what o'clock, your Excellency, do you desire us to ring for Mass to-morrow?' And he said: 'As you think best. Only, couldn't it be as short and quick as possible without a choir.' Without a choir! Er . . . do you understand, without, without a choir. . . ."

Alexey Alexeitch turned crimson. He would rather have spent two hours on his knees again than have heard those words! He did not sleep all night. He was not so much mortified at the waste of his labours as at the fact that the deacon would give him no peace now with his jeers. The deacon was delighted at his discomfiture. Next day all through the service he was casting disdainful glances towards the choir where Alexey Alexeitch was booming responses in solitude. When he passed by the choir with the censer he muttered:

"Perform your music! Do your utmost! The Count will give a ten-rouble note to the choir!"

After the service the sacristan went home, crushed and ill with mortification. At the gate he was overtaken by the red-faced deacon.

"Stop a minute, Alyosha!" said the deacon. "Stop a minute, silly, don't be cross! You are not the only one, I am in for it too! Immediately after the Mass Father Kuzma went up to the Count and asked: 'And what did you think of the deacon's voice, your Excellency. He has a deep bass, hasn't he?' And the Count - do you know what he answered by way of compliment? 'Anyone can bawl,' he said. 'A man's voice is not as important as his brains.' A learned gentleman from Petersburg! An atheist is an atheist, and that's all about it! Come, brother in misfortune, let us go and have a drop to drown our troubles!"

And the enemies went out of the gate arm-in-arm.

THE ALBUM

Kraterov, the titular councillor, as thin and slender as the Admiralty spire, stepped forward and, addressing Zhmyhov, said:

"Your Excellency! Moved and touched to the bottom of our hearts by the way you have ruled us during long years, and by your fatherly care. . . ."

"During the course of more than ten years. . ." Zakusin prompted.

"During the course of more than ten years, we, your subordinates, on this so memorable for us . . . er . . . day, beg your Excellency to accept in token of our respect and profound gratitude this album with our portraits in it, and express our hope that for the duration of your distinguished life, that for long, long years to come, to your dying day you may not abandon us. . . ."

"With your fatherly guidance in the path of justice and progress. . ." added Zakusin, wiping from his brow the perspiration that had suddenly appeared on it; he was evidently longing to speak, and in all probability had a speech ready. "And," he wound up, "may your standard fly for long, long years in the career of genius, industry, and social self-consciousness."

A tear trickled down the wrinkled left cheek of Zhmyhov.

"Gentlemen!" he said in a shaking voice, "I did not expect, I had no idea that you were going to celebrate my modest jubilee. . . . I am touched indeed . . . very much so. . . . I shall not forget this moment to my dying day, and believe me . . . believe me, friends, that no one is so desirous of your welfare as I am . . . and if there has been anything . . . it was for your benefit."

Zhmyhov, the actual civil councillor, kissed the titular councillor Kraterov, who had not expected such an honour, and turned pale with delight. Then the chief made a gesture that signified that he could not speak for emotion, and shed tears as though an expensive album had not been presented to him, but on the contrary, taken from him. . . . Then when he had a little recovered and said a few more words full of feeling and given everyone his hand to shake, he went downstairs amid loud and joyful cheers, got into his carriage and drove off, followed by their blessings. As he sat in his carriage he was aware of a flood of joyous feelings such as he had never known before, and once more he shed tears.

At home new delights awaited him. There his family, his friends, and acquaintances had prepared him such an ovation that it seemed to him that he really had been of very great service to his country, and that if he had never existed his country would perhaps have been in a very bad way. The jubilee dinner was made up of toasts, speeches, and tears. In short, Zhmyhov had never expected that his merits would be so warmly appreciated.

"Gentlemen!" he said before the dessert, "two hours ago I was recompensed for all the sufferings a man has to undergo who is the servant, so to say, not of routine, not of the letter, but of duty! Through the whole duration of my service I have constantly adhered to the principle;- the public does not exist for us, but we for the public, and to-day I received the highest reward! My subordinates presented me with an album . . . see! I was touched."

Festive faces bent over the album and began examining it.

"It's a pretty album," said Zhmyhov's daughter Olya, "it must have cost fifty roubles, I do believe. Oh, it's charming! You must give me the album, papa, do you hear? I'll take care of it, it's so pretty."

After dinner Olya carried off the album to her room and shut it up in her table drawer. Next day she took the clerks out of it, flung them on the floor, and put her school friends in their place. The government uniforms made way for white pelerines. Kolya, his Excellency's little son, picked up the clerks and painted their clothes red. Those who had no moustaches he presented with green moustaches and added brown beards to the beardless. When there was nothing left to paint he cut the little men out of the card-board, pricked their eyes with a pin, and began playing soldiers with them. After cutting out the titular councillor Kraterov, he fixed him on a match-box and carried him in that state to his father's study.

"Papa, a monument, look!"

Zhmyhov burst out laughing, lurched forward, and, looking tenderly at the child, gave him a warm kiss on the cheek.

"There, you rogue, go and show mamma; let mamma look too."

MINDS IN FERMENT

The earth was like an oven. The afternoon sun blazed with such energy that even the thermometer hanging in the excise officer's room lost its head: it ran up to 112.5 and stopped there, irresolute. The inhabitants streamed with perspiration like overdriven horses, and were too lazy to mop their faces.

Two of the inhabitants were walking along the market-place in front of the closely shuttered houses. One was Potcheshihin, the local treasury clerk, and the other was Optimov, the agent, for many years a correspondent of the *Son of the Fatherland* newspaper. They walked in silence, speechless from the heat. Optimov felt tempted to find fault with the local authorities for the dust and disorder of the market-place, but, aware of the peace-loving disposition and moderate views of his companion, he said nothing.

In the middle of the market-place Potcheshihin suddenly halted and began gazing into the sky.

"What are you looking at?"

"Those starlings that flew up. I wonder where they have settled. Clouds and clouds of them. . . . If one were to go and take a shot at them, and if one were to pick them up . . . and if . . . They have settled in the Father Prebendary's garden!"

"Oh no! They are not in the Father Prebendary's, they are in the Father Deacon's. If you did have a shot at them from here you wouldn't kill anything. Fine shot won't carry so far; it loses its force. And why should you kill them, anyway? They're birds destructive of the fruit, that's true; still, they're fowls of the air, works of the Lord. The starling sings, you know. . . . And what does it sing, pray? A song of praise. . . . 'All ye fowls of the air, praise ye the Lord.' No. I do believe they have settled in the Father Prebendary's garden."

Three old pilgrim women, wearing bark shoes and carrying wallets, passed noiselessly by the speakers. Looking enquiringly at the gentlemen who were for some unknown reason staring at the Father Prebendary's house, they slackened their pace, and when they were a few yards off stopped, glanced at the friends once more, and then fell to gazing at the house themselves.

"Yes, you were right; they have settled in the Father Prebendary's," said Optimov. "His cherries are ripe now, so they have gone there to peck them."

From the garden gate emerged the Father Prebendary himself, accompanied by the sexton. Seeing the attention directed upon his abode and wondering what people were staring at, he stopped, and he, too, as well as the sexton, began looking upwards to find out.

"The father is going to a service somewhere, I suppose," said Potcheshihin. "The Lord be his succour!"

Some workmen from Purov's factory, who had been bathing in the river, passed between the friends and the priest. Seeing the latter absorbed in contemplation of the heavens and the pilgrim women, too, standing motionless with their eyes turned upwards, they stood still and stared in the same direction.

A small boy leading a blind beggar and a peasant, carrying a tub of stinking fish to throw into the market-place, did the same.

"There must be something the matter, I should think," said Potcheshihin, "a fire or something. But there's no sign of smoke anywhere. Hey! Kuzma!" he shouted to the peasant, "what's the matter?"

The peasant made some reply, but Potcheshihin and Optimov did not catch it. Sleepy-looking shopmen made their appearance at the doors of all the shops. Some plasterers at work on a warehouse near left their ladders and joined the workmen.

The fireman, who was describing circles with his bare feet, on the watch-tower, halted, and, after looking steadily at them for a few minutes, came down. The watch-tower was left deserted. This seemed suspicious.

"There must be a fire somewhere. Don't shove me! You damned swine!"

"Where do you see the fire? What fire? Pass on, gentlemen! I ask you civilly!"

"It must be a fire indoors!"

"Asks us civilly and keeps poking with his elbows. Keep your hands to yourself! Though you are a head constable, you have no sort of right to make free with your fists!"

"He's trodden on my corn! Ah! I'll crush you!"

"Crushed? Who's crushed? Lads! a man's been crushed!"

"What's the meaning of this crowd? What do you want?"

"A man's been crushed, please your honour!"

"Where? Pass on! I ask you civilly! I ask you civilly, you blockheads!"

"You may shove a peasant, but you daren't touch a gentleman! Hands off!"

"Did you ever know such people? There's no doing anything with them by fair words, the devils! Sidorov, run for Akim Danilitch! Look sharp! It'll be the worse for you, gentlemen! Akim Danilitch is coming, and he'll give it to you! You here, Parfen? A blind man, and at his age too! Can't see, but he must be like other people and won't do what he's told. Smirnov, put his name down!"

"Yes, sir! And shall I write down the men from Purov's? That man there with the swollen cheek, he's from Purov's works."

"Don't put down the men from Purov's. It's Purov's birthday to-morrow."

The starlings rose in a black cloud from the Father Prebendary's garden, but Potcheshihin and Optimov did not notice them. They stood staring into the air, wondering what could have attracted such a crowd, and what it was looking at.

Akim Danilitch appeared. Still munching and wiping his lips, he cut his way into the crowd, bellowing:

"Firemen, be ready! Disperse! Mr. Optimov, disperse, or it'll be the worse for you! Instead of writing all kinds of things about decent people in the papers, you had better try to behave yourself more conformably! No good ever comes of reading the papers!"

"Kindly refrain from reflections upon literature!" cried Optimov hotly. "I am a literary man, and I will allow no one to make reflections upon literature! though, as is the duty of a citizen, I respect you as a father and benefactor!"

"Firemen, turn the hose on them!"

"There's no water, please your honour!"

"Don't answer me! Go and get some! Look sharp!"

"We've nothing to get it in, your honour. The major has taken the fire-brigade horses to drive his aunt to the station.

"Disperse! Stand back, damnation take you! Is that to your taste? Put him down, the devil!"

"I've lost my pencil, please your honour!"

The crowd grew larger and larger. There is no telling what proportions it might have reached if the new organ just arrived from Moscow had not fortunately begun playing in the tavern close by. Hearing their favourite tune, the crowd gasped and rushed off to the tavern. So nobody ever knew why the crowd had assembled, and Potcheshihin and Optimov had by now forgotten the existence of the starlings who were innocently responsible for the proceedings.

An hour later the town was still and silent again, and only a solitary figure was to be seen-the fireman pacing round and round on the watch-tower.

The same evening Akim Danilitch sat in the grocer's shop drinking *limonade gaseuse* and brandy, and writing:

"In addition to the official report, I venture, your Excellency, to append a few supplementary observations of my own. Father and benefactor! In very truth, but for the prayers of your virtuous spouse in her salubrious villa near our town, there's no knowing what might not have come to pass. What I have been through to-day I can find no words to express. The efficiency of Krushensky and of the major of the fire brigade are beyond all praise! I am proud of such devoted servants of our country! As for me, I did all that a weak man could do, whose only desire is the welfare of his neighbour; and sitting now in the bosom of my family, with tears in my eyes I thank Him Who spared us bloodshed! In absence of evidence, the guilty parties remain in custody, but I propose to release them in a week or so. It was their ignorance that led them astray!"

A CHAMELEON

The police superintendent Otchumyelov is walking across the market square wearing a new overcoat and carrying a parcel under his arm. A red-haired policeman strides after him with a sieve full of confiscated gooseberries in his hands. There is silence all around. Not a soul in the square. . . . The open doors of the shops and taverns look out upon God's world disconsolately, like hungry mouths; there is not even a beggar near them.

"So you bite, you damned brute?" Otchumyelov hears suddenly. "Lads, don't let him go! Biting is prohibited nowadays! Hold him! ah . . . ah!"

There is the sound of a dog yelping. Otchumyelov looks in the direction of the sound and sees a dog, hopping on three legs and looking about her, run out of Pitchugin's timber-yard. A man in a starched cotton shirt, with his waistcoat unbuttoned, is chasing her. He runs after her, and throwing his body forward falls down and seizes the dog by her hind legs. Once more there is a yelping and a shout of "Don't let go!" Sleepy countenances are protruded from the shops, and soon a crowd, which seems to have sprung out of the earth, is gathered round the timber-yard.

"It looks like a row, your honour . . ." says the policeman.

Otchumyelov makes a half turn to the left and strides towards the crowd.

He sees the aforementioned man in the unbuttoned waistcoat standing close by the gate of the timber-yard, holding his right hand in the air and displaying a bleeding finger to the crowd. On his half-drunken face there is plainly written: "I'll pay you out, you rogue!" and indeed the very finger has the look of a flag of victory. In this man Otchumyelov recognises Hryukin, the goldsmith. The culprit who has caused the sensation, a white borzoy puppy with a sharp muzzle and a yellow patch on her back, is sitting on the ground with her fore-paws outstretched in the middle of the crowd, trembling all over. There is an expression of misery and terror in her tearful eyes.

"What's it all about?" Otchumyelov inquires, pushing his way through the crowd. "What are you here for? Why are you waving your finger . . . ? Who was it shouted?"

"I was walking along here, not interfering with anyone, your honour," Hryukin begins, coughing into his fist. "I was talking about firewood to Mitry Mitritch, when this low brute for no rhyme or reason bit my finger. . . . You must excuse me, I am a working man. . . . Mine is fine work. I must have damages, for I shan't be able to use this finger for a week, may be. . . . It's not even the law, your honour, that one should put up with it from a beast. . . . If everyone is going to be bitten, life won't be worth living. . . ."

"H'm. Very good," says Otchumyelov sternly, coughing and raising his eyebrows. "Very good. Whose dog is it? I won't let this pass! I'll teach them to let their dogs run all over the place! It's time these gentry were looked after, if they won't obey the regulations! When he's fined, the blackguard, I'll teach him what it means to keep dogs and such stray cattle! I'll give him a lesson! . . . Yeldyrin," cries the superintendent, addressing the policeman, "find out whose dog this is and draw up a report! And the dog must be strangled. Without delay! It's sure to be mad. . . . Whose dog is it, I ask?"

"I fancy it's General Zhigalov's," says someone in the crowd.

"General Zhigalov's, h'm. . . . Help me off with my coat, Yeldyrin . . . it's frightfully hot! It must be a sign of rain. . . . There's one thing I can't make out, how it came to bite you?" Otchumyelov turns to Hryukin. "Surely it couldn't reach your finger. It's a little dog, and you are a great hulking fellow! You must have scratched your finger with a nail, and then the idea struck you to get damages for it. We all know . . . your sort! I know you devils!"

"He put a cigarette in her face, your honour, for a joke, and she had the sense to snap at him. . . . He is a nonsensical fellow, your honour!"

"That's a lie, Squinteye! You didn't see, so why tell lies about it? His honour is a wise gentleman, and will see who is telling lies and who is telling the truth, as in God's sight. . . . And if I am lying let the court decide. It's written in the law. . . . We are all equal nowadays. My own brother is in the gendarmes . . . let me tell you. . . ."

"Don't argue!"

"No, that's not the General's dog," says the policeman, with profound conviction, "the General hasn't got one like that. His are mostly setters."

"Do you know that for a fact?"

"Yes, your honour."

"I know it, too. The General has valuable dogs, thoroughbred, and this is goodness knows what! No coat, no shape. . . . A low creature. And to keep a dog like that! . . . where's the sense of it. If a dog like that were to turn up in Petersburg or Moscow, do you know what would happen? They would not worry about the law, they would strangle it in a twinkling! You've been injured, Hryukin, and we can't let the matter drop. . . . We must give them a lesson! It is high time . . . . !"

"Yet maybe it is the General's," says the policeman, thinking aloud. "It's not written on its face. . . . I saw one like it the other day in his yard."

"It is the General's, that's certain!" says a voice in the crowd.

"H'm, help me on with my overcoat, Yeldyrin, my lad . . . the wind's getting up. . . . I am cold. . . . You take it to the General's, and inquire there. Say I found it and sent it. And tell them not to let it out into the street. . . . It may be a valuable dog, and if every swine goes sticking a cigar in its mouth, it will soon be ruined. A dog is a delicate animal. . . . And you put your hand down, you blockhead. It's no use your displaying your fool of a finger. It's your own fault. . . ."

"Here comes the General's cook, ask him. . . Hi, Prohor! Come here, my dear man! Look at this dog. . . . Is it one of yours?"

"What an idea! We have never had one like that!"

"There's no need to waste time asking," says Otchumyelov. "It's a stray dog! There's no need to waste time talking about it. . . . Since he says it's a stray dog, a stray dog it is. . . . It must be destroyed, that's all about it."

"It is not our dog," Prohor goes on. "It belongs to the General's brother, who arrived the other day. Our master does not care for hounds. But his honour is fond of them. . . ."

"You don't say his Excellency's brother is here? Vladimir Ivanitch?" inquires Otchumyelov, and his whole face beams with an ecstatic smile. "'Well, I never! And I didn't know! Has he come on a visit?

"Yes."

"Well, I never. . . . He couldn't stay away from his brother. . . . And there I didn't know! So this is his honour's dog? Delighted to hear it. . . . Take it. It's not a bad pup. . . . A lively creature. . . . Snapped at this fellow's finger! Ha-ha-ha. . . . Come, why are you shivering? Rrr . . . Rrrr. . . . The rogue's angry . . . a nice little pup."

Prohor calls the dog, and walks away from the timber-yard with her. The crowd laughs at Hryukin.

"I'll make you smart yet!" Otchumyelov threatens him, and wrapping himself in his greatcoat, goes on his way across the square.

IN THE GRAVEYARD

"The wind has got up, friends, and it is beginning to get dark. Hadn't we better take ourselves off before it gets worse?"

The wind was frolicking among the yellow leaves of the old birch trees, and a shower of thick drops fell upon us from the leaves. One of our party slipped on the clayey soil, and clutched at a big grey cross to save himself from falling.

"Yegor Gryaznorukov, titular councillor and cavalier . ." he read. "I knew that gentleman. He was fond of his wife, he wore the Stanislav ribbon, and read nothing. . . . His digestion worked well . . . . life was all right, wasn't it? One would have thought he had no reason to die, but alas! fate had its eye on him. . . . The poor fellow fell a victim to his habits of observation. On one occasion, when he was listening at a keyhole, he got such a bang on the head from the door that he sustained concussion of the brain (he had a brain), and died. And here, under this tombstone, lies a man who from his cradle detested verses and epigrams. . . . As though to mock him his whole tombstone is adorned with verses. . . . There is someone coming!"

A man in a shabby overcoat, with a shaven, bluish-crimson countenance, overtook us. He had a bottle under his arm and a parcel of sausage was sticking out of his pocket.

"Where is the grave of Mushkin, the actor?" he asked us in a husky voice.

We conducted him towards the grave of Mushkin, the actor, who had died two years before.

"You are a government clerk, I suppose?" we asked him.

"No, an actor. Nowadays it is difficult to distinguish actors from clerks of the Consistory. No doubt you have noticed that. . . . That's typical, but it's not very flattering for the government clerk."

It was with difficulty that we found the actor's grave. It had sunken, was overgrown with weeds, and had lost all appearance of a grave. A cheap, little cross that had begun to rot, and was covered with green moss blackened by the frost, had an air of aged dejection and looked, as it were, ailing.

". . . forgotten friend Mushkin . . ." we read.

Time had erased the *never*, and corrected the falsehood of man.

"A subscription for a monument to him was got up among actors and journalists, but they drank up the money, the dear fellows . . ." sighed the actor, bowing down to the ground and touching the wet earth with his knees and his cap.

"How do you mean, drank it?"

That's very simple. They collected the money, published a paragraph about it in the newspaper, and spent it on drink. . . . I don't say it to blame them. . . . I hope it did them good, dear things! Good health to them, and eternal memory to him."

"Drinking means bad health, and eternal memory nothing but sadness. God give us remembrance for a time, but eternal memory - what next!"

"You are right there. Mushkin was a well-known man, you see; there were a dozen wreaths on the coffin, and he is already forgotten. Those to whom he was dear have forgotten him, but those to whom he did harm remember him. I, for instance, shall never, never forget him, for I got nothing but harm from him. I have no love for the deceased."

"What harm did he do you?"

"Great harm," sighed the actor, and an expression of bitter resentment overspread his face. "To me he was a villain and a scoundrel - the Kingdom of Heaven be his! It was through looking at him and listening to him that I became an actor. By his art he lured me from the parental home, he enticed me with the excitements of an actor's life, promised me all sorts of things - and brought tears and sorrow. . . . An actor's lot is a bitter one! I have lost youth, sobriety, and the divine semblance. . . . I haven't a half-penny to bless myself with, my shoes are down at heel, my breeches are frayed and patched, and my face looks as if it had been gnawed by dogs. . . . My head's full of freethinking and nonsense. . . . He robbed me of my faith - my evil genius! It would have been something if I had had talent, but as it is, I am ruined for nothing. . . . It's cold, honoured friends. . . . Won't you have some? There is enough for all. . . . B-r-r-r. . . . Let us drink to the rest of his soul! Though I don't like him and though he's dead, he was the only one I had in the world, the only one. It's the last time I shall visit him. . . . The doctors say I shall soon die of drink, so here I have come to say good-bye. One must forgive one's enemies."

We left the actor to converse with the dead Mushkin and went on. It began drizzling a fine cold rain.

At the turning into the principal avenue strewn with gravel, we met a funeral procession. Four bearers, wearing white calico sashes and muddy high boots with leaves sticking on them, carried the brown coffin. It was getting dark and they hastened, stumbling and shaking their burden. . . .

"We've only been walking here for a couple of hours and that is the third brought in already. . . . Shall we go home, friends?"

OYSTERS

I need no great effort of memory to recall, in every detail, the rainy autumn evening when I stood with my father in one of the more frequented streets of Moscow, and felt that I was gradually being overcome by a strange illness. I had no pain at all, but my legs were giving way under me, the words stuck in my throat, my head slipped weakly on one side . . . It seemed as though, in a moment, I must fall down and lose consciousness.

If I had been taken into a hospital at that minute, the doctors would have had to write over my bed: *Fames,* a disease which is not in the manuals of medicine.

Beside me on the pavement stood my father in a shabby summer overcoat and a serge cap, from which a bit of white wadding was sticking out. On his feet he had big heavy galoshes. Afraid, vain man, that people would see that his feet were bare under his galoshes, he had drawn the tops of some old boots up round the calves of his legs.

This poor, foolish, queer creature, whom I loved the more warmly the more ragged and dirty his smart summer overcoat became, had come to Moscow, five months before, to look for a job as copying-clerk. For those five months he had been trudging about Moscow looking for work, and it was only on that day that he had brought himself to go into the street to beg for alms.

Before us was a big house of three storeys, adorned with a blue signboard with the word "Restaurant" on it. My head was drooping feebly backwards and on one side, and I could not help looking upwards at the lighted windows of the restaurant. Human figures were flitting about at the windows. I could see the right side of the orchestrion, twooleographs, hanging lamps . . . . Staring into one window, I saw a patch of white. The patch was motionless, and its rectangular outlines stood out sharply against the dark, brown background. I looked intently and made out of the patch a white placard on the wall. Something was written on it, but what it was, I could not see. . .

For half an hour I kept my eyes on the placard. Its white attracted my eyes, and, as it were, hypnotised my brain. I tried to read it, but my efforts were in vain.

At last the strange disease got the upper hand.

The rumble of the carriages began to seem like thunder, in the stench of the street I distinguished a thousand smells. The restaurant lights and the lamps dazzled my eyes like lightning. My five senses were overstrained and sensitive beyond the normal. I began to see what I had not seen before.

"Oysters . . ." I made out on the placard.

A strange word! I had lived in the world eight years and three months, but had never come across that word. What did it mean? Surely it was not the name of the restaurant-keeper? But signboards with names on them always hang outside, not on the walls indoors!

"Papa, what does 'oysters' mean?" I asked in a husky voice, making an effort to turn my face towards my father.

My father did not hear. He was keeping a watch on the movements of the crowd, and following every passer-by with his eyes. . . . From his eyes I saw that he wanted to say something to the passers-by, but the fatal word hung like a heavy weight on his trembling lips and could not be flung off. He even took a step after one passer-by and touched him on the sleeve, but when he turned round, he said, "I beg your pardon," was overcome with confusion, and staggered back.

"Papa, what does 'oysters' mean?" I repeated.

"It is an animal . . . that lives in the sea."

I instantly pictured to myself this unknown marine animal. . . . I thought it must be something midway between a fish and a crab. As it was from the sea they made of it, of course, a very nice hot fish soup with savoury pepper and laurel leaves, or broth with vinegar and fricassee of fish and cabbage, or crayfish sauce, or served it cold with horse-radish. . . . I vividly imagined it being brought from the market, quickly cleaned, quickly put in the pot, quickly, quickly, for everyone was hungry . . . awfully hungry! From the kitchen rose the smell of hot fish and crayfish soup.

I felt that this smell was tickling my palate and nostrils, that it was gradually taking possession of my whole body. . . . The restaurant, my father, the white placard, my sleeves were all smelling of it, smelling so strongly that I began to chew. I moved my jaws and swallowed as though I really had a piece of this marine animal in my mouth . . .

My legs gave way from the blissful sensation I was feeling, and I clutched at my father's arm to keep myself from falling, and leant against his wet summer overcoat. My father was trembling and shivering. He was cold . . .

"Papa, are oysters a Lenten dish?" I asked.

"They are eaten alive . . . " said my father. "They are in shells like tortoises, but . . . in two halves."

The delicious smell instantly left off affecting me, and the illusion vanished. . . . Now I understood it all!

"How nasty," I whispered, "how nasty!"

So that's what "oysters" meant! I imagined to myself a creature like a frog. A frog sitting in a shell, peeping out from it with big, glittering eyes, and moving its revolting jaws. I imagined this creature in a shell with claws, glittering eyes, and a slimy skin, being brought from the market. . . . The children would all hide while the cook, frowning with an air of disgust, would take the creature by its claw, put it on a plate, and carry it into the dining-room. The grown-ups would take it and eat it, eat it alive with its eyes, its teeth, its legs! While it squeaked and tried to bite their lips. . . .

I frowned, but . . . but why did my teeth move as though I were munching? The creature was loathsome, disgusting, terrible, but I ate it, ate it greedily, afraid of distinguishing its taste or smell. As soon as I had eaten one, I saw the glittering eyes of a second, a third . . . I ate them too. . . . At last I ate the table-napkin, the plate, my father's goloshes, the white placard . . . I ate everything that caught my eye, because I felt that nothing but eating would take away my illness. The oysters had a terrible look in their eyes and were loathsome. I shuddered at the thought of them, but I wanted to eat! To eat!

"Oysters! Give me some oysters!" was the cry that broke from me and I stretched out my hand.

"Help us, gentlemen!" I heard at that moment my father say, in a hollow and shaking voice. "I am ashamed to ask but - my God! - I can bear no more!"

"Oysters!" I cried, pulling my father by the skirts of his coat.

"Do you mean to say you eat oysters? A little chap like you!" I heard laughter close to me.

Two gentlemen in top hats were standing before us, looking into my face and laughing.

"Do you really eat oysters, youngster? That's interesting! How do you eat them?"

I remember that a strong hand dragged me into the lighted restaurant. A minute later there was a crowd round me, watching me with curiosity and amusement. I sat at a table and ate something slimy, salt with a flavour of dampness and mouldiness. I ate greedily without chewing, without looking and trying to discover what I was eating. I fancied that if I opened my eyes I should see glittering eyes, claws, and sharp teeth.

All at once I began biting something hard, there was a sound of a scrunching.

"Ha, ha! He is eating the shells," laughed the crowd. "Little silly, do you suppose you can eat that?"

After that I remember a terrible thirst. I was lying in my bed, and could not sleep for heartburn and the strange taste in my parched mouth. My father was walking up and down, gesticulating with his hands.

"I believe I have caught cold," he was muttering. "I've a feeling in my head as though someone were sitting on it. . . . Perhaps it is because I have not . . . er . . . eaten anything to-day. . . . I really am a queer, stupid creature. . . . I saw those gentlemen pay ten roubles for the oysters.

Why didn't I go up to them and ask them . . . to lend me something? They would have given something."

Towards morning, I fell asleep and dreamt of a frog sitting in a shell, moving its eyes. At midday I was awakened by thirst, and looked for my father: he was still walking up and down and gesticulating.

THE MARSHAL'S WIDOW

On the first of February every year, St. Trifon's day, there is an extraordinary commotion on the estate of Madame Zavzyatov, the widow of Trifon Lvovitch, the late marshal of the district. On that day, the nameday of the deceased marshal, the widow Lyubov Petrovna has a requiem service celebrated in his memory, and after the requiem a thanksgiving to the Lord. The whole district assembles for the service. There you will see Hrumov the present marshal, Marfutkin, the president of the Zemstvo, Potrashkov, the permanent member of the Rural Board, the two justices of the peace of the district, the police captain, Krinolinov, two police-superintendents, the district doctor, Dvornyagin, smelling of iodoform, all the landowners, great and small, and so on. There are about fifty people assembled in all.

Precisely at twelve o'clock, the visitors, with long faces, make their way from all the rooms to the big hall. There are carpets on the floor and their steps are noiseless, but the solemnity of the occasion makes them instinctively walk on tip-toe, holding out their hands to balance themselves. In the hall everything is already prepared. Father Yevmeny, a little old man in a high faded cap, puts on his black vestments. Konkordiev, the deacon, already in his vestments, and as red as a crab, is noiselessly turning over the leaves of his missal and putting slips of paper in it. At the door leading to the vestibule, Luka, the sacristan, puffing out his cheeks and making round eyes, blows up the censer. The hall is gradually filled with bluish transparent smoke and the smell of incense.

Gelikonsky, the elementary schoolmaster, a young man with big pimples on his frightened face, wearing a new greatcoat like a sack, carries round wax candles on a silver-plated tray. The hostess, Lyubov Petrovna, stands in the front by a little table with a dish of funeral rice on it, and holds her handkerchief in readiness to her face. There is a profound stillness, broken from time to time by sighs. Everybody has a long, solemn face. . . .

The requiem service begins. The blue smoke curls up from the censer and plays in the slanting sunbeams, the lighted candles faintly splutter. The singing, at first harsh and deafening, soon becomes quiet and musical as the choir gradually adapt themselves to the acoustic conditions of the rooms. . . . The tunes are all mournful and sad. . . . The guests are gradually brought to a melancholy mood and grow pensive. Thoughts of the brevity of human life, of mutability, of worldly vanity stray through their brains. . . . They recall the deceased Zavzyatov, a thick-set, red-cheeked man who used to drink off a bottle of champagne at one gulp and smash looking-glasses with his forehead. And when they sing "With Thy Saints, O Lord," and the sobs of their hostess are audible, the guests shift uneasily from one foot to the other. The more emotional begin to feel a tickling in their throat and about their eyelids. Marfutkin, the president of the Zemstvo, to stifle the unpleasant feeling, bends down to the police captain's ear and whispers:

"I was at Ivan Fyodoritch's yesterday. . . . Pyotr Petrovitch and I took all the tricks, playing no trumps. . . . Yes, indeed. . . . Olga Andreyevna was so exasperated that her false tooth fell out of her mouth."

But at last the "Eternal Memory" is sung. Gelikonsky respectfully takes away the candles, and the memorial service is over. Thereupon there follows a momentary commotion; there is a changing of vestments and a thanksgiving service. After the thanksgiving, while Father Yevmeny is disrobing, the visitors rub their hands and cough, while their hostess tells some anecdote of the good-heartedness of the deceased Trifon Lvovitch.

"Pray come to lunch, friends," she says, concluding her story with a sigh.

The visitors, trying not to push or tread on each other's feet, hasten into the dining-room. . . . There the luncheon is awaiting them. The repast is so magnificent that the deacon Konkordiev thinks it his duty every year to fling up his hands as he looks at it and, shaking his head in amazement, say:

"Supernatural! It's not so much like human fare, Father Yevmeny, as offerings to the gods."

The lunch is certainly exceptional. Everything that the flora and fauna of the country can furnish is on the table, but the only thing supernatural about it, perhaps, is that on the table there is everything except . . . alcoholic beverages. Lyubov Petrovna has taken a vow never to have in her house cards or spirituous liquors - the two sources of her husband's ruin. And the only bottles contain oil and vinegar, as though in mockery and chastisement of the guests who are to a man desperately fond of the bottle, and given to tippling.

Please help yourselves, gentlemen!" the marshal's widow presses them. "Only you must excuse me, I have no vodka. . . . I have none in the house."

The guests approach the table and hesitatingly attack the pie. But the progress with eating is slow. In the plying of forks, in the cutting up and munching, there is a certain sloth and apathy. . . . Evidently something is wanting.

"I feel as though I had lost something," one of the justices of the peace whispers to the other. "I feel as I did when my wife ran away with the engineer. . . . I can't eat."

Marfutkin, before beginning to eat, fumbles for a long time in his pocket and looks for his handkerchief.

"Oh, my handkerchief must be in my greatcoat," he recalls in a loud voice, "and here I am looking for it," and he goes into the vestibule where the fur coats are hanging up.

He returns from the vestibule with glistening eyes, and at once attacks the pie with relish.

"I say, it's horrid munching away with a dry mouth, isn't it?" he whispers to Father Yevmeny. "Go into the vestibule, Father. There's a bottle there in my fur coat. . . . Only mind you are careful; don't make a clatter with the bottle."

Father Yevmeny recollects that he has some direction to give to Luka, and trips off to the vestibule.

"Father, a couple of words in confidence," says Dvornyagin, overtaking him.

"You should see the fur coat I've bought myself, gentlemen," Hrumov boasts. "It's worth a thousand, and I gave . . . you won't believe it . . . two hundred and fifty! Not a farthing more."

At any other time the guests would have greeted this information with indifference, but now they display surprise and incredulity. In the end they all troop out into the vestibule to look at the fur coat, and go on looking at it till the doctor's man Mikeshka carries five empty bottles out on the sly. When the steamed sturgeon is served, Marfutkin remembers that he has left his cigar case in his sledge and goes to the stable. That he may not be lonely on this expedition, he takes with him the deacon, who appropriately feels it necessary to have a look at his horse. . . .

On the evening of the same day, Lyubov Petrovna is sitting in her study, writing a letter to an old friend in Petersburg:

"To-day, as in past years," she writes among other things, "I had a memorial service for my dear husband. All my neighbours came to the service. They are a simple, rough set, but what hearts! I gave them a splendid lunch, but of course, as in previous years, without a drop of alcoholic liquor. Ever since he died from excessive drinking I have vowed to establish temperance in this district and thereby to expiate his sins. I have begun the campaign for temperance at my own house. Father Yevmeny is delighted with my efforts, and helps me both in word and deed. Oh, *ma chère,* if you knew how fond my bears are of me! The president of the Zemstvo, Marfutkin, kissed my hand after lunch, held it a long while to his lips, and, wagging his head in an absurd way, burst into tears: so much feeling but no words! Father Yevmeny, that delightful little old man, sat down by me, and looking tearfully at me kept babbling something like a child. I did not understand what he said, but I know how to understand true feeling. The police captain, the handsome man of whom I wrote to you, went down on his knees to me, tried to read me some verses of his own composition (he is a poet), but . . . his feelings were too much for him, he lurched and fell over . . . that huge giant went into hysterics, you can imagine my delight! The day did not pass without a hitch, however. Poor Alalykin, the president of the judges' assembly, a stout and apoplectic man, was overcome by illness and lay on the sofa in a state of unconsciousness for two hours. We had to pour water on him. . . . I am thankful to Doctor Dvornyagin: he had brought a bottle of brandy from his dispensary and he moistened the patient's temples, which quickly revived him, and he was able to be moved. . . ."

SMALL FRY

"Honored Sir, Father and Benefactor!" a petty clerk called Nevyrazimov was writing a rough copy of an Easter congratulatory letter. "I trust that you may spend this Holy Day even as many more to come, in good health and prosperity. And to your family also I . . ."

The lamp, in which the kerosene was getting low, was smoking and smelling. A stray cockroach was running about the table in alarm near Nevyrazimov's writing hand. Two rooms away from the office Paramon the porter was for the third time cleaning his best boots, and with such energy that the sound of the blacking-brush and of his expectorations was audible in all the rooms.

"What else can I write to him, the rascal?" Nevyrazimov wondered, raising his eyes to the smutty ceiling.

On the ceiling he saw a dark circle - the shadow of the lamp-shade. Below it was the dusty cornice, and lower still the wall, which had once been painted a bluish muddy color. And the office seemed to him such a place of desolation that he felt sorry, not only for himself, but even for the cockroach.

"When I am off duty I shall go away, but he'll be on duty here all his cockroach-life," he thought, stretching. "I am bored! Shall I clean my boots?"

And stretching once more, Nevyrazimov slouched lazily to the porter's room. Paramon had finished cleaning his boots. Crossing himself with one hand and holding the brush in the other, he was standing at the open window-pane, listening.

"They're ringing," he whispered to Nevyrazimov, looking at him with eyes intent and wide open. "Already!"

Nevyrazimov put his ear to the open pane and listened. The Easter chimes floated into the room with a whiff of fresh spring air. The booming of the bells mingled with the rumble of carriages, and above the chaos of sounds rose the brisk tenor tones of the nearest church and a loud shrill laugh.

"What a lot of people!" sighed Nevyrazimov, looking down into the street, where shadows of men flitted one after another by the illumination lamps. "They're all hurrying to the midnight service. . . . Our fellows have had a drink by now, you may be sure, and are strolling about the town. What a lot of laughter, what a lot of talk! I'm the only unlucky one, to have to sit here on such a day: And I have to do it every year!"

"Well, nobody forces you to take the job. It's not your turn to be on duty today, but Zastupov hired you to take his place. When other folks are enjoying themselves you hire yourself out. It's greediness!"

"Devil a bit of it! Not much to be greedy over - two roubles is all he gives me; a necktie as an extra. . . . It's poverty, not greediness. And it would be jolly, now, you know, to be going with a party to the service, and then to break the fast. . . . To drink and to have a bit of supper and tumble off to sleep. . . . One sits down to the table, there's an Easter cake and the samovar hissing, and some charming little thing beside you. . . . You drink a glass and chuck her under the chin, and it's first-rate. . . . You feel you're somebody. . . . Ech h-h! . . . I've made a mess of things! Look at that hussy driving by in her carriage, while I have to sit here and brood."

"We each have our lot in life, Ivan Danilitch. Please God, you'll be promoted and drive about in your carriage one day."

"I? No, brother, not likely. I shan't get beyond a 'titular,' not if I try till I burst. I'm not an educated man."

"Our General has no education either, but . . ."

"Well, but the General stole a hundred thousand before he got his position. And he's got very different manners and deportment from me, brother. With my manners and deportment one can't get far! And such a scoundrelly surname, Nevyrazimov! It's a hopeless position, in fact. One may go on as one is, or one may hang oneself . . ."

He moved away from the window and walked wearily about the rooms. The din of the bells grew louder and louder. . . . There was no need to stand by the window to hear it. And the better he could hear the bells and the louder the roar of the carriages, the darker seemed the muddy walls and the smutty cornice and the more the lamp smoked.

"Shall I hook it and leave the office?" thought Nevyrazimov.

But such a flight promised nothing worth having. . . . After coming out of the office and wandering about the town, Nevyrazimov would have gone home to his lodging, and in his lodging it was even grayer and more depressing than in the office. . . . Even supposing he were to spend that day pleasantly and with comfort, what had he beyond? Nothing but the same gray walls, the same stop-gap duty and complimentary letters. . . .

Nevyrazimov stood still in the middle of the office and sank into thought. The yearning for a new, better life gnawed at his heart with an intolerable ache. He had a passionate longing to find himself suddenly in the street, to mingle with the living crowd, to take part in the solemn festivity for the sake of which all those bells were clashing and those carriages were rumbling. He longed for what he had known in childhood - the family circle, the festive faces of his own people, the white cloth, light, warmth . . . ! He thought of the carriage in which the lady had just driven by, the overcoat in which the head clerk was so smart, the gold chain that adorned the secretary's chest. . . . He thought of a warm bed, of the Stanislav order, of new boots, of a uniform without holes in the elbows. . . . He thought of all those things because he had none of them.

"Shall I steal?" he thought. "Even if stealing is an easy matter, hiding is what's difficult. Men run away to America, they say, with what they've stolen, but the devil knows where that blessed America is. One must have education even to steal, it seems."

The bells died down. He heard only a distant noise of carriages and Paramon's cough, while his depression and anger grew more and more intense and unbearable. The clock in the office struck half-past twelve.

"Shall I write a secret report? Proshkin did, and he rose rapidly."

Nevyrazimov sat down at his table and pondered. The lamp in which the kerosene had quite run dry was smoking violently and threatening to go out. The stray cockroach was still running about the table and had found no resting-place.

"One can always send in a secret report, but how is one to make it up? I should want to make all sorts of innuendoes and insinuations, like Proshkin, and I can't do it. If I made up anything I should be the first to get into trouble for it. I'm an ass, damn my soul!"

And Nevyrazimov, racking his brain for a means of escape from his hopeless position, stared at the rough copy he had written. The letter was written to a man whom he feared and hated with his whole soul, and from whom he had for the last ten years been trying to wring a post worth eighteen roubles a month, instead of the one he had at sixteen roubles.

"Ah, I'll teach you to run here, you devil!" He viciously slapped the palm of his hand on the cockroach, who had the misfortune to catch his eye. "Nasty thing!"

The cockroach fell on its back and wriggled its legs in despair. Nevyrazimov took it by one leg and threw it into the lamp. The lamp flared up and spluttered.

And Nevyrazimov felt better.

IN A HOTEL

"LET me tell you, my good man," began Madame Nashatyrin, the colonel's lady at No. 47, crimson and spluttering, as she pounced on the hotel-keeper. "Either give me other apartments, or I shall leave your confounded hotel altogether! It's a sink of iniquity! Mercy on us, I have grown-up daughters and one hears nothing but abominations day and night! It's beyond everything! Day and night! Sometimes he fires off such things that it simply makes one's ears blush! Positively like a cabman. It's a good thing that my poor girls don't understand or I should have to fly out into the street with them... He's saying something now! You listen!"

"I know a thing better than that, my boy," a husky bass floated in from the next room. "Do you remember Lieutenant Druzhkov? Well, that same Druzhkov was one day making a drive with the yellow into the pocket and as he usually did, you know, flung up his leg.... All at once something went crrr-ack! At first they thought he had torn the cloth of the billiard table, but when they looked, my dear fellow, his United States had split at every seam! He had made such a high kick, the beast, that not a seam was left.... Ha-ha-ha, and there were ladies present, too... among others the wife of that drivelling Lieutenant Okurin.... Okurin was furious.... 'How dare the fellow,' said he, 'behave with impropriety in the presence of my wife?' One thing led to another... you know our fellows!... Okurin sent seconds to Druzhkov, and Druzhkov said 'don't be a fool'... ha-ha-ha, 'but tell him he had better send seconds not to me but to the tailor who made me those breeches; it is his fault, you know.' Ha-ha-ha! Ha-ha-ha...."

Lilya and Mila, the colonel's daughters, who were sitting in the window with their round cheeks propped on their fists, flushed crimson and dropped their eyes that looked buried in their plump faces.

"Now you have heard him, haven't you?" Madame Nashatyrin went on, addressing the hotel-keeper. "And that, you consider, of no consequence, I suppose? I am the wife of a colonel, sir! My husband is a commanding officer. I will not permit some cabman to utter such infamies almost in my presence!"

"He is not a cabman, madam, but the staff-captain Kikin. . . . A gentleman born."

"If he has so far forgotten his station as to express himself like a cabman, then he is even more deserving of contempt! In short, don't answer me, but kindly take steps!"

"But what can I do, madam? You are not the only one to complain, everybody's complaining, but what am I to do with him? One goes to his room and begins putting him to shame, saying: 'Hannibal Ivanitch, have some fear of God! It's shameful! and he'll punch you in the face with his fists and say all sorts of things: 'there, put that in your pipe and smoke it,' and such like. It's a disgrace! He wakes up in the morning and sets to walking about the corridor in nothing, saving your presence, but his underclothes. And when he has had a drop he will pick up a revolver and set to putting bullets into the wall. By day he is swilling liquor and at night he plays cards like mad, and after cards it is fighting. . . . I am ashamed for the other lodgers to see it!"

"Why don't you get rid of the scoundrel?"

"Why, there's no getting him out! He owes me for three months, but we don't ask for our money, we simply ask him to get out as a favour. . . . The magistrate has given him an order to clear out of the rooms, but he's taking it from one court to another, and so it drags on. . . . He's a perfect nuisance, that's what he is. And, good Lord, such a man, too! Young, good-looking and intellectual. . . . When he hasn't had a drop you couldn't wish to see a nicer gentleman. The other day he wasn't drunk and he spent the whole day writing letters to his father and mother."

"Poor father and mother!" sighed the colonel's lady.

"They are to be pitied, to be sure! There's no comfort in having such a scamp! He's sworn at and turned out of his lodgings, and not a day passes but he is in trouble over some scandal. It's sad!"

"His poor unhappy wife!" sighed the lady.

"He has no wife, madam. A likely idea! She would have to thank God if her head were not broken. . . ."

The lady walked up and down the room.

"He is not married, you say?"

"Certainly not, madam."

The lady walked up and down the room again and mused a little.

"H'm, not married . . ." she pronounced meditatively. "H'm. Lilya and Mila, don't sit at the window, there's a draught! What a pity! A young man and to let himself sink to this! And all owing to what? The lack of good influence! There is no mother who would. . . . Not married? Well . . . there it is. . . . Please be so good," the lady continued suavely after a moment's thought, "as to go to him and ask him in my name to . . . refrain from using expressions. . . . Tell him that Madame Nashatyrin begs him. . . . Tell him she is staying with her daughters in No. 47 . . . that she has come up from her estate in the country. . . ."

"Certainly."

"Tell him, a colonel's lady and her daughters. He might even come and apologize. . . . We are always at home after dinner. Oh, Mila, shut the window!"

"Why, what do you want with that . . . black sheep, mamma?" drawled Lilya when the hotel-keeper had retired. "A queer person to invite! A drunken, rowdy rascal!"

"Oh, don't say so, ma chère! You always talk like that; and there . . . sit down! Why, whatever he may be, we ought not to despise him. . . . There's something good in everyone. Who knows," sighed the colonel's lady, looking her daughters up and down anxiously, "perhaps your fate is here. Change your dresses anyway. . . ."

BOOTS

A piano-tuner called Murkin, a close-shaven man with a yellow face, with a nose stained with snuff, and cotton-wool in his ears, came out of his hotel-room into the passage, and in a cracked voice cried: "Semyon! Waiter!"

And looking at his frightened face one might have supposed that the ceiling had fallen in on him or that he had just seen a ghost in his room.

"Upon my word, Semyon!" he cried, seeing the attendant running towards him. "What is the meaning of it? I am a rheumatic, delicate man and you make me go barefoot! Why is it you don't give me my boots all this time? Where are they?"

Semyon went into Murkin's room, looked at the place where he was in the habit of putting the boots he had cleaned, and scratched his head: the boots were not there.

"Where can they be, the damned things?" Semyon brought out. "I fancy I cleaned them in the evening and put them here. . . . H'm! . . . Yesterday, I must own, I had a drop. . . . I must have put them in another room, I suppose. That must be it, Afanasy Yegoritch, they are in another room! There are lots of boots, and how the devil is one to know them apart when one is drunk and does not know what one is doing? . . . I must have taken them in to the lady that's next door . . . the actress. . . ."

"And now, if you please, I am to go in to a lady and disturb her all through you! Here, if you please, through this foolishness I am to wake up a respectable woman."

Sighing and coughing, Murkin went to the door of the next room and cautiously tapped.

"Who's there?" he heard a woman's voice a minute later.

"It's I!" Murkin began in a plaintive voice, standing in the attitude of a cavalier addressing a lady of the highest society. "Pardon my disturbing you, madam, but I am a man in delicate health, rheumatic. . . . The doctors, madam, have ordered me to keep my feet warm, especially as I have to go at once to tune the piano at Madame la Générale Shevelitsyn's. I can't go to her barefoot."

"But what do you want? What piano?"

"Not a piano, madam; it is in reference to boots! Semyon, stupid fellow, cleaned my boots and put them by mistake in your room. Be so extremely kind, madam, as to give me my boots!"

There was a sound of rustling, of jumping off the bed and the flapping of slippers, after which the door opened slightly and a plump feminine hand flung at Murkin's feet a pair of boots. The piano-tuner thanked her and went into his own room.

"Odd . . ." he muttered, putting on the boots, it seems as though this is not the right boot. Why, here are two left boots! Both are for the left foot! I say, Semyon, these are not my boots! My boots have red tags and no patches on them, and these are in holes and have no tags."

Semyon picked up the boots, turned them over several times before his eyes, and frowned.

"Those are Pavel Alexandritch's boots," he grumbled, squinting at them. He squinted with the left eye.

"What Pavel Alexandritch?"

"The actor; he comes here every Tuesday. . . . He must have put on yours instead of his own. . . . So I must have put both pairs in her room, his and yours. Here's a go!"

"Then go and change them!"

"That's all right!" sniggered Semyon, "go and change them. . . . Where am I to find him now? He went off an hour ago. . . . Go and look for the wind in the fields!"

"Where does he live then?"

"Who can tell? He comes here every Tuesday, and where he lives I don't know. He comes and stays the night, and then you may wait till next Tuesday...."

"There, do you see, you brute, what you have done? Why, what am I to do now? It is time I was at Madame la Générale Shevelitsyn's, you anathema! My feet are frozen!"

"You can change the boots before long. Put on these boots, go about in them till the evening, and in the evening go to the theatre.... Ask there for Blistanov, the actor.... If you don't care to go to the theatre, you will have to wait till next Tuesday; he only comes here on Tuesdays...."

"But why are there two boots for the left foot?" asked the piano-tuner, picking up the boots with an air of disgust.

"What God has sent him, that he wears. Through poverty ... where is an actor to get boots? I said to him 'What boots, Pavel Alexandritch! They are a positive disgrace!' and he said: 'Hold your peace,' says he, 'and turn pale! In those very boots,' says he, 'I have played counts and princes.' A queer lot! Artists, that's the only word for them! If I were the governor or anyone in command, I would get all these actors together and clap them all in prison."

Continually sighing and groaning and knitting his brows, Murkin drew the two left boots on to his feet, and set off, limping, to Madame la Générale Shevelitsyn's. He went about the town all day long tuning pianos, and all day long it seemed to him that everyone was looking at his feet and seeing his patched boots with heels worn down at the sides! Apart from his moral agonies he had to suffer physically also; the boots gave him a corn.

In the evening he was at the theatre. There was a performance of *Bluebeard*. It was only just before the last act, and then only thanks to the good offices of a man he knew who played a flute in the orchestra, that he gained admittance behind the scenes. Going to the men's dressing-room, he found there all the male performers. Some were changing their clothes, others were painting their faces, others were smoking. Bluebeard was standing with King Bobesh, showing him a revolver.

"You had better buy it," said Bluebeard. "I bought it at Kursk, a bargain, for eight roubles, but, there! I will let you have it for six. . . . A wonderfully good one!"

"Steady. . . . It's loaded, you know!"

"Can I see Mr. Blistanov?" the piano-tuner asked as he went in.

"I am he!" said Bluebeard, turning to him. "What do you want?"

"Excuse my troubling you, sir," began the piano-tuner in an imploring voice, "but, believe me, I am a man in delicate health, rheumatic. The doctors have ordered me to keep my feet warm . . ."

"But, speaking plainly, what do you want?"

"You see," said the piano-tuner, addressing Bluebeard. "Er . . . you stayed last night at Buhteyev's furnished apartments . . . No. 64 . . ."

"What's this nonsense?" said King Bobesh with a grin. "My wife is at No. 64."

"Your wife, sir? Delighted. . . ." Murkin smiled. "It was she, your good lady, who gave me this gentleman's boots. . . . After this gentleman - the piano-tuner indicated Blistanov-"had gone away I missed my boots. . . . I called the waiter, you know, and he said: 'I left your boots in the next room!' By mistake, being in a state of intoxication, he left my boots as well as yours at 64," said Murkin, turning to Blistanov, "and when you left this gentleman's lady you put on mine."

"What are you talking about?" said Blistanov, and he scowled. " Have you come here to libel me?"

"Not at all, sir - God forbid! You misunderstand me. What am I talking about? About boots! You did stay the night at No. 64, didn't you?"

"When?"

"Last night!"

"Why, did you see me there?"

"No, sir, I didn't see you," said Murkin in great confusion, sitting down and taking off the boots. "I did not see you, but this gentleman's lady threw out your boots here to me . . . instead of mine."

"What right have you, sir, to make such assertions? I say nothing about myself, but you are slandering a woman, and in the presence of her husband, too!"

A fearful hubbub arose behind the scenes. King Bobesh, the injured husband, suddenly turned crimson and brought his fist down upon the table with such violence that two actresses in the next dressing-room felt faint.

"And you believe it?" cried Bluebeard. "You believe this worthless rascal? O-oh! Would you like me to kill him like a dog? Would you like it? I will turn him into a beefsteak! I'll blow his brains out!"

And all the persons who were promenading that evening in the town park by the Summer theatre describe to this day how just before the fourth act they saw a man with bare feet, a yellow face, and terror-stricken eyes dart out of the theatre and dash along the principal avenue. He was pursued by a man in the costume of Bluebeard, armed with a revolver. What happened later no one saw. All that is known is that Murkin was confined to his bed for a fortnight after his acquaintance with Blistanov, and that to the words "I am a man in delicate health, rheumatic" he took to adding, "I am a wounded man. . ."

NERVES

Dmitri Osipovitch Vaxin, the architect, returned from town to his holiday cottage greatly impressed by the spiritualistic séance at which he had been present. As he undressed and got into his solitary bed (Madame Vaxin had gone to an all-night service) he could not help remembering all he had seen and heard. It had not, properly speaking, been a séance at all, but the whole evening had been spent in terrifying conversation. A young lady had begun it by talking, apropos of nothing, about thought-reading. From thought-reading they had passed imperceptibly to spirits, and from spirits to ghosts, from ghosts to people buried alive. . . . A gentleman had read a horrible story of a corpse turning round in the coffin. Vaxin himself had asked for a saucer and shown the young ladies how to converse with spirits. He had called up among others the spirit of his deceased uncle, Klavdy Mironitch, and had mentally asked him:

"Has not the time come for me to transfer the ownership of our house to my wife?"

To which his uncle's spirit had replied:

"All things are good in their season."

"There is a great deal in nature that is mysterious and . . . terrible . . ." thought Vaxin, as he got into bed. "It's not the dead but the unknown that's so horrible."

It struck one o'clock. Vaxin turned over on the other side and peeped out from beneath the bedclothes at the blue light of the lamp burning before the holy ikon. The flame flickered and cast a faint light on the ikon-stand and the big portrait of Uncle Klavdy that hung facing his bed.

"And what if the ghost of Uncle Klavdy should appear this minute?" flashed through Vaxin's mind. "But, of course, that's impossible."

Ghosts are, we all know, a superstition, the offspring of undeveloped intelligence, but Vaxin, nevertheless, pulled the bed-clothes over his head, and shut his eyes very tight. The corpse that turned round in its coffin came back to his mind, and the figures of his deceased mother-in-law, of a colleague who had hanged himself, and of a girl who had drowned herself, rose before his imagination. . . . Vaxin began trying to dispel these gloomy ideas, but the more he tried to drive them away the more haunting the figures and fearful fancies became. He began to feel frightened.

"Hang it all!" he thought. "Here I am afraid in the dark like a child! Idiotic!"

Tick . . . tick . . . tick . . . he heard the clock in the next room. The church-bell chimed the hour in the churchyard close by. The bell tolled slowly, depressingly, mournfully. . . . A cold chill ran down Vaxin's neck and spine. He fancied he heard someone breathing heavily over his head, as though Uncle Klavdy had stepped out of his frame and was bending over his nephew. . . . Vaxin felt unbearably frightened. He clenched his teeth and held his breath in terror.

At last, when a cockchafer flew in at the open window and began buzzing over his bed, he could bear it no longer and gave a violent tug at the bellrope.

"Dmitri Osipitch, *was wollen Sie?*" he heard the voice of the German governess at his door a moment later.

"Ah, it's you, Rosalia Karlovna!" Vaxin cried, delighted. "Why do you trouble? Gavrila might just . . ."

"Yourself Gavrila to the town sent. And Glafira is somewhere all the evening gone. . . . There's nobody in the house. . . . *Was wollen Sie doch?*"

"Well, what I wanted . . . it's . . . but, please, come in . . . you needn't mind! . . . it's dark."

Rosalia Karlovna, a stout red-cheeked person, came in to the bedroom and stood in an expectant attitude at the door.

"Sit down, please . . . you see, it's like this. . . . What on earth am I to ask her for?" he wondered, stealing a glance at Uncle Klavdy's portrait and feeling his soul gradually returning to tranquility.

"What I really wanted to ask you was . . . Oh, when the man goes to town, don't forget to tell him to . . . er . . . er . . . to get some cigarette-papers. . . . But do, please sit down."

"Cigarette-papers? good. . . . *Was wollen Sie noch?*"

"*Ich will* . . . there's nothing I will, but. . . But do sit down! I shall think of something else in a minute."

"It is shocking for a maiden in a man's room to remain. . . . Mr. Vaxin, you are, I see, a naughty man. . . . I understand. . . . To order cigarette-papers one does not a person wake. . . . I understand you. . . ."

Rosalia Karlovna turned and went out of the room.

Somewhat reassured by his conversation with her and ashamed of his cowardice, Vaxin pulled the bedclothes over his head and shut his eyes. For about ten minutes he felt fairly comfortable, then the same nonsense came creeping back into his mind. . . . He swore to himself, felt for the matches, and without opening his eyes lighted a candle.

But even the light was no use. To Vaxin's excited imagination it seemed as though someone were peeping round the corner and that his uncle's eyes were moving.

"I'll ring her up again . . . damn the woman!" he decided. "I'll tell her I'm unwell and ask for some drops."

Vaxin rang. There was no response. He rang again, and as though answering his ring, he heard the church-bell toll the hour.

Overcome with terror, cold all over, he jumped out of bed, ran headlong out of his bedroom, and making the sign of the cross and cursing himself for his cowardice, he fled barefoot in his night-shirt to the governess's room.

"Rosalia Karlovna!" he began in a shaking voice as he knocked at her door, "Rosalia Karlovna! . . . Are you asleep? . . . I feel . . . so . . . er . . . er . . . unwell. . . . Drops! . . ."

There was no answer. Silence reigned.

"I beg you . . . do you understand? I beg you! Why this squeamishness, I can't understand . . . especially when a man . . . is ill . . . How absurdly *zierlich manierlich* you are really . . . at your age. . . ."

"I to your wife shall tell. . . . Will not leave an honest maiden in peace. . . . When I was at Baron Anzig's, and the baron try to come to me for matches, I understand at once what his matches mean and tell to the baroness. . . . I am an honest maiden."

"Hang your honesty! I am ill I tell you . . . and asking you for drops. Do you understand? I'm ill!"

"Your wife is an honest, good woman, and you ought her to love! *Ja!* She is noble! . . . I will not be her foe!"

"You are a fool! simply a fool! Do you understand, a fool?"

Vaxin leaned against the door-post, folded his arms and waited for his panic to pass off. To return to his room where the lamp flickered and his uncle stared at him from his frame was more than he could face, and to stand at the governess's door in nothing but his night-shirt was inconvenient from every point of view. What could he do?

It struck two o'clock and his terror had not left him. There was no light in the passage and something dark seemed to be peeping out from every corner. Vaxin turned so as to face the door-post, but at that instant it seemed as though somebody tweaked his night-shirt from behind and touched him on the shoulder.

"Damnation! . . . Rosalia Karlovna!"

No answer. Vaxin hesitatingly opened the door and peeped into the room. The virtuous German was sweetly slumbering. The tiny flame of a night-light threw her solid buxom person into relief. Vaxin stepped into the room and sat down on a wickerwork trunk near the door. He felt better in the presence of a living creature, even though that creature was asleep.

"Let the German idiot sleep," he thought, "I'll sit here, and when it gets light I'll go back. . . . It's daylight early now."

Vaxin curled up on the trunk and put his arm under his head to await the coming of dawn.

"What a thing it is to have nerves!" he reflected. "An educated, intelligent man! . . . Hang it all! . . . It's a perfect disgrace!"

As he listened to the gentle, even breathing of Rosalia Karlovna, he soon recovered himself completely.

At six o'clock, Vaxin's wife returned from the all-night service, and not finding her husband in their bedroom, went to the governess to ask her for some change for the cabman.

On entering the German's room, a strange sight met her eyes.

On the bed lay stretched Rosalia Karlovna fast asleep, and a couple of yards from her was her husband curled up on the trunk sleeping the sleep of the just and snoring loudly.

What she said to her husband, and how he looked when he woke, I leave to others to describe. It is beyond my powers.

A COUNTRY COTTAGE

Two young people who had not long been married were walking up and down the platform of a little country station. His arm was round her waist, her head was almost on his shoulder, and both were happy.

The moon peeped up from the drifting cloudlets and frowned, as it seemed, envying their happiness and regretting her tedious and utterly superfluous virginity. The still air was heavy with the fragrance of lilac and wild cherry. Somewhere in the distance beyond the line a corncrake was calling.

"How beautiful it is, Sasha, how beautiful!" murmured the young wife. "It all seems like a dream. See, how sweet and inviting that little copse looks! How nice those solid, silent telegraph posts are! They add a special note to the landscape, suggesting humanity, civilization in the distance. . . . Don't you think it's lovely when the wind brings the rushing sound of a train?"

"Yes. . . . But what hot little hands you've got. . . That's because you're excited, Varya. . . . What have you got for our supper to-night?"

"Chicken and salad. . . . It's a chicken just big enough for two. . . . Then there is the salmon and sardines that were sent from town."

The moon as though she had taken a pinch of snuff hid her face behind a cloud. Human happiness reminded her of her own loneliness, of her solitary couch beyond the hills and dales.

"The train is coming!" said Varya, "how jolly!"

Three eyes of fire could be seen in the distance. The stationmaster came out on the platform. Signal lights flashed here and there on the line.

"Let's see the train in and go home," said Sasha, yawning. "What a splendid time we are having together, Varya, it's so splendid, one can hardly believe it's true!"

The dark monster crept noiselessly alongside the platform and came to a standstill. They caught glimpses of sleepy faces, of hats and shoulders at the dimly lighted windows.

"Look! look!" they heard from one of the carriages. "Varya and Sasha have come to meet us! There they are! . . . Varya! . . . Varya. . . . Look!"

Two little girls skipped out of the train and hung on Varya's neck. They were followed by a stout, middle-aged lady, and a tall, lanky gentleman with grey whiskers; behind them came two schoolboys, laden with bags, and after the schoolboys, the governess, after the governess the grandmother.

"Here we are, here we are, dear boy!" began the whiskered gentleman, squeezing Sasha's hand. "Sick of waiting for us, I expect! You have been pitching into your old uncle for not coming down all this time, I daresay! Kolya, Kostya, Nina, Fifa . . . children! Kiss your cousin Sasha! We're all here, the whole troop of us, just for three or four days. . . . I hope we shan't be too many for you? You mustn't let us put you out!"

At the sight of their uncle and his family, the young couple were horror-stricken. While his uncle talked and kissed them, Sasha had a vision of their little cottage: he and Varya giving up their three little rooms, all the pillows and bedding to their guests; the salmon, the sardines, the chicken all devoured in a single instant; the cousins plucking the flowers in their little garden, spilling the ink, filled the cottage with noise and confusion; his aunt talking continually about her ailments and her papa's having been Baron von Fintich. . . .

And Sasha looked almost with hatred at his young wife, and whispered:

"It's you they've come to see! . . . Damn them!"

"No, it's you," answered Varya, pale with anger. "They're your relations! they're not mine!"

And turning to her visitors, she said with a smile of welcome: "Welcome to the cottage!"

The moon came out again. She seemed to smile, as though she were glad she had no relations. Sasha, turning his head away to hide his angry despairing face, struggled to give a note of cordial welcome to his voice as he said:

"It is jolly of you! Welcome to the cottage!"

MALINGERERS

Marfa Petrovna Petchonkin, the General's widow, who has been practising for ten years as a homeopathic doctor, is seeing patients in her study on one of the Tuesdays in May. On the table before her lie a chest of homeopathic drugs, a book on homeopathy, and bills from a homeopathic chemist. On the wall the letters from some Petersburg homeopath, in Marfa Petrovna's opinion a very celebrated and great man, hang under glass in a gilt frame, and there also is a portrait of Father Aristark, to whom the lady owes her salvation - that is, the renunciation of pernicious allopathy and the knowledge of the truth. In the vestibule patients are sitting waiting, for the most part peasants. All but two or three of them are barefoot, as the lady has given orders that their ill-smelling boots are to be left in the yard.

Marfa Petrovna has already seen ten patients when she calls the eleventh: "Gavrila Gruzd!"

The door opens and instead of Gavrila Gruzd, Zamuhrishen, a neighbouring landowner who has sunk into poverty, a little old man with sour eyes, and with a gentleman's cap under his arm, walks into the room. He puts down his stick in the corner, goes up to the lady, and without a word drops on one knee before her.

"What are you about, Kuzma Kuzmitch?" cries the lady in horror, flushing crimson. "For goodness sake!"

"While I live I will not rise," says Zamuhrishen, bending over her hand. "Let all the world see my homage on my knees, our guardian angel, benefactress of the human race! Let them! Before the good fairy who has given me life, guided me into the path of truth, and enlightened my scepticism I am ready not merely to kneel but to pass through fire, our miraculous healer, mother of the orphan and the widowed! I have recovered. I am a new man, enchantress!"

"I . . . I am very glad . . ." mutters the lady, flushing with pleasure. "It's so pleasant to hear that. . . Sit down please! Why, you were so seriously ill that Tuesday."

"Yes indeed, how ill I was! It's awful to recall it," says Zamuhrishen, taking a seat." I had rheumatism in every part and every organ. I have been in misery for eight years, I've had no rest from it . . . by day or by night, my benefactress. I have consulted doctors, and I went to professors at Kazan; I have tried all sorts of mud-baths, and drunk waters, and goodness knows what I haven't tried! I have wasted all my substance on doctors, my beautiful lady. The doctors did me nothing but harm. They drove the disease inwards. Drive in, that they did, but to drive out was beyond their science. All they care about is their fees, the brigands; but as for the benefit of humanity - for that they don't care a straw. They prescribe some quackery, and you have to drink it. Assassins, that's the only word for them. If it hadn't been for you, our angel, I should have been in the grave by now! I went home from you that Tuesday, looked at the pilules that you gave me then, and wondered what good there could be in them. Was it possible that those little grains, scarcely visible, could cure my immense, long-standing disease? That's what I thought - unbeliever that I was! - and I smiled; but when I took the pilule - it was instantaneous! It was as though I had not been ill, or as though it had been lifted off me. My wife looked at me with her eyes starting out of her head and couldn't believe it. 'Why, is it you, Kolya?' 'Yes, it is I,' I said. And we knelt down together before the ikon, and fell to praying for our angel: 'Send her, O Lord, all that we are feeling!' "

Zamuhrishen wipes his eyes with his sleeve gets up from his chair, and shows a disposition to drop on one knee again; but the lady checks him and makes him sit down.

"It's not me you must thank," she says, blushing with excitement and looking enthusiastically at the portrait of Father Aristark. "It's not my doing. . . . I am only the obedient instrument . . It's really a miracle. Rheumatism of eight years' standing by one pilule of scrofuloso!"

"Excuse me, you were so kind as to give me three pilules. One I took at dinner and the effect was instantaneous! Another in the evening, and the third next day; and since then not a touch! Not a twinge anywhere! And you know I thought I was dying, I had written to Moscow for my son to come! The Lord has given you wisdom, our lady of healing! Now I am walking, and feel as though I were in Paradise. The Tuesday I came to you I was hobbling, and now I am ready to run after a hare. . . . I could live for a hundred years. There's only one trouble, our lack of means. I'm well now, but what's the use of health if there's nothing to live on? Poverty weighs on me worse than illness. . . . For example, take this . . . It's the time to sow oats, and how is one to sow it if one has no seed? I ought to buy it, but the money . . . everyone knows how we are off for money. . . ."

"I will give you oats, Kuzma Kuzmitch. . . . Sit down, sit down. You have so delighted me, you have given me so much pleasure that it's not you but I that should say thank you!"

"You are our joy! That the Lord should create such goodness! Rejoice, Madam, looking at your good deeds! . . . While we sinners have no cause for rejoicing in ourselves. . . . We are paltry, poor-spirited, useless people . . . a mean lot. . . . We are only gentry in name, but in a material sense we are the same as peasants, only worse. . . . We live in stone houses, but it's a mere make-believe . . . for the roof leaks. And there is no money to buy wood to mend it with."

"I'll give you the wood, Kuzma Kuzmitch."

Zamuhrishen asks for and gets a cow too, a letter of recommendation for his daughter whom he wants to send to a boarding school, and . . . touched by the lady's liberality he whimpers with excess of feeling, twists his mouth, and feels in his pocket for his handkerchief. . . .

Marfa Petrovna sees a red paper slip out of his pocket with his handkerchief and fall noiselessly to the floor.

"I shall never forget it to all eternity . . ." he mutters, "and I shall make my children and my grandchildren remember it . . . from generation to generation. 'See, children,' I shall say, 'who has saved me from the grave, who . . .' "

When she has seen her patient out, the lady looks for a minute at Father Aristark with eyes full of tears, then turns her caressing, reverent gaze on the drug chest, the books, the bills, the armchair in which the man she had saved from death has just been sitting, and her eyes fall on the paper just dropped by her patient. She picks up the paper, unfolds it, and sees in it three pilules - the very pilules she had given Zamuhrishen the previous Tuesday.

"They are the very ones," she thinks puzzled. ". . . The paper is the same. . . . He hasn't even unwrapped them! What has he taken then? Strange. . . . Surely he wouldn't try to deceive me!"

And for the first time in her ten years of practice a doubt creeps into Marfa Petrovna's mind. . . . She summons the other patients, and while talking to them of their complaints notices what has hitherto slipped by her ears unnoticed. The patients, every one of them as though they were in a conspiracy, first belaud her for their miraculous cure, go into raptures over her medical skill, and abuse allopath doctors, then when she is flushed with excitement, begin holding forth on their needs. One asks for a bit of land to plough, another for wood, a third for permission to shoot in her forests, and so on. She looks at the broad, benevolent countenance of Father Aristark who has revealed the truth to her, and a new truth begins gnawing at her heart. An evil oppressive truth. . . .

The deceitfulness of man!

THE FISH

A summer morning. The air is still; there is no sound but the churring of a grasshopper on the river bank, and somewhere the timid cooing of a turtle-dove. Feathery clouds stand motionless in the sky, looking like snow scattered about. . . . Gerassim, the carpenter, a tall gaunt peasant, with a curly red head and a face overgrown with hair, is floundering about in the water under the green willow branches near an unfinished bathing shed. . . . He puffs and pants and, blinking furiously, is trying to get hold of something under the roots of the willows. His face is covered with perspiration. A couple of yards from him, Lubim, the carpenter, a young hunchback with a triangular face and narrow Chinese-looking eyes, is standing up to his neck in water. Both Gerassim and Lubim are in shirts and linen breeches. Both are blue with cold, for they have been more than an hour already in the water.

"But why do you keep poking with your hand?" cries the hunchback Lubim, shivering as though in a fever. "You blockhead! Hold him, hold him, or else he'll get away, the anathema! Hold him, I tell you!"

"He won't get away. . . . Where can he get to? He's under a root," says Gerassim in a hoarse, hollow bass, which seems to come not from his throat, but from the depths of his stomach. "He's slippery, the beggar, and there's nothing to catch hold of."

"Get him by the gills, by the gills!"

"There's no seeing his gills. . . . Stay, I've got hold of something. . . . I've got him by the lip. . . He's biting, the brute!"

"Don't pull him out by the lip, don't - or you'll let him go! Take him by the gills, take him by the gills. . . . You've begun poking with your hand again! You are a senseless man, the Queen of Heaven forgive me! Catch hold!"

"Catch hold!" Gerassim mimics him. "You're a fine one to give orders. . . . You'd better come and catch hold of him yourself, you hunchback devil. . . . What are you standing there for?"

"I would catch hold of him if it were possible. But can I stand by the bank, and me as short as I am? It's deep there."

"It doesn't matter if it is deep. . . . You must swim."

The hunchback waves his arms, swims up to Gerassim, and catches hold of the twigs. At the first attempt to stand up, he goes into the water over his head and begins blowing up bubbles.

"I told you it was deep," he says, rolling his eyes angrily. "Am I to sit on your neck or what?"

"Stand on a root . . . there are a lot of roots like a ladder." The hunchback gropes for a root with his heel, and tightly gripping several twigs, stands on it. . . . Having got his balance, and established himself in his new position, he bends down, and trying not to get the water into his mouth, begins fumbling with his right hand among the roots. Getting entangled among the weeds and slipping on the mossy roots he finds his hand in contact with the sharp pincers of a crayfish.

"As though we wanted to see you, you demon!" says Lubim, and he angrily flings the crayfish on the bank.

At last his hand feels Gerassim's arm, and groping its way along it comes to something cold and slimy.

"Here he is!" says Lubim with a grin. "A fine fellow! Move your fingers, I'll get him directly . . . by the gills. Stop, don't prod me with your elbow. . . . I'll have him in a minute, in a minute, only let me get hold of him. . . . The beggar has got a long way under the roots, there is nothing to get hold of. . . . One can't get to the head . . . one can only feel its belly . . . . kill that gnat on my neck - it's stinging! I'll get him by the gills, directly. . . . Come to one side and give him a push! Poke him with your finger!"

The hunchback puffs out his cheeks, holds his breath, opens his eyes wide, and apparently has already got his fingers in the gills, but at that moment the twigs to which he is holding on with his left hand break, and losing his balance he plops into the water! Eddies race away from the bank as though frightened, and little bubbles come up from the spot where he has fallen in. The hunchback swims out and, snorting, clutches at the twigs.

"You'll be drowned next, you stupid, and I shall have to answer for you," wheezes Gerassim." Clamber out, the devil take you! I'll get him out myself."

High words follow. . . . The sun is baking hot. The shadows begin to grow shorter and to draw in on themselves, like the horns of a snail. . . . The high grass warmed by the sun begins to give out a strong, heavy smell of honey. It will soon be midday, and Gerassim and Lubim are still floundering under the willow tree. The husky bass and the shrill, frozen tenor persistently disturb the stillness of the summer day.

"Pull him out by the gills, pull him out! Stay, I'll push him out! Where are you shoving your great ugly fist? Poke him with your finger - you pig's face! Get round by the side! get to the left, to the left, there's a big hole on the right! You'll be a supper for the water-devil! Pull it by the lip!"

There is the sound of the flick of a whip. . . . A herd of cattle, driven by Yefim, the shepherd, saunter lazily down the sloping bank to drink. The shepherd, a decrepit old man, with one eye and a crooked mouth, walks with his head bowed, looking at his feet. The first to reach the water are the sheep, then come the horses, and last of all the cows.

"Push him from below!" he hears Lubim's voice. "Stick your finger in! Are you deaf, fellow, or what? Tfoo!"

"What are you after, lads?" shouts Yefim.

"An eel-pout! We can't get him out! He's hidden under the roots. Get round to the side! To the side!"

For a minute Yefim screws up his eye at the fishermen, then he takes off his bark shoes, throws his sack off his shoulders, and takes off his shirt. He has not the patience to take off his breeches, but, making the sign of the cross, he steps into the water, holding out his thin dark arms to balance himself. . . . For fifty paces he walks along the slimy bottom, then he takes to swimming.

"Wait a minute, lads!" he shouts. "Wait! Don't be in a hurry to pull him out, you'll lose him. You must do it properly!"

Yefim joins the carpenters and all three, shoving each other with their knees and their elbows, puffing and swearing at one another, bustle about the same spot. Lubim, the hunchback, gets a mouthful of water, and the air rings with his hard spasmodic coughing.

"Where's the shepherd?" comes a shout from the bank. "Yefim! Shepherd! Where are you? The cattle are in the garden! Drive them out, drive them out of the garden! Where is he, the old brigand?"

First men's voices are heard, then a woman's. The master himself, Andrey Andreitch, wearing a dressing-gown made of a Persian shawl and carrying a newspaper in his hand, appears from behind the garden fence. He looks inquiringly towards the shouts which come from the river, and then trips rapidly towards the bathing shed.

"What's this? Who's shouting?" he asks sternly, seeing through the branches of the willow the three wet heads of the fishermen. "What are you so busy about there?"

"Catching a fish," mutters Yefim, without raising his head.

"I'll give it to you! The beasts are in the garden and he is fishing! . . . When will that bathing shed be done, you devils? You've been at work two days, and what is there to show for it?"

"It . . . will soon be done," grunts Gerassim; summer is long, you'll have plenty of time to wash, your honour. . . . Pfrrr! . . . We can't manage this eel-pout here anyhow. . . . He's got under a root and sits there as if he were in a hole and won't budge one way or another . . . ."

"An eel-pout?" says the master, and his eyes begin to glisten. "Get him out quickly then."

"You'll give us half a rouble for it presently if we oblige you. . . . A huge eel-pout, as fat as a merchant's wife. . . . It's worth half a rouble, your honour, for the trouble. . . . Don't squeeze him, Lubim, don't squeeze him, you'll spoil him! Push him up from below! Pull the root upwards, my good man . . . what's your name? Upwards, not downwards, you brute! Don't swing your legs!"

Five minutes pass, ten. . . . The master loses all patience.

"Vassily!" he shouts, turning towards the garden. "Vaska! Call Vassily to me!"

The coachman Vassily runs up. He is chewing something and breathing hard.

"Go into the water," the master orders him. "Help them to pull out that eel-pout. They can't get him out."

Vassily rapidly undresses and gets into the water.

"In a minute. . . . I'll get him in a minute," he mutters. "Where's the eel-pout? We'll have him out in a trice! You'd better go, Yefim. An old man like you ought to be minding his own business instead of being here. Where's that eel-pout? I'll have him in a minute. . . . Here he is! Let go."

"What's the good of saying that? We know all about that! You get it out!"

"But there is no getting it out like this! One must get hold of it by the head."

"And the head is under the root! We know that, you fool!"

"Now then, don't talk or you'll catch it! You dirty cur!"

"Before the master to use such language," mutters Yefim. "You won't get him out, lads! He's fixed himself much too cleverly!"

"Wait a minute, I'll come directly," says the master, and he begins hurriedly undressing. "Four fools, and can't get an eel-pout!"

When he is undressed, Andrey Andreitch gives himself time to cool and gets into the water. But even his interference leads to nothing.

"We must chop the root off," Lubim decides at last. "Gerassim, go and get an axe! Give me an axe!"

"Don't chop your fingers off," says the master, when the blows of the axe on the root under water are heard. "Yefim, get out of this! Stay, I'll get the eel-pout. . . . You'll never do it."

The root is hacked a little. They partly break it off, and Andrey Andreitch, to his immense satisfaction, feels his fingers under the gills of the fish.

"I'm pulling him out, lads! Don't crowd round . . . stand still. . . . I am pulling him out!"

The head of a big eel-pout, and behind it its long black body, nearly a yard long, appears on the surface of the water. The fish flaps its tail heavily and tries to tear itself away.

"None of your nonsense, my boy! Fiddlesticks! I've got you! Aha!"

A honied smile overspreads all the faces. A minute passes in silent contemplation.

"A famous eel-pout," mutters Yefim, scratching under his shoulder-blades. "I'll be bound it weighs ten pounds."

"Mm! . . . Yes," the master assents. "The liver is fairly swollen! It seems to stand out! A-ach!"

The fish makes a sudden, unexpected upward movement with its tail and the fishermen hear a loud splash . . . they all put out their hands, but it is too late; they have seen the last of the eel-pout.

GONE ASTRAY

A country village wrapped in the darkness of night. One o'clock strikes from the belfry. Two lawyers, called Kozyavkin and Laev, both in the best of spirits and a little unsteady on their legs, come out of the wood and turn towards the cottages.

"Well, thank God, we've arrived," says Kozyavkin, drawing a deep breath. "Tramping four miles from the station in our condition is a feat. I am fearfully done up! And, as ill-luck would have it, not a fly to be seen."

"Petya, my dear fellow. . . . I can't. . . . I feel like dying if I'm not in bed in five minutes."

"In bed! Don't you think it, my boy! First we'll have supper and a glass of red wine, and then you can go to bed. Verotchka and I will wake you up. . . . Ah, my dear fellow, it's a fine thing to be married! You don't understand it, you cold-hearted wretch! I shall be home in a minute, worn out and exhausted. . . . A loving wife will welcome me, give me some tea and something to eat, and repay me for my hard work and my love with such a fond and loving look out of her darling black eyes that I shall forget how tired I am, and forget the burglary and the law courts and the appeal division. . . . It's glorious!"

"Yes - I say, I feel as though my legs were dropping off, I can scarcely get along. . . . I am frightfully thirsty. . . ."

"Well, here we are at home."

The friends go up to one of the cottages, and stand still under the nearest window.

"It's a jolly cottage," said Kozyavkin. "You will see to-morrow what views we have! There's no light in the windows. Verotchka must have gone to bed, then; she must have got tired of sitting up. She's in bed, and must be worrying at my not having turned up." (He pushes the window with his stick, and it opens.) "Plucky girl! She goes to bed without bolting the window." (He takes off his cape and flings it with his portfolio in at the window.) "I am hot! Let us strike up a serenade and make her laugh!" (He sings.) "The moon floats in the midnight sky.

. . . Faintly stir the tender breezes. . . . Faintly rustle in the treetops. . . . Sing, sing, Alyosha! Verotchka, shall we sing you Schubert's Serenade?" (He sings.)

His performance is cut short by a sudden fit of coughing. "Tphoo! Verotchka, tell Aksinya to unlock the gate for us!" (A pause.) "Verotchka! don't be lazy, get up, darling!" (He stands on a stone and looks in at the window.) "Verotchka, my dumpling; Verotchka, my poppet . . . my little angel, my wife beyond compare, get up and tell Aksinya to unlock the gate for us! You are not asleep, you know. Little wife, we are really so done up and exhausted that we're not in the mood for jokes. We've trudged all the way from the station! Don't you hear? Ah, hang it all!" (He makes an effort to climb up to the window and falls down.) "You know this isn't a nice trick to play on a visitor! I see you are just as great a schoolgirl as ever, Vera, you are always up to mischief!"

"Perhaps Vera Stepanovna is asleep," says Laev.

"She isn't asleep! I bet she wants me to make an outcry and wake up the whole neighbourhood. I'm beginning to get cross, Vera! Ach, damn it all! Give me a leg up, Alyosha; I'll get in. You are a naughty girl, nothing but a regular schoolgirl. . . Give me a hoist."

Puffing and panting, Laev gives him a leg up, and Kozyavkin climbs in at the window and vanishes into the darkness within.

"Vera!" Laev hears a minute later, "where are you? . . . D-damnation! Tphoo! I've put my hand into something! Tphoo!"

There is a rustling sound, a flapping of wings, and the desperate cackling of a fowl.

"A nice state of things," Laev hears. "Vera, where on earth did these chickens come from? Why, the devil, there's no end of them! There's a basket with a turkey in it. . . . It pecks, the nasty creature."

Two hens fly out of the window, and cackling at the top of their voices, flutter down the village street.

"Alyosha, we've made a mistake!" says Kozyavkin in a lachrymose voice. "There are a lot of hens here.... I must have mistaken the house. Confound you, you are all over the place, you cursed brutes!"

"Well, then, make haste and come down. Do you hear? I am dying of thirst!"

"In a minute.... I am looking for my cape and portfolio."

"Light a match."

"The matches are in the cape.... I was a crazy idiot to get into this place. The cottages are exactly alike; the devil himself couldn't tell them apart in the dark. Aie, the turkey's pecked my cheek, nasty creature!"

"Make haste and get out or they'll think we are stealing the chickens."

"In a minute.... I can't find my cape anywhere.... There are lots of old rags here, and I can't tell where the cape is. Throw me a match."

"I haven't any."

"We are in a hole, I must say! What am I to do? I can't go without my cape and my portfolio. I must find them."

"I can't understand a man's not knowing his own cottage," says Laev indignantly. " Drunken beast.... If I'd known I was in for this sort of thing I would never have come with you. I should have been at home and fast asleep by now, and a nice fix I'm in here.... I'm fearfully done up and thirsty, and my head is going round."

"In a minute, in a minute.... You won't expire."

A big cock flies crowing over Laev's head. Laev heaves a deep sigh, and with a hopeless gesture sits down on a stone. He is beset with a burning thirst, his eyes are closing, his head drops forward.... Five minutes pass, ten, twenty, and Kozyavkin is still busy among the hens.

"Petya, will you be long?"

"A minute. I found the portfolio, but I have lost it again."

Laev lays his head on his fists, and closes his eyes. The cackling of the fowls grows louder and louder. The inhabitants of the empty cottage fly out of the window and flutter round in circles, he fancies, like owls over his head. His ears ring with their cackle, he is overwhelmed with terror.

"The beast!" he thinks. "He invited me to stay, promising me wine and junket, and then he makes me walk from the station and listen to these hens...."

In the midst of his indignation his chin sinks into his collar, he lays his head on his portfolio, and gradually subsides. Weariness gets the upper hand and he begins to doze.

"I've found the portfolio!" he hears Kozyavkin cry triumphantly. "I shall find the cape in a minute and then off we go!"

Then through his sleep he hears the barking of dogs. First one dog barks, then a second, and a third. . . . And the barking of the dogs blends with the cackling of the fowls into a sort of savage music. Someone comes up to Laev and asks him something. Then he hears someone climb over his head into the window, then a knocking and a shouting. . . . A woman in a red apron stands beside him with a lantern in her hand and asks him something.

"You've no right to say so," he hears Kozyavkin's voice. "I am a lawyer, a bachelor of laws - Kozyavkin - here's my visiting card."

"What do I want with your card?" says someone in a husky bass. "You've disturbed all my fowls, you've smashed the eggs! Look what you've done. The turkey poults were to have come out to-day or to-morrow, and you've smashed them. What's the use of your giving me your card, sir?"

"How dare you interfere with me! No! I won't have it!"

"I am thirsty," thinks Laev, trying to open his eyes, and he feels somebody climb down from the window over his head.

"My name is Kozyavkin! I have a cottage here. Everyone knows me."

"We don't know anyone called Kozyavkin."

"What are you saying? Call the elder. He knows me."

"Don't get excited, the constable will be here directly. . . . We know all the summer visitors here, but I've never seen you in my life."

"I've had a cottage in Rottendale for five years."

"Whew! Do you take this for the Dale? This is Sicklystead, but Rottendale is farther to the right, beyond the match factory. It's three miles from here."

"Bless my soul! Then I've taken the wrong turning!"

The cries of men and fowls mingle with the barking of dogs, and the voice of Kozyavkin rises above the chaos of confused sounds:

"You shut up! I'll pay. I'll show you whom you have to deal with!"

Little by little the voices die down. Laev feels himself being shaken by the shoulder. . . .

THE HUNTSMAN

A sultry, stifling midday. Not a cloudlet in the sky. . . . The sun-baked grass had a disconsolate, hopeless look: even if there were rain it could never be green again. . . . The forest stood silent, motionless, as though it were looking at something with its tree-tops or expecting something.

At the edge of the clearing a tall, narrow-shouldered man of forty in a red shirt, in patched trousers that had been a gentleman's, and in high boots, was slouching along with a lazy, shambling step. He was sauntering along the road. On the right was the green of the clearing, on the left a golden sea of ripe rye stretched to the very horizon. He was red and perspiring, a white cap with a straight jockey peak, evidently a gift from some open-handed young gentleman, perched jauntily on his handsome flaxen head. Across his shoulder hung a game-bag with a blackcock lying in it. The man held a double-barrelled gun cocked in his hand, and screwed up his eyes in the direction of his lean old dog who was running on ahead sniffing the bushes. There was stillness all round, not a sound . . . everything living was hiding away from the heat.

"Yegor Vlassitch!" the huntsman suddenly heard a soft voice.

He started and, looking round, scowled. Beside him, as though she had sprung out of the earth, stood a pale-faced woman of thirty with a sickle in her hand. She was trying to look into his face, and was smiling diffidently.

"Oh, it is you, Pelagea!" said the huntsman, stopping and deliberately uncocking the gun. "H'm! . . . How have you come here?"

"The women from our village are working here, so I have come with them. . . . As a labourer, Yegor Vlassitch."

"Oh . . ." growled Yegor Vlassitch, and slowly walked on.

Pelagea followed him. They walked in silence for twenty paces.

"I have not seen you for a long time, Yegor Vlassitch . . ." said Pelagea looking tenderly at the huntsman's moving shoulders. "I have not seen you since you came into our hut at Easter for a drink of water . . . you came in at Easter for a minute and then God knows how . . . drunk . . . you scolded and beat me and went away . . . I have been waiting and waiting . . . I've tired my eyes out looking for you. Ah, Yegor Vlassitch, Yegor Vlassitch! you might look in just once!"

"What is there for me to do there?"

"Of course there is nothing for you to do . . . though to be sure . . . there is the place to look after. . . . To see how things are going. . . . You are the master. . . . I say, you have shot a blackcock, Yegor Vlassitch! You ought to sit down and rest!"

As she said all this Pelagea laughed like a silly girl and looked up at Yegor's face. Her face was simply radiant with happiness.

"Sit down? If you like . . ." said Yegor in a tone of indifference, and he chose a spot between two fir-trees. "Why are you standing? You sit down too."

Pelagea sat a little way off in the sun and, ashamed of her joy, put her hand over her smiling mouth. Two minutes passed in silence.

"You might come for once," said Pelagea.

"What for?" sighed Yegor, taking off his cap and wiping his red forehead with his hand. "There is no object in my coming. To go for an hour or two is only waste of time, it's simply upsetting you, and to live continually in the village my soul could not endure. . . . You know yourself I am a pampered man. . . . I want a bed to sleep in, good tea to drink, and refined conversation. . . . I want all the niceties, while you live in poverty and dirt in the village. . . . I couldn't stand it for a day. Suppose there were an edict that I must live with you, I should either set fire to the hut or lay hands on myself. From a boy I've had this love for ease; there is no help for it."

"Where are you living now?"

"With the gentleman here, Dmitry Ivanitch, as a huntsman. I furnish his table with game, but he keeps me . . . more for his pleasure than anything."

"That's not proper work you're doing, Yegor Vlassitch. . . . For other people it's a pastime, but with you it's like a trade . . . like real work."

"You don't understand, you silly," said Yegor, gazing gloomily at the sky. "You have never understood, and as long as you live you will never understand what sort of man I am. . . . You think of me as a foolish man, gone to the bad, but to anyone who understands I am the best shot there is in the whole district. The gentry feel that, and they have even printed things about me in a magazine. There isn't a man to be compared with me as a sportsman. . . . And it is not because I am pampered and proud that I look down upon your village work. From my childhood, you know, I have never had any calling apart from guns and dogs. If they took away my gun, I used to go out with the fishing-hook, if they took the hook I caught things with my hands. And I went in for horse-dealing too, I used to go to the fairs when I had the money, and you know that if a peasant goes in for being a sportsman, or a horse-dealer, it's good-bye to the plough. Once the spirit of freedom has taken a man you will never root it out of him. In the same way, if a gentleman goes in for being an actor or for any other art, he will never make an official or a landowner. You are a woman, and you do not understand, but one must understand that."

"I understand, Yegor Vlassitch."

"You don't understand if you are going to cry. . . ."

"I . . . I'm not crying," said Pelagea, turning away. "It's a sin, Yegor Vlassitch! You might stay a day with luckless me, anyway. It's twelve years since I was married to you, and . . . and . . . there has never once been love between us! . . . I . . . I am not crying."

"Love . . ." muttered Yegor, scratching his hand. "There can't be any love. It's only in name we are husband and wife; we aren't really. In your eyes I am a wild man, and in mine you are a simple peasant woman with no understanding. Are we well matched? I am a free, pampered, profligate man, while you are a working woman, going in bark shoes and never straightening your back. The way I think of myself is that I am the foremost man in every kind of sport, and you look at me with pity. . . . Is that being well matched?"

"But we are married, you know, Yegor Vlassitch," sobbed Pelagea.

"Not married of our free will. . . . Have you forgotten? You have to thank Count Sergey Paylovitch and yourself. Out of envy, because I shot better than he did, the Count kept giving me wine for a whole month, and when a man's drunk you could make him change his religion, let alone getting married. To pay me out he married me to you when I was drunk. . . . A huntsman to a herd-girl! You saw I was drunk, why did you marry me? You were not a serf, you know; you could have resisted. Of course it was a bit of luck for a herd-girl to marry a huntsman, but you ought to have thought about it. Well, now be miserable, cry. It's a joke for the Count, but a crying matter for you. . . . Beat yourself against the wall."

A silence followed. Three wild ducks flew over the clearing. Yegor followed them with his eyes till, transformed into three scarcely visible dots, they sank down far beyond the forest.

"How do you live?" he asked, moving his eyes from the ducks to Pelagea.

"Now I am going out to work, and in the winter I take a child from the Foundling Hospital and bring it up on the bottle. They give me a rouble and a half a month."

"Oh. . . ."

Again a silence. From the strip that had been reaped floated a soft song which broke off at the very beginning. It was too hot to sing.

"They say you have put up a new hut for Akulina," said Pelagea.

Yegor did not speak.

"So she is dear to you. . . ."

"It's your luck, it's fate!" said the huntsman, stretching. "You must put up with it, poor thing. But good-bye, I've been chattering long enough. . . . I must be at Boltovo by the evening."

Yegor rose, stretched himself, and slung his gun over his shoulder; Pelagea got up.

"And when are you coming to the village?" she asked softly.

"I have no reason to, I shall never come sober, and you have little to gain from me drunk; I am spiteful when I am drunk. Good-bye!"

"Good-bye, Yegor Vlassitch."

Yegor put his cap on the back of his head and, clicking to his dog, went on his way. Pelagea stood still looking after him. . . . She saw his moving shoulder-blades, his jaunty cap, his lazy, careless step, and her eyes were full of sadness and tender affection. . . . Her gaze flitted over her husband's tall, lean figure and caressed and fondled it. . . . He, as though he felt that gaze, stopped and looked round. . . . He did not speak, but from his face, from his shrugged shoulders, Pelagea could see that he wanted to say something to her. She went up to him timidly and looked at him with imploring eyes.

"Take it," he said, turning round.

He gave her a crumpled rouble note and walked quickly away.

"Good-bye, Yegor Vlassitch," she said, mechanically taking the rouble.

He walked by a long road, straight as a taut strap. She, pale and motionless as a statue, stood, her eyes seizing every step he took. But the red of his shirt melted into the dark colour of his trousers, his step could not be seen, and the dog could not be distinguished from the boots. Nothing could be seen but the cap, and . . . suddenly Yegor turned off sharply into the clearing and the cap vanished in the greenness.

"Good-bye, Yegor Vlassitch," whispered Pelagea, and she stood on tiptoe to see the white cap once more.

A MALEFACTOR

An exceedingly lean little peasant, in a striped hempen shirt and patched drawers, stands facing the investigating magistrate. His face overgrown with hair and pitted with smallpox, and his eyes scarcely visible under thick, overhanging eyebrows have an expression of sullen moroseness. On his head there is a perfect mop of tangled, unkempt hair, which gives him an even more spider-like air of moroseness. He is barefooted.

"Denis Grigoryev!" the magistrate begins. "Come nearer, and answer my questions. On the seventh of this July the railway watchman, Ivan Semyonovitch Akinfov, going along the line in the morning, found you at the hundred-and-forty-first mile engaged in unscrewing a nut by which the rails are made fast to the sleepers. Here it is, the nut! . . . With the aforesaid nut he detained you. Was that so?"

"Wha-at?"

"Was this all as Akinfov states?"

"To be sure, it was."

"Very good; well, what were you unscrewing the nut for?"

"Wha-at?"

"Drop that 'wha-at' and answer the question; what were you unscrewing the nut for?"

"If I hadn't wanted it I shouldn't have unscrewed it," croaks Denis, looking at the ceiling.

"What did you want that nut for?"

"The nut? We make weights out of those nuts for our lines."

"Who is 'we'?"

"We, people. . . . The Klimovo peasants, that is."

"Listen, my man; don't play the idiot to me, but speak sensibly. It's no use telling lies here about weights!"

"I've never been a liar from a child, and now I'm telling lies . . ." mutters Denis, blinking. "But can you do without a weight, your honour? If you put live bait or maggots on a hook, would it go to the bottom without a weight? . . . I am telling lies," grins Denis. . . . "What the devil is the use of the worm if it swims on the surface! The perch and the pike and the eel-pout always go to the bottom, and a bait on the surface is only taken by a shillisper, not very often then, and there are no shillispers in our river. . . . That fish likes plenty of room."

"Why are you telling me about shillispers?"

"Wha-at? Why, you asked me yourself! The gentry catch fish that way too in our parts. The silliest little boy would not try to catch a fish without a weight. Of course anyone who did not understand might go to fish without a weight. There is no rule for a fool."

"So you say you unscrewed this nut to make a weight for your fishing line out of it?"

"What else for? It wasn't to play knuckle-bones with!"

"But you might have taken lead, a bullet . . . a nail of some sort. . . ."

"You don't pick up lead in the road, you have to buy it, and a nail's no good. You can't find anything better than a nut. . . . It's heavy, and there's a hole in it."

"He keeps pretending to be a fool! as though he'd been born yesterday or dropped from heaven! Don't you understand, you blockhead, what unscrewing these nuts leads to? If the watchman had not noticed it the train might have run off the rails, people would have been killed - you would have killed people."

"God forbid, your honour! What should I kill them for? Are we heathens or wicked people? Thank God, good gentlemen, we have lived all our lives without ever dreaming of such a thing. . . . Save, and have mercy on us, Queen of Heaven! . . . What are you saying?"

"And what do you suppose railway accidents do come from? Unscrew two or three nuts and you have an accident."

Denis grins, and screws up his eye at the magistrate incredulously.

"Why! how many years have we all in the village been unscrewing nuts, and the Lord has been merciful; and you talk of accidents, killing people. If I had carried away a rail or put a log across the line, say, then maybe it might have upset the train, but... pouf! a nut!"

"But you must understand that the nut holds the rail fast to the sleepers!"

"We understand that.... We don't unscrew them all... we leave some. ... We don't do it thoughtlessly ... we understand...."

Denis yawns and makes the sign of the cross over his mouth.

"Last year the train went off the rails here," says the magistrate. "Now I see why!"

"What do you say, your honour?"

"I am telling you that now I see why the train went off the rails last year.... I understand!"

"That's what you are educated people for, to understand, you kind gentlemen. The Lord knows to whom to give understanding.... Here you have reasoned how and what, but the watchman, a peasant like ourselves, with no understanding at all, catches one by the collar and hauls one along.... You should reason first and then haul me off. It's a saying that a peasant has a peasant's wit.... Write down, too, your honour, that he hit me twice - in the jaw and in the chest."

"When your hut was searched they found another nut.... At what spot did you unscrew that, and when?"

"You mean the nut which lay under the red box?"

"I don't know where it was lying, only it was found. When did you unscrew it?"

"I didn't unscrew it; Ignashka, the son of one-eyed Semyon, gave it me. I mean the one which was under the box, but the one which was in the sledge in the yard Mitrofan and I unscrewed together."

"What Mitrofan?"

"Mitrofan Petrov.... Haven't you heard of him? He makes nets in our village and sells them to the gentry. He needs a lot of those nuts. Reckon a matter of ten for each net."

"Listen. Article 1081 of the Penal Code lays down that every wilful damage of the railway line committed when it can expose the traffic on that line to danger, and the guilty party knows that an accident must be caused by it... (Do you understand? Knows! And you could not help knowing what this unscrewing would lead to...) is liable to penal servitude."

"Of course, you know best.... We are ignorant people.... What do we understand?"

"You understand all about it! You are lying, shamming!"

"What should I lie for? Ask in the village if you don't believe me. Only a bleak is caught without a weight, and there is no fish worse than a gudgeon, yet even that won't bite without a weight."

"You'd better tell me about the shillisper next," said the magistrate, smiling.

"There are no shillispers in our parts.... We cast our line without a weight on the top of the water with a butterfly; a mullet may be caught that way, though that is not often."

"Come, hold your tongue."

A silence follows. Denis shifts from one foot to the other, looks at the table with the green cloth on it, and blinks his eyes violently as though what was before him was not the cloth but the sun. The magistrate writes rapidly.

"Can I go?" asks Denis after a long silence.

"No. I must take you under guard and send you to prison."

Denis leaves off blinking and, raising his thick eyebrows, looks inquiringly at the magistrate.

"How do you mean, to prison? Your honour! I have no time to spare, I must go to the fair; I must get three roubles from Yegor for some tallow! . . ."

"Hold your tongue; don't interrupt."

"To prison. . . . If there was something to go for, I'd go; but just to go for nothing! What for? I haven't stolen anything, I believe, and I've not been fighting. . . . If you are in doubt about the arrears, your honour, don't believe the elder. . . . You ask the agent . . . he's a regular heathen, the elder, you know."

"Hold your tongue."

I am holding my tongue, as it is," mutters Denis; "but that the elder has lied over the account, I'll take my oath for it. . . . There are three of us brothers: Kuzma Grigoryev, then Yegor Grigoryev, and me, Denis Grigoryev."

"You are hindering me. . . . Hey, Semyon," cries the magistrate, "take him away!"

"There are three of us brothers," mutters Denis, as two stalwart soldiers take him and lead him out of the room. "A brother is not responsible for a brother. Kuzma does not pay, so you, Denis, must answer for it. . . . Judges indeed! Our master the general is dead - the Kingdom of Heaven be his - or he would have shown you judges. . . . You ought to judge sensibly, not at random. . . . Flog if you like, but flog someone who deserves it, flog with conscience."

THE HEAD OF THE FAMILY

It is, as a rule, after losing heavily at cards or after a drinking-bout when an attack of dyspepsia is setting in that Stepan Stepanitch Zhilin wakes up in an exceptionally gloomy frame of mind. He looks sour, rumpled, and dishevelled; there is an expression of displeasure on his grey face, as though he were offended or disgusted by something. He dresses slowly, sips his Vichy water deliberately, and begins walking about the rooms.

"I should like to know what b-b-beast comes in here and does not shut the door!" he grumbles angrily, wrapping his dressing-gown about him and spitting loudly. "Take away that paper! Why is it lying about here? We keep twenty servants, and the place is more untidy than a pot-house. Who was that ringing? Who the devil is that?"

"That's Anfissa, the midwife who brought our Fedya into the world," answers his wife.

"Always hanging about . . . these cadging toadies!"

"There's no making you out, Stepan Stepanitch. You asked her yourself, and now you scold."

"I am not scolding; I am speaking. You might find something to do, my dear, instead of sitting with your hands in your lap trying to pick a quarrel. Upon my word, women are beyond my comprehension! Beyond my comprehension! How can they waste whole days doing nothing? A man works like an ox, like a b-beast, while his wife, the partner of his life, sits like a pretty doll, sits and does nothing but watch for an opportunity to quarrel with her husband by way of diversion. It's time to drop these schoolgirlish ways, my dear. You are not a schoolgirl, not a young lady; you are a wife and mother! You turn away? Aha! It's not agreeable to listen to the bitter truth!"

"It's strange that you only speak the bitter truth when your liver is out of order."

"That's right; get up a scene."

"Have you been out late? Or playing cards?"

"What if I have? Is that anybody's business? Am I obliged to give an account of my doings to anyone? It's my own money I lose, I suppose? What I spend as well as what is spent in this house belongs to me - me. Do you hear? To me!"

And so on, all in the same style. But at no other time is Stepan Stepanitch so reasonable, virtuous, stern or just as at dinner, when all his household are sitting about him. It usually begins with the soup. After swallowing the first spoonful Zhilin suddenly frowns and puts down his spoon.

"Damn it all!" he mutters; "I shall have to dine at a restaurant, I suppose."

"What's wrong?" asks his wife anxiously. "Isn't the soup good?"

"One must have the taste of a pig to eat hogwash like that! There's too much salt in it; it smells of dirty rags . . . more like bugs than onions. . . . It's simply revolting, Anfissa Ivanovna," he says, addressing the midwife. "Every day I give no end of money for housekeeping. . . . I deny myself everything, and this is what they provide for my dinner! I suppose they want me to give up the office and go into the kitchen to do the cooking myself."

"The soup is very good to-day," the governess ventures timidly.

"Oh, you think so?" says Zhilin, looking at her angrily from under his eyelids. "Every one to his taste, of course. It must be confessed our tastes are very different, Varvara Vassilyevna. You, for instance, are satisfied with the behaviour of this boy" (Zhilin with a tragic gesture points to his son Fedya); "you are delighted with him, while I . . . I am disgusted. Yes!"

Fedya, a boy of seven with a pale, sickly face, leaves off eating and drops his eyes. His face grows paler still.

"Yes, you are delighted, and I am disgusted. Which of us is right, I cannot say, but I venture to think as his father, I know my own son better than you do. Look how he is sitting! Is that the way decently brought up children sit? Sit properly."

Fedya tilts his chin up, cranes his neck, and fancies that he is holding himself better. Tears come into his eyes.

"Eat your dinner! Hold your spoon properly! You wait. I'll show you, you horrid boy! Don't dare to whimper! Look straight at me!"

Fedya tries to look straight at him, but his face is quivering and his eyes fill with tears.

"A-ah! . . . you cry? You are naughty and then you cry? Go and stand in the corner, you beast!"

"But . . . let him have his dinner first," his wife intervenes.

"No dinner for him! Such bla . . . such rascals don't deserve dinner!"

Fedya, wincing and quivering all over, creeps down from his chair and goes into the corner.

"You won't get off with that!" his parent persists. "If nobody else cares to look after your bringing up, so be it; I must begin. . . . I won't let you be naughty and cry at dinner, my lad! Idiot! You must do your duty! Do you understand? Do your duty! Your father works and you must work, too! No one must eat the bread of idleness! You must be a man! A m-man!"

"For God's sake, leave off," says his wife in French. "Don't nag at us before outsiders, at least. . . . The old woman is all ears; and now, thanks to her, all the town will hear of it."

I am not afraid of outsiders," answers Zhilin in Russian. "Anfissa Ivanovna sees that I am speaking the truth. Why, do you think I ought to be pleased with the boy? Do you know what he costs me? Do you know, you nasty boy, what you cost me? Or do you imagine that I coin money, that I get it for nothing? Don't howl! Hold your tongue! Do you hear what I say? Do you want me to whip you, you young ruffian?"

Fedya wails aloud and begins to sob.

"This is insufferable," says his mother, getting up from the table and flinging down her dinner-napkin. "You never let us have dinner in peace! Your bread sticks in my throat."

And putting her handkerchief to her eyes, she walks out of the dining-room.

"Now she is offended," grumbles Zhilin, with a forced smile. "She's been spoilt. . . . That's how it is, Anfissa Ivanovna; no one likes to hear the truth nowadays. . . . It's all my fault, it seems."

Several minutes of silence follow. Zhilin looks round at the plates, and noticing that no one has yet touched their soup, heaves a deep sigh, and stares at the flushed and uneasy face of the governess.

"Why don't you eat, Varvara Vassilyevna?" he asks. "Offended, I suppose? I see. . . . You don't like to be told the truth. You must forgive me, it's my nature; I can't be a hypocrite. . . . I always blurt out the plain truth" (a sigh). "But I notice that my presence is unwelcome. No one can eat or talk while I am here. . . . Well, you should have told me, and I would have gone away. . . . I will go."

Zhilin gets up and walks with dignity to the door. As he passes the weeping Fedya he stops.

"After all that has passed here, you are free," he says to Fedya, throwing back his head with dignity. "I won't meddle in your bringing up again. I wash my hands of it! I humbly apologise that as a father, from a sincere desire for your welfare, I have disturbed you and your mentors. At the same time, once for all I disclaim all responsibility for your future. . . ."

Fedya wails and sobs more loudly than ever. Zhilin turns with dignity to the door and departs to his bedroom.

When he wakes from his after-dinner nap he begins to feel the stings of conscience. He is ashamed to face his wife, his son, Anfissa Ivanovna, and even feels very wretched when he recalls the scene at dinner, but his amour-propre is too much for him; he has not the manliness to be frank, and he goes on sulking and grumbling.

Waking up next morning, he feels in excellent spirits, and whistles gaily as he washes. Going into the dining-room to breakfast, he finds there Fedya, who, at the sight of his father, gets up and looks at him helplessly.

"Well, young man?" Zhilin greets him good-humouredly, sitting down to the table. "What have you got to tell me, young man? Are you all right? Well, come, chubby; give your father a kiss."

With a pale, grave face Fedya goes up to his father and touches his cheek with his quivering lips, then walks away and sits down in his place without a word.

A DEAD BODY

A still August night. A mist is rising slowly from the fields and casting an opaque veil over everything within eyesight. Lighted up by the moon, the mist gives the impression at one moment of a calm, boundless sea, at the next of an immense white wall. The air is damp and chilly. Morning is still far off. A step from the bye-road which runs along the edge of the forest a little fire is gleaming. A dead body, covered from head to foot with new white linen, is lying under a young oak-tree. A wooden ikon is lying on its breast. Beside the corpse almost on the road sits the "watch" - two peasants performing one of the most disagreeable and uninviting of peasants' duties. One, a tall young fellow with a scarcely perceptible moustache and thick black eyebrows, in a tattered sheepskin and bark shoes, is sitting on the wet grass, his feet stuck out straight in front of him, and is trying to while away the time with work. He bends his long neck, and breathing loudly through his nose, makes a spoon out of a big crooked bit of wood; the other - a little scraggy, pock-marked peasant with an aged face, a scanty moustache, and a little goat's beard - sits with his hands dangling loose on his knees, and without moving gazes listlessly at the light. A small camp-fire is lazily burning down between them, throwing a red glow on their faces. There is perfect stillness. The only sounds are the scrape of the knife on the wood and the crackling of damp sticks in the fire.

"Don't you go to sleep, Syoma . . ." says the young man.

"I . . . I am not asleep . . ." stammers the goat-beard.

"That's all right. . . . It would be dreadful to sit here alone, one would be frightened. You might tell me something, Syoma."

"You are a queer fellow, Syomushka! Other people will laugh and tell a story and sing a song, but you - there is no making you out. You sit like a scarecrow in the garden and roll your eyes at the fire. You can't say anything properly . . . when you speak you seem frightened. I dare say you are fifty, but you have less sense than a child. Aren't you sorry that you are a simpleton?"

"I am sorry," the goat-beard answers gloomily.

"And we are sorry to see your foolishness, you may be sure. You are a good-natured, sober peasant, and the only trouble is that you have no sense in your head. You should have picked up some sense for yourself if the Lord has afflicted you and given you no understanding. You must make an effort, Syoma. . . . You should listen hard when anything good's being said, note it well, and keep thinking and thinking. . . . If there is any word you don't understand, you should make an effort and think over in your head in what meaning the word is used. Do you see? Make an effort! If you don't gain some sense for yourself you'll be a simpleton and of no account at all to your dying day."

All at once a long drawn-out, moaning sound is heard in the forest. Something rustles in the leaves as though torn from the very top of the tree and falls to the ground. All this is faintly repeated by the echo. The young man shudders and looks enquiringly at his companion.

"It's an owl at the little birds," says Syoma, gloomily.

"Why, Syoma, it's time for the birds to fly to the warm countries!"

"To be sure, it is time."

"It is chilly at dawn now. It is co-old. The crane is a chilly creature, it is tender. Such cold is death to it. I am not a crane, but I am frozen. . . . Put some more wood on!"

Syoma gets up and disappears in the dark undergrowth. While he is busy among the bushes, breaking dry twigs, his companion puts his hand over his eyes and starts at every sound. Syoma brings an armful of wood and lays it on the fire. The flame irresolutely licks the black twigs with its little tongues, then suddenly, as though at the word of command, catches them and throws a crimson light on the faces, the road, the white linen with its prominences where the hands and feet of the corpse raise it, the ikon. The "watch" is silent. The young man bends his neck still lower and sets to work with still more nervous haste. The goat-beard sits motionless as before and keeps his eyes fixed on the fire. . . .

"Ye that love not Zion . . . shall be put to shame by the Lord." A falsetto voice is suddenly heard singing in the stillness of the night, then slow footsteps are audible, and the dark figure of a man in a short monkish cassock and a broad-brimmed hat, with a wallet on his shoulders, comes into sight on the road in the crimson firelight.

"Thy will be done, O Lord! Holy Mother!" the figure says in a husky falsetto. "I saw the fire in the outer darkness and my soul leapt for joy. . . . . At first I thought it was men grazing a drove of horses, then I thought it can't be that, since no horses were to be seen. 'Aren't they thieves,' I wondered, 'aren't they robbers lying in wait for a rich Lazarus? Aren't they the gypsy people offering sacrifices to idols? And my soul leapt for joy. 'Go, Feodosy, servant of God,' I said to myself, 'and win a martyr's crown!' And I flew to the fire like a light-winged moth. Now I stand before you, and from your outer aspect I judge of your souls: you are not thieves and you are not heathens. Peace be to you!"

"Good-evening."

"Good orthodox people, do you know how to reach the Makuhinsky Brickyards from here?"

"It's close here. You go straight along the road; when you have gone a mile and a half there will be Ananova, our village. From the village, father, you turn to the right by the river-bank, and so you will get to the brickyards. It's two miles from Ananova."

"God give you health. And why are you sitting here?

"We are sitting here watching. You see, there is a dead body. . . ."

"What? what body? Holy Mother!"

The pilgrim sees the white linen with the ikon on it, and starts so violently that his legs give a little skip. This unexpected sight has an overpowering effect upon him. He huddles together and stands as though rooted to the spot, with wide-open mouth and staring eyes. For three minutes he is silent as though he could not believe his eyes, then begins muttering:

"O Lord! Holy Mother! I was going along not meddling with anyone, and all at once such an affliction."

"What may you be?" enquires the young man. "Of the clergy?"

"No . . . no. . . . I go from one monastery to another. . . . Do you know Mi . . . Mihail Polikarpitch, the foreman of the brickyard? Well, I am his nephew. . . . Thy will be done, O Lord! Why are you here?"

"We are watching . . . we are told to."

"Yes, yes . . ." mutters the man in the cassock, passing his hand over his eyes. "And where did the deceased come from?"

"He was a stranger."

"Such is life! But I'll . . . er . . . be getting on, brothers. . . . I feel flustered. I am more afraid of the dead than of anything, my dear souls! And only fancy! while this man was alive he wasn't noticed, while now when he is dead and given over to corruption we tremble before him as before some famous general or a bishop. . . . Such is life; was he murdered, or what?"

"The Lord knows! Maybe he was murdered, or maybe he died of himself."

"Yes, yes. . . . Who knows, brothers? Maybe his soul is now tasting the joys of Paradise."

"His soul is still hovering here, near his body," says the young man. "It does not depart from the body for three days."

"H'm, yes! . . . How chilly the nights are now! It sets one's teeth chattering. . . . So then I am to go straight on and on? . . ."

"Till you get to the village, and then you turn to the right by the river-bank."

"By the river-bank. . . . To be sure. . . . Why am I standing still? I must go on. Farewell, brothers."

The man in the cassock takes five steps along the road and stops.

"I've forgotten to put a kopeck for the burying," he says. "Good orthodox friends, can I give the money?"

"You ought to know best, you go the round of the monasteries. If he died a natural death it would go for the good of his soul; if it's a suicide it's a sin."

"That's true. . . . And maybe it really was a suicide! So I had better keep my money. Oh, sins, sins! Give me a thousand roubles and I would not consent to sit here. . . . Farewell, brothers."

The cassock slowly moves away and stops again.

"I can't make up my mind what I am to do," he mutters. "To stay here by the fire and wait till daybreak. . . . I am frightened; to go on is dreadful, too. The dead man will haunt me all the way in the darkness. . . . The Lord has chastised me indeed! Over three hundred miles I have come on foot and nothing happened, and now I am near home and there's trouble. I can't go on. . . ."

"It is dreadful, that is true."

"I am not afraid of wolves, of thieves, or of darkness, but I am afraid of the dead. I am afraid of them, and that is all about it. Good orthodox brothers, I entreat you on my knees, see me to the village."

"We've been told not to go away from the body."

"No one will see, brothers. Upon my soul, no one will see! The Lord will reward you a hundredfold! Old man, come with me, I beg! Old man! Why are you silent?"

"He is a bit simple," says the young man.

"You come with me, friend; I will give you five kopecks."

"For five kopecks I might," says the young man, scratching his head, "but I was told not to. If Syoma here, our simpleton, will stay alone, I will take you. Syoma, will you stay here alone?"

"I'll stay," the simpleton consents.

"Well, that's all right, then. Come along! The young man gets up, and goes with the cassock. A minute later the sound of their steps and their talk dies away. Syoma shuts his eyes and gently dozes. The fire begins to grow dim, and a big black shadow falls on the dead body.

THE COOK'S WEDDING

Grisha, a fat, solemn little person of seven, was standing by the kitchen door listening and peeping through the keyhole. In the kitchen something extraordinary, and in his opinion never seen before, was taking place. A big, thick-set, red-haired peasant, with a beard, and a drop of perspiration on his nose, wearing a cabman's full coat, was sitting at the kitchen table on which they chopped the meat and sliced the onions. He was balancing a saucer on the five fingers of his right hand and drinking tea out of it, and crunching sugar so loudly that it sent a shiver down Grisha's back. Aksinya Stepanovna, the old nurse, was sitting on the dirty stool facing him, and she, too, was drinking tea. Her face was grave, though at the same time it beamed with a kind of triumph. Pelageya, the cook, was busy at the stove, and was apparently trying to hide her face. And on her face Grisha saw a regular illumination: it was burning and shifting through every shade of colour, beginning with a crimson purple and ending with a deathly white. She was continually catching hold of knives, forks, bits of wood, and rags with trembling hands, moving, grumbling to herself, making a clatter, but in reality doing nothing. She did not once glance at the table at which they were drinking tea, and to the questions put to her by the nurse she gave jerky, sullen answers without turning her face.

"Help yourself, Danilo Semyonitch," the nurse urged him hospitably. "Why do you keep on with tea and nothing but tea? You should have a drop of vodka!"

And nurse put before the visitor a bottle of vodka and a wine-glass, while her face wore a very wily expression.

"I never touch it. . . . No . . ." said the cabman, declining. "Don't press me, Aksinya Stepanovna."

"What a man! . . . A cabman and not drink! . . . A bachelor can't get on without drinking. Help yourself!"

The cabman looked askance at the bottle, then at nurse's wily face, and his own face assumed an expression no less cunning, as much as to say, "You won't catch me, you old witch!"

"I don't drink; please excuse me. Such a weakness does not do in our calling. A man who works at a trade may drink, for he sits at home, but we cabmen are always in view of the public. Aren't we? If one goes into a pothouse one finds one's horse gone; if one takes a drop too much it is worse still; before you know where you are you will fall asleep or slip off the box. That's where it is."

"And how much do you make a day, Danilo Semyonitch?"

"That's according. One day you will have a fare for three roubles, and another day you will come back to the yard without a farthing. The days are very different. Nowadays our business is no good. There are lots and lots of cabmen as you know, hay is dear, and folks are paltry nowadays and always contriving to go by tram. And yet, thank God, I have nothing to complain of. I have plenty to eat and good clothes to wear, and . . . we could even provide well for another. . ." (the cabman stole a glance at Pelageya) "if it were to their liking. . . ."

Grisha did not hear what was said further. His mamma came to the door and sent him to the nursery to learn his lessons.

"Go and learn your lesson. It's not your business to listen here!"

When Grisha reached the nursery, he put "My Own Book" in front of him, but he did not get on with his reading. All that he had just seen and heard aroused a multitude of questions in his mind.

"The cook's going to be married," he thought. "Strange - I don't understand what people get married for. Mamma was married to papa, Cousin Verotchka to Pavel Andreyitch. But one might be married to papa and Pavel Andreyitch after all: they have gold watch-chains and nice suits, their boots are always polished; but to marry that dreadful cabman with a red nose and felt boots. . . . Fi! And why is it nurse wants poor Pelageya to be married?"

When the visitor had gone out of the kitchen, Pelageya appeared and began clearing away. Her agitation still persisted. Her face was red and looked scared. She scarcely touched the floor with the broom, and swept every corner five times over. She lingered for a long time in the room where mamma was sitting. She was evidently oppressed by her isolation, and she was longing to express herself, to share her impressions with someone, to open her heart.

"He's gone," she muttered, seeing that mamma would not begin the conversation.

"One can see he is a good man," said mamma, not taking her eyes off her sewing. "Sober and steady."

"I declare I won't marry him, mistress!" Pelageya cried suddenly, flushing crimson. "I declare I won't!"

"Don't be silly; you are not a child. It's a serious step; you must think it over thoroughly, it's no use talking nonsense. Do you like him?"

"What an idea, mistress!" cried Pelageya, abashed. "They say such things that . . . my goodness. . . ."

"She should say she doesn't like him!" thought Grisha.

"What an affected creature you are. . . . Do you like him?"

"But he is old, mistress!"

"Think of something else," nurse flew out at her from the next room. "He has not reached his fortieth year; and what do you want a young man for? Handsome is as handsome does. . . . Marry him and that's all about it!"

"I swear I won't," squealed Pelageya.

"You are talking nonsense. What sort of rascal do you want? Anyone else would have bowed down to his feet, and you declare you won't marry him. You want to be always winking at the postmen and tutors. That tutor that used to come to Grishenka, mistress . . . she was never tired of making eyes at him. O-o, the shameless hussy!"

"Have you seen this Danilo before?" mamma asked Pelageya.

"How could I have seen him? I set eyes on him to-day for the first time. Aksinya picked him up and brought him along . . . the accursed devil. . . . And where has he come from for my undoing!"

At dinner, when Pelageya was handing the dishes, everyone looked into her face and teased her about the cabman. She turned fearfully red, and went off into a forced giggle.

"It must be shameful to get married," thought Grisha. "Terribly shameful."

All the dishes were too salt, and blood oozed from the half-raw chickens, and, to cap it all, plates and knives kept dropping out of Pelageya's hands during dinner, as though from a shelf that had given way; but no one said a word of blame to her, as they all understood the state of her feelings. Only once papa flicked his table-napkin angrily and said to mamma:

"What do you want to be getting them all married for? What business is it of yours? Let them get married of themselves if they want to."

After dinner, neighbouring cooks and maidservants kept flitting into the kitchen, and there was the sound of whispering till late evening. How they had scented out the matchmaking, God knows. When Grisha woke in the night he heard his nurse and the cook whispering together in the nursery. Nurse was talking persuasively, while the cook alternately sobbed and giggled. When he fell asleep after this, Grisha dreamed of Pelageya being carried off by Tchernomor and a witch.

Next day there was a calm. The life of the kitchen went on its accustomed way as though the cabman did not exist. Only from time to time nurse put on her new shawl, assumed a solemn and austere air, and went off somewhere for an hour or two, obviously to conduct negotiations. . . . Pelageya did not see the cabman, and when his name was mentioned she flushed up and cried:

"May he be thrice damned! As though I should be thinking of him! Tfoo!"

In the evening mamma went into the kitchen, while nurse and Pelageya were zealously mincing something, and said:

"You can marry him, of course - that's your business - but I must tell you, Pelageya, that he cannot live here. . . . You know I don't like to have anyone sitting in the kitchen. Mind now, remember.... And I can't let you sleep out."

"Goodness knows! What an idea, mistress!" shrieked the cook. "Why do you keep throwing him up at me? Plague take him! He's a regular curse, confound him!..."

Glancing one Sunday morning into the kitchen, Grisha was struck dumb with amazement. The kitchen was crammed full of people. Here were cooks from the whole courtyard, the porter, two policemen, a non-commissioned officer with good-conduct stripes, and the boy Filka.... This Filka was generally hanging about the laundry playing with the dogs; now he was combed and washed, and was holding an ikon in a tinfoil setting. Pelageya was standing in the middle of the kitchen in a new cotton dress, with a flower on her head. Beside her stood the cabman. The happy pair were red in the face and perspiring and blinking with embarrassment.

"Well... I fancy it is time," said the non-commissioned officer, after a prolonged silence.

Pelageya's face worked all over and she began blubbering....

The soldier took a big loaf from the table, stood beside nurse, and began blessing the couple. The cabman went up to the soldier, flopped down on his knees, and gave a smacking kiss on his hand. He did the same before nurse. Pelageya followed him mechanically, and she too bowed down to the ground. At last the outer door was opened, there was a whiff of white mist, and the whole party flocked noisily out of the kitchen into the yard.

"Poor thing, poor thing," thought Grisha, hearing the sobs of the cook. "Where have they taken her? Why don't papa and mamma protect her?"

After the wedding there was singing and concertina-playing in the laundry till late evening. Mamma was cross all the evening because nurse smelt of vodka, and owing to the wedding there was no one to heat the samovar. Pelageya had not come back by the time Grisha went to bed.

"The poor thing is crying somewhere in the dark!" he thought. "While the cabman is saying to her 'shut up!' "

Next morning the cook was in the kitchen again. The cabman came in for a minute. He thanked mamma, and glancing sternly at Pelageya, said:

"Will you look after her, madam? Be a father and a mother to her. And you, too, Aksinya Stepanovna, do not forsake her, see that everything is as it should be . . . without any nonsense. . . . And also, madam, if you would kindly advance me five roubles of her wages. I have got to buy a new horse-collar."

Again a problem for Grisha: Pelageya was living in freedom, doing as she liked, and not having to account to anyone for her actions, and all at once, for no sort of reason, a stranger turns up, who has somehow acquired rights over her conduct and her property! Grisha was distressed. He longed passionately, almost to tears, to comfort this victim, as he supposed, of man's injustice. Picking out the very biggest apple in the store-room he stole into the kitchen, slipped it into Pelageya's hand, and darted headlong away.

IN A STRANGE LAND

Sunday, midday. A landowner, called Kamyshev, is sitting in his dining-room, deliberately eating his lunch at a luxuriously furnished table. Monsieur Champoun, a clean, neat, smoothly-shaven, old Frenchman, is sharing the meal with him. This Champoun had once been a tutor in Kamyshev's household, had taught his children good manners, the correct pronunciation of French, and dancing: afterwards when Kamyshev's children had grown up and become lieutenants, Champoun had become something like a *bonne* of the male sex. The duties of the former tutor were not complicated. He had to be properly dressed, to smell of scent, to listen to Kamyshev's idle babble, to eat and drink and sleep - and apparently that was all. For this he received a room, his board, and an indefinite salary.

Kamyshev eats and as usual babbles at random.

"Damnation!" he says, wiping away the tears that have come into his eyes after a mouthful of ham thickly smeared with mustard. "Ough! It has shot into my head and all my joints. Your French mustard would not do that, you know, if you ate the whole potful."

"Some like the French, some prefer the Russian. . ." Champoun assents mildly.

"No one likes French mustard except Frenchmen. And a Frenchman will eat anything, whatever you give him - frogs and rats and black beetles. . . brrr! You don't like that ham, for instance, because it is Russian, but if one were to give you a bit of baked glass and tell you it was French, you would eat it and smack your lips. . . . To your thinking everything Russian is nasty."

"I don't say that."

"Everything Russian is nasty, but if it's French - o say tray zholee! To your thinking there is no country better than France, but to my mind. . . Why, what is France, to tell the truth about it? A little bit of land. Our police captain was sent out there, but in a month he asked to be transferred: there was nowhere to turn round! One can drive round the whole of your France in one day, while here when you drive out of the gate - you can see no end to the land, you can ride on and on. . ."

"Yes, monsieur, Russia is an immense country."

"To be sure it is! To your thinking there are no better people than the French. Well-educated, clever people! Civilization! I agree, the French are all well-educated with elegant manners. . . that is true. . . . A Frenchman never allows himself to be rude: he hands a lady a chair at the right minute, he doesn't eat crayfish with his fork, he doesn't spit on the floor, but . . . there's not the same spirit in him! not the spirit in him! I don't know how to explain it to you but, however one is to express it, there's nothing in a Frenchman of . . . something . . . (the speaker flourishes his fingers) . . . of something . . . fanatical. I remember I have read somewhere that all of you have intelligence acquired from books, while we Russians have innate intelligence. If a Russian studies the sciences properly, none of your French professors is a match for him."

"Perhaps," says Champoun, as it were reluctantly.

"No, not perhaps, but certainly! It's no use your frowning, it's the truth I am speaking. The Russian intelligence is an inventive intelligence. Only of course he is not given a free outlet for it, and he is no hand at boasting. He will invent something - and break it or give it to the children to play with, while your Frenchman will invent some nonsensical thing and make an uproar for all the world to hear it. The other day Iona the coachman carved a little man out of wood, if you pull the little man by a thread he plays unseemly antics. But Iona does not brag of it. . . . I don't like Frenchmen as a rule. I am not referring to you, but speaking generally. . . . They are an immoral people! Outwardly they look like men, but they live like dogs. Take marriage for instance. With us, once you are married, you stick to your wife, and there is no talk about it, but goodness knows how it is with you. The husband is sitting all day long in a café, while his wife fills the house with Frenchmen, and sets to dancing the can-can with them."

"That's not true!" Champoun protests, flaring up and unable to restrain himself. "The principle of the family is highly esteemed in France."

"We know all about that principle! You ought to be ashamed to defend it: one ought to be impartial: a pig is always a pig. . . . We must thank the Germans for having beaten them. . . . Yes indeed, God bless them for it."

"In that case, monsieur, I don't understand. . ." says the Frenchman leaping up with flashing eyes, "if you hate the French why do you keep me?"

"What am I to do with you?"

"Let me go, and I will go back to France."

"Wha-at? But do you suppose they would let you into France now? Why, you are a traitor to your country! At one time Napoleon's your great man, at another Gambetta. . . . Who the devil can make you out?"

"Monsieur," says Champoun in French, spluttering and crushing up his table napkin in his hands, "my worst enemy could not have thought of a greater insult than the outrage you have just done to my feelings! All is over!"

And with a tragic wave of his arm the Frenchman flings his dinner napkin on the table majestically, and walks out of the room with dignity.

Three hours later the table is laid again, and the servants bring in the dinner. Kamyshev sits alone at the table. After the preliminary glass he feels a craving to babble. He wants to chatter, but he has no listener.

"What is Alphonse Ludovikovitch doing?" he asks the footman.

"He is packing his trunk, sir."

"What a noodle! Lord forgive us!" says Kamyshev, and goes in to the Frenchman.

Champoun is sitting on the floor in his room, and with trembling hands is packing in his trunk his linen, scent bottles, prayer-books, braces, ties. . . . All his correct figure, his trunk, his bedstead and the table - all have an air of elegance and effeminacy. Great tears are dropping from his big blue eyes into the trunk.

"Where are you off to?" asks Kamyshev, after standing still for a little.

The Frenchman says nothing.

"Do you want to go away?" Kamyshev goes on. "Well, you know, but . . . I won't venture to detain you. But what is queer is, how are you going to travel without a passport? I wonder! You know I have lost your passport. I thrust it in somewhere between some papers, and it is lost. . . . And they are strict about passports among us. Before you have gone three or four miles they pounce upon you."

Champoun raises his head and looks mistrustfully at Kamyshev.

"Yes. . . . You will see! They will see from your face you haven't a passport, and ask at once: Who is that? Alphonse Champoun. We know that Alphonse Champoun. Wouldn't you like to go under police escort somewhere nearer home!"

"Are you joking?"

"What motive have I for joking? Why should I? Only mind now; it's a compact, don't you begin whining then and writing letters. I won't stir a finger when they lead you by in fetters!"

Champoun jumps up and, pale and wide-eyed, begins pacing up and down the room.

"What are you doing to me? " he says in despair, clutching at his head. "My God! accursed be that hour when the fatal thought of leaving my country entered my head! . . ."

"Come, come, come . . . I was joking!" says Kamyshev in a lower tone. "Queer fish he is; he doesn't understand a joke. One can't say a word!"

"My dear friend!" shrieks Champoun, reassured by Kamyshev's tone. "I swear I am devoted to Russia, to you and your children. . . . To leave you is as bitter to me as death itself! But every word you utter stabs me to the heart!"

"Ah, you queer fish! If I do abuse the French, what reason have you to take offence? You are a queer fish really! You should follow the example of Lazar Isaakitch, my tenant. I call him one thing and another, a Jew, and a scurvy rascal, and I make a pig's ear out of my coat tail, and catch him by his Jewish curls. He doesn't take offence."

"But he is a slave! For a kopeck he is ready to put up with any insult!"

"Come, come, come . . . that's enough! Peace and concord!"

Champoun powders his tear-stained face and goes with Kamyshev to the dining-room. The first course is eaten in silence, after the second the same performance begins over again, and so Champoun's sufferings have no end.

OVERDOING IT

Glyeb Gavrilovitch Smirnov, a land surveyor, arrived at the station of Gnilushki. He had another twenty or thirty miles to drive before he would reach the estate which he had been summoned to survey. (If the driver were not drunk and the horses were not bad, it would hardly be twenty miles, but if the driver had had a drop and his steeds were worn out it would mount up to a good forty.)

"Tell me, please, where can I get post-horses here?" the surveyor asked of the station gendarme.

"What? Post-horses? There's no finding a decent dog for seventy miles round, let alone post-horses. . . . But where do you want to go?"

"To Dyevkino, General Hohotov's estate."

"Well," yawned the gendarme, "go outside the station, there are sometimes peasants in the yard there, they will take passengers."

The surveyor heaved a sigh and made his way out of the station.

There, after prolonged enquiries, conversations, and hesitations, he found a very sturdy, sullen-looking pock-marked peasant, wearing a tattered grey smock and bark-shoes.

"You have got a queer sort of cart!" said the surveyor, frowning as he clambered into the cart. "There is no making out which is the back and which is the front."

"What is there to make out? Where the horse's tail is, there's the front, and where your honour's sitting, there's the back."

The little mare was young, but thin, with legs planted wide apart and frayed ears. When the driver stood up and lashed her with a whip made of cord, she merely shook her head; when he swore at her and lashed her once more, the cart squeaked and shivered as though in a fever. After the third lash the cart gave a lurch, after the fourth, it moved forward.

"Are we going to drive like this all the way?" asked the surveyor, violently jolted and marvelling at the capacity of Russian drivers for combining a slow tortoise-like pace with a jolting that turns the soul inside out.

"We shall ge-et there!" the peasant reassured him. "The mare is young and frisky. . . . Only let her get running and then there is no stopping her. . . . No-ow, cur-sed brute!"

It was dusk by the time the cart drove out of the station. On the surveyor's right hand stretched a dark frozen plain, endless and boundless. If you drove over it you would certainly get to the other side of beyond. On the horizon, where it vanished and melted into the sky, there was the languid glow of a cold autumn sunset. . . . On the left of the road, mounds of some sort, that might be last year's stacks or might be a village, rose up in the gathering darkness. The surveyor could not see what was in front as his whole field of vision on that side was covered by the broad clumsy back of the driver. The air was still, but it was cold and frosty.

"What a wilderness it is here," thought the surveyor, trying to cover his ears with the collar of his overcoat. "Neither post nor paddock. If, by ill-luck, one were attacked and robbed no one would hear you, whatever uproar you made. . . . And the driver is not one you could depend on. . . . Ugh, what a huge back! A child of nature like that has only to move a finger and it would be all up with one! And his ugly face is suspicious and brutal-looking."

"Hey, my good man!" said the surveyor, "What is your name?"

"Mine? Klim."

"Well, Klim, what is it like in your parts here? Not dangerous? Any robbers on the road?"

"It is all right, the Lord has spared us. . . . Who should go robbing on the road?"

"It's a good thing there are no robbers. But to be ready for anything I have got three revolvers with me," said the surveyor untruthfully. "And it doesn't do to trifle with a revolver, you know. One can manage a dozen robbers. . . ."

It had become quite dark. The cart suddenly began creaking, squeaking, shaking, and, as though unwillingly, turned sharply to the left.

"Where is he taking me to?" the surveyor wondered. "He has been driving straight and now all at once to the left. I shouldn't wonder if he'll take me, the rascal, to some den of thieves . . . and. . . . Things like that do happen."

"I say," he said, addressing the driver, "so you tell me it's not dangerous here? That's a pity. . . I like a fight with robbers. . . . I am thin and sickly-looking, but I have the strength of a bull. . . . Once three robbers attacked me and what do you think? I gave one such a dressing that. . . that he gave up his soul to God, you understand, and the other two were sent to penal servitude in Siberia. And where I got the strength I can't say. . . . One grips a strapping fellow of your sort with one hand and . . . wipes him out."

Klim looked round at the surveyor, wrinkled up his whole face, and lashed his horse.

"Yes . . ." the surveyor went on. "God forbid anyone should tackle me. The robber would have his bones broken, and, what's more, he would have to answer for it in the police court too. . . . I know all the judges and the police captains, I am a man in the Government, a man of importance. Here I am travelling and the authorities know . . . they keep a regular watch over me to see no one does me a mischief. There are policemen and village constables stuck behind bushes all along the road. . . . Sto . . . sto . . . . stop!" the surveyor bawled suddenly. "Where have you got to? Where are you taking me to?"

"Why, don't you see? It's a forest!"

"It certainly is a forest," thought the surveyor. "I was frightened! But it won't do to betray my feelings. . . . He has noticed already that I am in a funk. Why is it he has taken to looking round at me so often? He is plotting something for certain. . . . At first he drove like a snail and now how he is dashing along!"

"I say, Klim, why are you making the horse go like that?"

"I am not making her go. She is racing along of herself. . . . Once she gets into a run there is no means of stopping her. It's no pleasure to her that her legs are like that."

"You are lying, my man, I see that you are lying. Only I advise you not to drive so fast. Hold your horse in a bit. . . . Do you hear? Hold her in!"

"What for?"

"Why . . . why, because four comrades were to drive after me from the station. We must let them catch us up. . . . They promised to overtake us in this forest. It will be more cheerful in their company. . . . They are a strong, sturdy set of fellows. . . . And each of them has got a pistol. Why do you keep looking round and fidgeting as though you were sitting on thorns? eh? I, my good fellow, er . . . my good fellow . . . there is no need to look around at me . . . there is nothing interesting about me. . . . Except perhaps the revolvers. Well, if you like I will take them out and show you. . . ."

The surveyor made a pretence of feeling in his pockets and at that moment something happened which he could not have expected with all his cowardice. Klim suddenly rolled off the cart and ran as fast as he could go into the forest.

"Help!" he roared. "Help! Take the horse and the cart, you devil, only don't take my life. Help!"

There was the sound of footsteps hurriedly retreating, of twigs snapping - and all was still. . . . The surveyor had not expected such a *dénouement*. He first stopped the horse and then settled himself more comfortably in the cart and fell to thinking.

"He has run off . . . he was scared, the fool. Well, what's to be done now? I can't go on alone because I don't know the way; besides they may think I have stolen his horse. . . . What's to be done?"

"Klim! Klim," he cried.

"Klim," answered the echo.

At the thought that he would have to sit through the whole night in the cold and dark forest and hear nothing but the wolves, the echo, and the snorting of the scraggy mare, the surveyor began to have twinges down his spine as though it were being rasped with a cold file.

"Klimushka," he shouted. "Dear fellow! Where are you, Klimushka?"

For two hours the surveyor shouted, and it was only after he was quite husky and had resigned himself to spending the night in the forest that a faint breeze wafted the sound of a moan to him.

"Klim, is it you, dear fellow? Let us go on."

"You'll mu-ur-der me!"

"But I was joking, my dear man! I swear to God I was joking! As though I had revolvers! I told a lie because I was frightened. For goodness sake let us go on, I am freezing!"

Klim, probably reflecting that a real robber would have vanished long ago with the horse and cart, came out of the forest and went hesitatingly up to his passenger.

"Well, what were you frightened of, stupid? I . . . I was joking and you were frightened. Get in!"

"God be with you, sir," Klim muttered as he clambered into the cart, "if I had known I wouldn't have taken you for a hundred roubles. I almost died of fright. . . ."

Klim lashed at the little mare. The cart swayed. Klim lashed once more and the cart gave a lurch. After the fourth stroke of the whip when the cart moved forward, the surveyor hid his ears in his collar and sank into thought.

The road and Klim no longer seemed dangerous to him.

OLD AGE

Uzelkov, an architect with the rank of civil councillor, arrived in his native town, to which he had been invited to restore the church in the cemetery. He had been born in the town, had been at school, had grown up and married in it. But when he got out of the train he scarcely recognized it. Everything was changed. . . . Eighteen years ago when he had moved to Petersburg the street-boys used to catch marmots, for instance, on the spot where now the station was standing; now when one drove into the chief street, a hotel of four storeys stood facing one; in old days there was an ugly grey fence just there; but nothing - neither fences nor houses - had changed as much as the people. From his enquiries of the hotel waiter Uzelkov learned that more than half of the people he remembered were dead, reduced to poverty, forgotten.

"And do you remember Uzelkov?" he asked the old waiter about himself. "Uzelkov the architect who divorced his wife? He used to have a house in Svirebeyevsky Street . . . you must remember."

"I don't remember, sir."

"How is it you don't remember? The case made a lot of noise, even the cabmen all knew about it. Think, now! Shapkin the attorney managed my divorce for me, the rascal . . . the notorious cardsharper, the fellow who got a thrashing at the club. . . ."

"Ivan Nikolaitch?"

"Yes, yes. . . . Well, is he alive? Is he dead?"

"Alive, sir, thank God. He is a notary now and has an office. He is very well off. He has two houses in Kirpitchny Street. . . . His daughter was married the other day."

Uzelkov paced up and down the room, thought a bit, and in his boredom made up his mind to go and see Shapkin at his office. When he walked out of the hotel and sauntered slowly towards Kirpitchny Street it was midday. He found Shapkin at his office and scarcely recognized him. From the once well-made, adroit attorney with a mobile, insolent, and always drunken face Shapkin had changed into a modest, grey-headed, decrepit old man.

"You don't recognize me, you have forgotten me," began Uzelkov. "I am your old client, Uzelkov."

"Uzelkov, what Uzelkov? Ah!" Shapkin remembered, recognized, and was struck all of a heap. There followed a shower of exclamations, questions, recollections.

"This is a surprise! This is unexpected!" cackled Shapkin. "What can I offer you? Do you care for champagne? Perhaps you would like oysters? My dear fellow, I have had so much from you in my time that I can't offer you anything equal to the occasion. . . ."

"Please don't put yourself out . . ." said Uzelkov. "I have no time to spare. I must go at once to the cemetery and examine the church; I have undertaken the restoration of it."

"That's capital! We'll have a snack and a drink and drive together. I have capital horses. I'll take you there and introduce you to the church-warden; I will arrange it all. . . . But why is it, my angel, you seem to be afraid of me and hold me at arm's length? Sit a little nearer! There is no need for you to be afraid of me nowadays. He-he! . . . At one time, it is true, I was a cunning blade, a dog of a fellow . . . no one dared approach me; but now I am stiller than water and humbler than the grass. I have grown old, I am a family man, I have children. It's time I was dead."

The friends had lunch, had a drink, and with a pair of horses drove out of the town to the cemetery.

"Yes, those were times!" Shapkin recalled as he sat in the sledge. "When you remember them you simply can't believe in them. Do you remember how you divorced your wife? It's nearly twenty years ago, and I dare say you have forgotten it all; but I remember it as though I'd divorced you yesterday. Good Lord, what a lot of worry I had over it! I was a sharp fellow, tricky and cunning, a desperate character. . . . Sometimes I was burning to tackle some ticklish business, especially if the fee were a good one, as, for instance, in your case. What did you pay me then? Five or six thousand! That was worth taking trouble for, wasn't it? You went off to Petersburg and left the whole thing in my hands to do the best I could, and, though Sofya Mihailovna, your wife, came only of a merchant family, she was proud and dignified. To bribe her to take the guilt on herself was difficult, awfully difficult! I would go to negotiate with her, and as soon as she saw me she called to her maid: 'Masha, didn't I tell you not to admit that scoundrel?' Well, I tried one thing and another. . . . I wrote her letters and contrived to meet her accidentally - it was no use! I had to act through a third person. I had a lot of trouble with her for a long time, and she only gave in when you agreed to give her ten thousand. . . . She couldn't resist ten thousand, she couldn't hold out. . . . She cried, she spat in my face, but she consented, she took the guilt on herself!"

"I thought it was fifteen thousand she had from me, not ten," said Uzelkov.

"Yes, yes . . . fifteen - I made a mistake," said Shapkin in confusion. "It's all over and done with, though, it's no use concealing it. I gave her ten and the other five I collared for myself. I deceived you both. . . . It's all over and done with, it's no use to be ashamed. And indeed, judge for yourself, Boris Petrovitch, weren't you the very person for me to get money out of? . . . You were a wealthy man and had everything you wanted. . . . Your marriage was an idle whim, and so was your divorce. You were making a lot of money. . . . I remember you made a scoop of twenty thousand over one contract. Whom should I have fleeced if not you? And I must own I envied you. If you grabbed anything they took off their caps to you, while they would thrash me for a rouble and slap me in the face at the club. . . . But there, why recall it? It is high time to forget it."

"Tell me, please, how did Sofya Mihailovna get on afterwards?"

"With her ten thousand? Very badly. God knows what it was - she lost her head, perhaps, or maybe her pride and her conscience tormented her at having sold her honour, or perhaps she loved you; but, do you know, she took to drink. . . . As soon as she got her money she was off driving about with officers. It was drunkenness, dissipation, debauchery. . . . When she went to a restaurant with officers she was not content with port or anything light, she must have strong brandy, fiery stuff to stupefy her."

"Yes, she was eccentric. . . . I had a lot to put up with from her . . . sometimes she would take offence at something and begin being hysterical. . . . And what happened afterwards?"

"One week passed and then another. . . . I was sitting at home, writing something. All at once the door opened and she walked in . . . drunk. 'Take back your cursed money,' she said, and flung a roll of notes in my face. . . . So she could not keep it up. I picked up the notes and counted them. It was five hundred short of the ten thousand, so she had only managed to get through five hundred."

"Where did you put the money?"

"It's all ancient history . . . there's no reason to conceal it now. . . . In my pocket, of course. Why do you look at me like that? Wait a bit for what will come later. . . . It's a regular novel, a pathological study. A couple of months later I was going home one night in a nasty drunken condition. . . . I lighted a candle, and lo and behold! Sofya Mihailovna was sitting on my sofa, and she was drunk, too, and in a frantic state - as wild as though she had run out of Bedlam. 'Give me back my money,' she said, 'I have changed my mind; if I must go to ruin I won't do it by halves, I'll have my fling! Be quick, you scoundrel, give me my money! ' A disgraceful scene!"

"And you . . . gave it her?"

"I gave her, I remember, ten roubles."

"Oh! How could you?" cried Uzelkov, frowning. "If you couldn't or wouldn't have given it her, you might have written to me. . . . And I didn't know! I didn't know!"

"My dear fellow, what use would it have been for me to write, considering that she wrote to you herself when she was lying in the hospital afterwards?"

"Yes, but I was so taken up then with my second marriage. I was in such a whirl that I had no thoughts to spare for letters. . . . But you were an outsider, you had no antipathy for Sofya. . . why didn't you give her a helping hand? . . ."

"You can't judge by the standards of to-day, Boris Petrovitch; that's how we look at it now, but at the time we thought very differently.... Now maybe I'd give her a thousand roubles, but then even that ten-rouble note I did not give her for nothing. It was a bad business! ... We must forget it.... But here we are...."

The sledge stopped at the cemetery gates. Uzelkov and Shapkin got out of the sledge, went in at the gate, and walked up a long, broad avenue. The bare cherry-trees and acacias, the grey crosses and tombstones, were silvered with hoar-frost, every little grain of snow reflected the bright, sunny day. There was the smell there always is in cemeteries, the smell of incense and freshly dug earth....

"Our cemetery is a pretty one," said Uzelkov, "quite a garden!"

"Yes, but it is a pity thieves steal the tombstones.... And over there, beyond that iron monument on the right, Sofya Mihailovna is buried. Would you like to see?"

The friends turned to the right and walked through the deep snow to the iron monument.

"Here it is," said Shapkin, pointing to a little slab of white marble. "A lieutenant put the stone on her grave."

Uzelkov slowly took off his cap and exposed his bald head to the sun. Shapkin, looking at him, took off his cap too, and another bald patch gleamed in the sunlight. There was the stillness of the tomb all around as though the air, too, were dead. The friends looked at the grave, pondered, and said nothing.

"She sleeps in peace," said Shapkin, breaking the silence. "It's nothing to her now that she took the blame on herself and drank brandy. You must own, Boris Petrovitch...."

"Own what?" Uzelkov asked gloomily.

"Why.... However hateful the past, it was better than this."

And Shapkin pointed to his grey head.

"I used not to think of the hour of death. . . . I fancied I could have given death points and won the game if we had had an encounter; but now. . . . But what's the good of talking!"

Uzelkov was overcome with melancholy. He suddenly had a passionate longing to weep, as once he had longed for love, and he felt those tears would have tasted sweet and refreshing. A moisture came into his eyes and there was a lump in his throat, but . . . Shapkin was standing beside him and Uzelkov was ashamed to show weakness before a witness. He turned back abruptly and went into the church.

Only two hours later, after talking to the churchwarden and looking over the church, he seized a moment when Shapkin was in conversation with the priest and hastened away to weep. . . . He stole up to the grave secretly, furtively, looking round him every minute. The little white slab looked at him pensively, mournfully, and innocently as though a little girl lay under it instead of a dissolute, divorced wife.

"To weep, to weep!" thought Uzelkov.

But the moment for tears had been missed; though the old man blinked his eyes, though he worked up his feelings, the tears did not flow nor the lump come in his throat. After standing for ten minutes, with a gesture of despair, Uzelkov went to look for Shapkin.

SORROW

The turner, Grigory Petrov, who had been known for years past as a splendid craftsman, and at the same time as the most senseless peasant in the Galtchinskoy district, was taking his old woman to the hospital. He had to drive over twenty miles, and it was an awful road. A government post driver could hardly have coped with it, much less an incompetent sluggard like Grigory. A cutting cold wind was blowing straight in his face. Clouds of snowflakes were whirling round and round in all directions, so that one could not tell whether the snow was falling from the sky or rising from the earth. The fields, the telegraph posts, and the forest could not be seen for the fog of snow. And when a particularly violent gust of wind swooped down on Grigory, even the yoke above the horse's head could not be seen. The wretched, feeble little nag crawled slowly along. It took all its strength to drag its legs out of the snow and to tug with its head. The turner was in a hurry. He kept restlessly hopping up and down on the front seat and lashing the horse's back.

"Don't cry, Matryona, . . ." he muttered. "Have a little patience. Please God we shall reach the hospital, and in a trice it will be the right thing for you. . . . Pavel Ivanitch will give you some little drops, or tell them to bleed you; or maybe his honor will be pleased to rub you with some sort of spirit - it'll . . . draw it out of your side. Pavel Ivanitch will do his best. He will shout and stamp about, but he will do his best. . . . He is a nice gentleman, affable, God give him health! As soon as we get there he will dart out of his room and will begin calling me names. 'How? Why so?' he will cry. 'Why did you not come at the right time? I am not a dog to be hanging about waiting on you devils all day. Why did you not come in the morning? Go away! Get out of my sight. Come again to-morrow.' And I shall say: 'Mr. Doctor! Pavel Ivanitch! Your honor!' Get on, do! plague take you, you devil! Get on!"

The turner lashed his nag, and without looking at the old woman went on muttering to himself:

" 'Your honor! It's true as before God. . . . Here's the Cross for you, I set off almost before it was light. How could I be here in time if the Lord. . . .The Mother of God . . . is wroth, and has sent such a snowstorm? Kindly look for yourself. . . . Even a first-rate horse could not do it, while mine - you can see for yourself - is not a horse but a disgrace.' And Pavel Ivanitch will frown and shout: 'We know you! You always find some excuse! Especially you, Grishka; I know you of old! I'll be bound you have stopped at half a dozen taverns!' And I shall say: 'Your honor! am I a criminal or a heathen? My old woman is giving up her soul to God, she is dying, and am I going to run from tavern to tavern! What an idea, upon my word! Plague take them, the taverns!' Then Pavel Ivanitch will order you to be taken into the hospital, and I shall fall at his feet.... 'Pavel Ivanitch! Your honor, we thank you most humbly! Forgive us fools and anathemas, don't be hard on us peasants! We deserve a good kicking, while you graciously put yourself out and mess your feet in the snow!' And Pavel Ivanitch will give me a look as though he would like to hit me, and will say: 'You'd much better not be swilling vodka, you fool, but taking pity on your old woman instead of falling at my feet. You want a thrashing!' 'You are right there - a thrashing, Pavel Ivanitch, strike me God! But how can we help bowing down at your feet if you are our benefactor, and a real father to us? Your honor! I give you my word, ... here as before God, ... you may spit in my face if I deceive you: as soon as my Matryona, this same here, is well again and restored to her natural condition, I'll make anything for your honor that you would like to order! A cigarette-case, if you like, of the best birchwood, ... balls for croquet, skittles of the most foreign pattern I can turn.... I will make anything for you! I won't take a farthing from you. In Moscow they would charge you four roubles for such a cigarette-case, but I won't take a farthing.' The doctor will laugh and say: 'Oh, all right, all right.... I see! But it's a pity you are a drunkard....' I know how to manage the gentry, old girl. There isn't a gentleman I couldn't talk to. Only God grant we don't get off the road. Oh, how it is blowing! One's eyes are full of snow."

And the turner went on muttering endlessly. He prattled on mechanically to get a little relief from his depressing feelings. He had plenty of words on his tongue, but the thoughts and questions in his brain were even more numerous. Sorrow had come upon the turner unawares, unlooked-for, and unexpected, and now he could not get over it, could not recover himself. He had lived hitherto in unruffled calm, as though in drunken half-consciousness, knowing neither grief nor joy, and now he was suddenly aware of a dreadful pain in his heart. The careless idler and drunkard found himself quite suddenly in the position of a busy man, weighed down by anxieties and haste, and even struggling with nature.

The turner remembered that his trouble had begun the evening before. When he had come home yesterday evening, a little drunk as usual, and from long-established habit had begun swearing and shaking his fists, his old woman had looked at her rowdy spouse as she had never looked at him before. Usually, the expression in her aged eyes was that of a martyr, meek like that of a dog frequently beaten and badly fed; this time she had looked at him sternly and immovably, as saints in the holy pictures or dying people look. From that strange, evil look in her eyes the trouble had begun. The turner, stupefied with amazement, borrowed a horse from a neighbor, and now was taking his old woman to the hospital in the hope that, by means of powders and ointments, Pavel Ivanitch would bring back his old woman's habitual expression.

"I say, Matryona, . . ." the turner muttered, "if Pavel Ivanitch asks you whether I beat you, say, 'Never!' and I never will beat you again. I swear it. And did I ever beat you out of spite? I just beat you without thinking. I am sorry for you. Some men wouldn't trouble, but here I am taking you. . . . I am doing my best. And the way it snows, the way it snows! Thy Will be done, O Lord! God grant we don't get off the road. . . . Does your side ache, Matryona, that you don't speak? I ask you, does your side ache?"

It struck him as strange that the snow on his old woman's face was not melting; it was queer that the face itself looked somehow drawn, and had turned a pale gray, dingy waxen hue and had grown grave and solemn.

"You are a fool!" muttered the turner. . . . "I tell you on my conscience, before God, . . . and you go and . . . Well, you are a fool! I have a good mind not to take you to Pavel Ivanitch!"

The turner let the reins go and began thinking. He could not bring himself to look round at his old woman: he was frightened. He was afraid, too, of asking her a question and not getting an answer. At last, to make an end of uncertainty, without looking round he felt his old woman's cold hand. The lifted hand fell like a log.

"She is dead, then! What a business!"

And the turner cried. He was not so much sorry as annoyed. He thought how quickly everything passes in this world! His trouble had hardly begun when the final catastrophe had happened. He had not had time to live with his old woman, to show her he was sorry for her before she died. He had lived with her for forty years, but those forty years had passed by as it were in a fog. What with drunkenness, quarreling, and poverty, there had been no feeling of life. And, as though to spite him, his old woman died at the very time when he felt he was sorry for her, that he could not live without her, and that he had behaved dreadfully badly to her.

"Why, she used to go the round of the village," he remembered. "I sent her out myself to beg for bread. What a business! She ought to have lived another ten years, the silly thing; as it is I'll be bound she thinks I really was that sort of man. . . . Holy Mother! but where the devil am I driving? There's no need for a doctor now, but a burial. Turn back!"

Grigory turned back and lashed the horse with all his might. The road grew worse and worse every hour. Now he could not see the yoke at all. Now and then the sledge ran into a young fir tree, a dark object scratched the turner's hands and flashed before his eyes, and the field of vision was white and whirling again.

"To live over again," thought the turner.

He remembered that forty years ago Matryona had been young, handsome, merry, that she had come of a well-to-do family. They had married her to him because they had been attracted by his handicraft. All the essentials for a happy life had been there, but the trouble was that, just as he had got drunk after the wedding and lay sprawling on the stove, so he had gone on without waking up till now. His wedding he remembered, but of what happened after the wedding - for the life of him he could remember nothing, except perhaps that he had drunk, lain on the stove, and quarreled. Forty years had been wasted like that.

The white clouds of snow were beginning little by little to turn gray. It was getting dusk.

"Where am I going?" the turner suddenly bethought him with a start. "I ought to be thinking of the burial, and I am on the way to the hospital. . . . It as is though I had gone crazy."

Grigory turned round again, and again lashed his horse. The little nag strained its utmost and, with a snort, fell into a little trot. The turner lashed it on the back time after time. . . . A knocking was audible behind him, and though he did not look round, he knew it was the dead woman's head knocking against the sledge. And the snow kept turning darker and darker, the wind grew colder and more cutting. . . .

"To live over again!" thought the turner. "I should get a new lathe, take orders, . . . give the money to my old woman. . . ."

And then he dropped the reins. He looked for them, tried to pick them up, but could not - his hands would not work. . . .

"It does not matter," he thought, "the horse will go of itself, it knows the way. I might have a little sleep now. . . . Before the funeral or the requiem it would be as well to get a little rest. . . ."

The turner closed his eyes and dozed. A little later he heard the horse stop; he opened his eyes and saw before him something dark like a hut or a haystack. . . .

He would have got out of the sledge and found out what it was, but he felt overcome by such inertia that it seemed better to freeze than move, and he sank into a peaceful sleep.

He woke up in a big room with painted walls. Bright sunlight was streaming in at the windows. The turner saw people facing him, and his first feeling was a desire to show himself a respectable man who knew how things should be done.

"A requiem, brothers, for my old woman," he said. "The priest should be told. . . ."

"Oh, all right, all right; lie down," a voice cut him short.

"Pavel Ivanitch!" the turner cried in surprise, seeing the doctor before him. "Your honor, benefactor! "

He wanted to leap up and fall on his knees before the doctor, but felt that his arms and legs would not obey him.

"Your honor, where are my legs, where are my arms!"

"Say good-by to your arms and legs.... They've been frozen off. Come, come!... What are you crying for? You've lived your life, and thank God for it! I suppose you have had sixty years of it - that's enough for you!..."

"I am grieving.... Graciously forgive me! If I could have another five or six years!..."

"What for?"

"The horse isn't mine, I must give it back.... I must bury my old woman.... How quickly it is all ended in this world! Your honor, Pavel Ivanitch! A cigarette-case of birchwood of the best! I'll turn you croquet balls...."

The doctor went out of the ward with a wave of his hand. It was all over with the turner.

OH! THE PUBLIC

"Here goes, I've done with drinking! Nothing... n-o-thing shall tempt me to it. It's time to take myself in hand; I must buck up and work... You're glad to get your salary, so you must do your work honestly, heartily, conscientiously, regardless of sleep and comfort. Chuck taking it easy. You've got into the way of taking a salary for nothing, my boy - that's not the right thing... not the right thing at all...."

After administering to himself several such lectures Podtyagin, the head ticket collector, begins to feel an irresistible impulse to get to work. It is past one o'clock at night, but in spite of that he wakes the ticket collectors and with them goes up and down the railway carriages, inspecting the tickets.

"T-t-t-ickets... P-p-p-please!" he keeps shouting, briskly snapping the clippers.

Sleepy figures, shrouded in the twilight of the railway carriages, start, shake their heads, and produce their tickets.

"T-t-t-tickets, please!" Podtyagin addresses a second-class passenger, a lean, scraggy-looking man, wrapped up in a fur coat and a rug and surrounded with pillows. "Tickets, please!"

The scraggy-looking man makes no reply. He is buried in sleep. The head ticket-collector touches him on the shoulder and repeats impatiently: "T-t-tickets, p-p-please!"

The passenger starts, opens his eyes, and gazes in alarm at Podtyagin.

"What?... Who?... Eh?"

"You're asked in plain language: t-t-tickets, p-p-please! If you please!"

"My God!" moans the scraggy-looking man, pulling a woebegone face. "Good Heavens! I'm suffering from rheumatism.... I haven't slept for three nights! I've just taken morphia on purpose to get to sleep, and you... with your tickets! It's merciless, it's inhuman! If you knew how hard it is for me to sleep you wouldn't disturb me for such nonsense.... It's cruel, it's absurd! And what do you want with my ticket! It's positively stupid!"

Podtyagin considers whether to take offence or not - and decides to take offence.

"Don't shout here! This is not a tavern!"

"No, in a tavern people are more humane. . ." coughs the passenger. "Perhaps you'll let me go to sleep another time! It's extraordinary: I've travelled abroad, all over the place, and no one asked for my ticket there, but here you're at it again and again, as though the devil were after you. . . ."

"Well, you'd better go abroad again since you like it so much."

"It's stupid, sir! Yes! As though it's not enough killing the passengers with fumes and stuffiness and draughts, they want to strangle us with red tape, too, damn it all! He must have the ticket! My goodness, what zeal! If it were of any use to the company - but half the passengers are travelling without a ticket!"

"Listen, sir!" cries Podtyagin, flaring up. "If you don't leave off shouting and disturbing the public, I shall be obliged to put you out at the next station and to draw up a report on the incident!"

"This is revolting!" exclaims "the public," growing indignant. "Persecuting an invalid! Listen, and have some consideration!"

"But the gentleman himself was abusive!" says Podtyagin, a little scared. "Very well. . . . I won't take the ticket . . . as you like. . . . Only, of course, as you know very well, it's my duty to do so. . . . If it were not my duty, then, of course. . . You can ask the station-master . . . ask anyone you like. . . ."

Podtyagin shrugs his shoulders and walks away from the invalid. At first he feels aggrieved and somewhat injured, then, after passing through two or three carriages, he begins to feel a certain uneasiness not unlike the pricking of conscience in his ticket-collector's bosom.

"There certainly was no need to wake the invalid," he thinks, "though it was not my fault. . . .They imagine I did it wantonly, idly. They don't know that I'm bound in duty . . . if they don't believe it, I can bring the station-master to them." A station. The train stops five minutes. Before the third bell, Podtyagin enters the same second-class carriage. Behind him stalks the station-master in a red cap.

"This gentleman here," Podtyagin begins, "declares that I have no right to ask for his ticket and . . . and is offended at it. I ask you, Mr. Station-master, to explain to him. . . . Do I ask for tickets according to regulation or to please myself? Sir," Podtyagin addresses the scraggy-looking man, "sir! you can ask the station-master here if you don't believe me."

The invalid starts as though he had been stung, opens his eyes, and with a woebegone face sinks back in his seat.

"My God! I have taken another powder and only just dozed off when here he is again. . . again! I beseech you have some pity on me!"

"You can ask the station-master . . . whether I have the right to demand your ticket or not."

"This is insufferable! Take your ticket. . . take it! I'll pay for five extra if you'll only let me die in peace! Have you never been ill yourself? Heartless people!"

"This is simply persecution!" A gentleman in military uniform grows indignant. "I can see no other explanation of this persistence."

"Drop it . . ." says the station-master, frowning and pulling Podtyagin by the sleeve.

Podtyagin shrugs his shoulders and slowly walks after the station-master.

"There's no pleasing them!" he thinks, bewildered. "It was for his sake I brought the station-master, that he might understand and be pacified, and he . . . swears!"

Another station. The train stops ten minutes. Before the second bell, while Podtyagin is standing at the refreshment bar, drinking seltzer water, two gentlemen go up to him, one in the uniform of an engineer, and the other in a military overcoat.

"Look here, ticket-collector!" the engineer begins, addressing Podtyagin. "Your behaviour to that invalid passenger has revolted all who witnessed it. My name is Puzitsky; I am an engineer, and this gentleman is a colonel. If you do not apologize to the passenger, we shall make a complaint to the traffic manager, who is a friend of ours."

"Gentlemen! Why of course I . . . why of course you . . ." Podtyagin is panic-stricken.

"We don't want explanations. But we warn you, if you don't apologize, we shall see justice done to him."

Certainly I . . . I'll apologize, of course. . . To be sure. . . ."

Half an hour later, Podtyagin having thought of an apologetic phrase which would satisfy the passenger without lowering his own dignity, walks into the carriage. "Sir," he addresses the invalid. "Listen, sir. . . ."

The invalid starts and leaps up: "What?"

"I . . . what was it? . . . You mustn't be offended. . . ."

"Och! Water . . ." gasps the invalid, clutching at his heart. "I'd just taken a third dose of morphia, dropped asleep, and . . . again! Good God! when will this torture cease!"

"I only . . . you must excuse . . ."

"Oh! . . . Put me out at the next station! I can't stand any more. . . . I . . . I am dying. . . ."

"This is mean, disgusting!" cry the "public," revolted. "Go away! You shall pay for such persecution. Get away!"

Podtyagin waves his hand in despair, sighs, and walks out of the carriage. He goes to the attendants' compartment, sits down at the table, exhausted, and complains:

"Oh, the public! There's no satisfying them! It's no use working and doing one's best! One's driven to drinking and cursing it all. . . . If you do nothing - they're angry; if you begin doing your duty, they're angry too. There's nothing for it but drink!"

Podtyagin empties a bottle straight off and thinks no more of work, duty, and honesty!

MARI D'ELLE

It was a free night. Natalya Andreyevna Bronin (her married name was Nikitin), the opera singer, is lying in her bedroom, her whole being abandoned to repose. She lies, deliciously drowsy, thinking of her little daughter who lives somewhere far away with her grandmother or aunt. . . . The child is more precious to her than the public, bouquets, notices in the papers, adorers . . . and she would be glad to think about her till morning. She is happy, at peace, and all she longs for is not to be prevented from lying undisturbed, dozing and dreaming of her little girl.

All at once the singer starts, and opens her eyes wide: there is a harsh abrupt ring in the entry. Before ten seconds have passed the bell tinkles a second time and a third time. The door is opened noisily and someone walks into the entry stamping his feet like a horse, snorting and puffing with the cold.

"Damn it all, nowhere to hang one's coat!" the singer hears a husky bass voice. "Celebrated singer, look at that! Makes five thousand a year, and can't get a decent hat-stand!"

"My husband!" thinks the singer, frowning. "And I believe he has brought one of his friends to stay the night too. . . . Hateful!"

No more peace. When the loud noise of someone blowing his nose and putting off his goloshes dies away, the singer hears cautious footsteps in her bedroom. . . . It is her husband, *mari d'elle*, Denis Petrovitch Nikitin. He brings a whiff of cold air and a smell of brandy. For a long while he walks about the bedroom, breathing heavily, and, stumbling against the chairs in the dark, seems to be looking for something. . . .

"What do you want?" his wife moans, when she is sick of his fussing about. "You have woken me."

"I am looking for the matches, my love. You . . . you are not asleep then? I have brought you a message. . . . Greetings from that . . . what's-his-name? . . . red-headed fellow who is always sending you bouquets. . . . Zagvozdkin. . . . I have just been to see him."

"What did you go to him for?"

"Oh, nothing particular.... We sat and talked and had a drink. Say what you like, Nathalie, I dislike that individual - I dislike him awfully! He is a rare blockhead. He is a wealthy man, a capitalist; he has six hundred thousand, and you would never guess it. Money is no more use to him than a radish to a dog. He does not eat it himself nor give it to others. Money ought to circulate, but he keeps tight hold of it, is afraid to part with it.... What's the good of capital lying idle? Capital lying idle is no better than grass."

Mari d'elle gropes his way to the edge of the bed and, puffing, sits down at his wife's feet.

"Capital lying idle is pernicious," he goes on. "Why has business gone downhill in Russia? Because there is so much capital lying idle among us; they are afraid to invest it. It's very different in England.... There are no such queer fish as Zagvozdkin in England, my girl.... There every farthing is in circulation.... Yes.... They don't keep it locked up in chests there...."

"Well, that's all right. I am sleepy."

"Directly.... Whatever was it I was talking about? Yes.... In these hard times hanging is too good for Zagvozdkin.... He is a fool and a scoundrel.... No better than a fool. If I asked him for a loan without security - why, a child could see that he runs no risk whatever. He doesn't understand, the ass! For ten thousand he would have got a hundred. In a year he would have another hundred thousand. I asked, I talked ... but he wouldn't give it me, the blockhead."

"I hope you did not ask him for a loan in my name."

"H'm.... A queer question...." *Mari d'elle* is offended. "Anyway he would sooner give me ten thousand than you. You are a woman, and I am a man anyway, a business-like person. And what a scheme I propose to him! Not a bubble, not some chimera, but a sound thing, substantial! If one could hit on a man who would understand, one might get twenty thousand for the idea alone! Even you would understand if I were to tell you about it. Only you ... don't chatter about it . . . not a word . . . but I fancy I have talked to you about it already. Have I talked to you about sausage-skins?"

"M'm . . . by and by."

"I believe I have. . . . Do you see the point of it? Now the provision shops and the sausage-makers get their sausage-skins locally, and pay a high price for them. Well, but if one were to bring sausage-skins from the Caucasus where they are worth nothing, and where they are thrown away, then . . . where do you suppose the sausage-makers would buy their skins, here in the slaughterhouses or from me? From me, of course! Why, I shall sell them ten times as cheap! Now let us look at it like this: every year in Petersburg and Moscow and in other centres these same skins would be bought to the. . . to the sum of five hundred thousand, let us suppose. That's the minimum. Well, and if. . . ."

"You can tell me to-morrow . . . later on. . . ."

"Yes, that's true. You are sleepy, *pardon*, I am just going . . . say what you like, but with capital you can do good business everywhere, wherever you go. . . . With capital even out of cigarette ends one may make a million. . . . Take your theatrical business now. Why, for example, did Lentovsky come to grief? It's very simple. He did not go the right way to work from the very first. He had no capital and he went headlong to the dogs. . . . He ought first to have secured his capital, and then to have gone slowly and cautiously. . . . Nowadays, one can easily make money by a theatre, whether it is a private one or a people's one. . . . If one produces the right plays, charges a low price for admission, and hits the public fancy, one may put a hundred thousand in one's pocket the first year. . . . You don't understand, but I am talking sense. . . . You see you are fond of hoarding capital; you are no better than that fool Zagvozdkin, you heap it up and don't know what for. . . . You won't listen, you don't want to. . . . If you were to put it into circulation, you wouldn't have to be rushing all over the place . . . . You see for a private theatre, five thousand would be enough for a beginning. . . . Not like Lentovsky, of course, but on a modest scale in a small way. I have got a manager already, I have looked at a suitable building. . . . It's only the money I haven't got. . . . If only you understood things you would have parted with your Five per cents . . . your Preference shares. . . ."

"No, *merci*. . . . You have fleeced me enough already. . . . Let me alone, I have been punished already. . . ."

"If you are going to argue like a woman, then of course . . ." sighs Nikitin, getting up. "Of course. . . ."

"Let me alone. . . . Come, go away and don't keep me awake. . . . I am sick of listening to your nonsense."

"H'm. . . . To be sure . . . of course! Fleeced. . . plundered. . . . What we give we remember, but we don't remember what we take."

"I have never taken anything from you."

"Is that so? But when we weren't a celebrated singer, at whose expense did we live then? And who, allow me to ask, lifted you out of beggary and secured your happiness? Don't you remember that?"

"Come, go to bed. Go along and sleep it off."

"Do you mean to say you think I am drunk? . . . if I am so low in the eyes of such a grand lady. . . I can go away altogether."

"Do. A good thing too."

"I will, too. I have humbled myself enough. And I will go."

"Oh, my God! Oh, do go, then! I shall be delighted!"

"Very well, we shall see."

Nikitin mutters something to himself, and, stumbling over the chairs, goes out of the bedroom. Then sounds reach her from the entry of whispering, the shuffling of goloshes and a door being shut. *Mari d'elle* has taken offence in earnest and gone out.

"Thank God, he has gone!" thinks the singer. "Now I can sleep."

And as she falls asleep she thinks of her *mari d'elle*, what sort of a man he is, and how this affliction has come upon her. At one time he used to live at Tchernigov, and had a situation there as a book-keeper. As an ordinary obscure individual and not the *mari d'elle*, he had been quite endurable: he used to go to his work and take his salary, and all his whims and projects went no further than a new guitar, fashionable trousers, and an amber cigarette-holder. Since he had become "the husband of a celebrity" he was completely transformed. The singer remembered that when first she told him she was going on the stage he had made a fuss, been indignant, complained to her parents, turned her out of the house. She had been obliged to go on the stage without his permission. Afterwards, when he learned from the papers and from various people that she was earning big sums, he had 'forgiven her,' abandoned book-keeping, and become her hanger-on. The singer was overcome with amazement when she looked at her hanger-on: when and where had he managed to pick up new tastes, polish, and airs and graces? Where had he learned the taste of oysters and of different Burgundies? Who had taught him to dress and do his hair in the fashion and call her 'Nathalie' instead of Natasha?"

"It's strange," thinks the singer. "In old days he used to get his salary and put it away, but now a hundred roubles a day is not enough for him. In old days he was afraid to talk before schoolboys for fear of saying something silly, and now he is overfamiliar even with princes . . . wretched, contemptible little creature!"

But then the singer starts again; again there is the clang of the bell in the entry. The housemaid, scolding and angrily flopping with her slippers, goes to open the door. Again someone comes in and stamps like a horse.

"He has come back!" thinks the singer. "When shall I be left in peace? It's revolting!" She is overcome by fury.

"Wait a bit. . . . I'll teach you to get up these farces! You shall go away. I'll make you go away!"

The singer leaps up and runs barefoot into the little drawing-room where her *mari* usually sleeps. She comes at the moment when he is undressing, and carefully folding his clothes on a chair.

"You went away!" she says, looking at him with bright eyes full of hatred. "What did you come back for?"

Nikitin remains silent, and merely sniffs.

"You went away! Kindly take yourself off this very minute! This very minute! Do you hear?"

Mari d'elle coughs and, without looking at his wife, takes off his braces.

"If you don't go away, you insolent creature, I shall go," the singer goes on, stamping her bare foot, and looking at him with flashing eyes. "I shall go! Do you hear, insolent . . . worthless wretch, flunkey, out you go!"

"You might have some shame before outsiders," mutters her husband. . . .

The singer looks round and only then sees an unfamiliar countenance that looks like an actor's. . . . The countenance, seeing the singer's uncovered shoulders and bare feet, shows signs of embarrassment, and looks ready to sink through the floor.

"Let me introduce . . ." mutters Nikitin, "Bezbozhnikov, a provincial manager."

The singer utters a shriek, and runs off into her bedroom.

"There, you see . . ." says *mari d'elle,* as he stretches himself on the sofa, "it was all honey just now . . . my love, my dear, my darling, kisses and embraces . . . but as soon as money is touched upon, then. . . . As you see . . . money is the great thing. . . . Good night!"

A minute later there is a snore.

THE LOOKING-GLASS

New Year's Eve. Nellie, the daughter of a landowner and general, a young and pretty girl, dreaming day and night of being married, was sitting in her room, gazing with exhausted, half-closed eyes into the looking-glass. She was pale, tense, and as motionless as the looking-glass.

The non-existent but apparent vista of a long, narrow corridor with endless rows of candles, the reflection of her face, her hands, of the frame - all this was already clouded in mist and merged into a boundless grey sea. The sea was undulating, gleaming and now and then flaring crimson. . . .

Looking at Nellie's motionless eyes and parted lips, one could hardly say whether she was asleep or awake, but nevertheless she was seeing. At first she saw only the smile and soft, charming expression of someone's eyes, then against the shifting grey background there gradually appeared the outlines of a head, a face, eyebrows, beard. It was he, the destined one, the object of long dreams and hopes. The destined one was for Nellie everything, the significance of life, personal happiness, career, fate. Outside him, as on the grey background of the looking-glass, all was dark, empty, meaningless. And so it was not strange that, seeing before her a handsome, gently smiling face, she was conscious of bliss, of an unutterably sweet dream that could not be expressed in speech or on paper. Then she heard his voice, saw herself living under the same roof with him, her life merged into his. Months and years flew by against the grey background. And Nellie saw her future distinctly in all its details.

Picture followed picture against the grey background. Now Nellie saw herself one winter night knocking at the door of Stepan Lukitch, the district doctor. The old dog hoarsely and lazily barked behind the gate. The doctor's windows were in darkness. All was silence.

"For God's sake, for God's sake!" whispered Nellie.

But at last the garden gate creaked and Nellie saw the doctor's cook.

"Is the doctor at home?"

"His honour's asleep," whispered the cook into her sleeve, as though afraid of waking her master.

"He's only just got home from his fever patients, and gave orders he was not to be waked."

But Nellie scarcely heard the cook. Thrusting her aside, she rushed headlong into the doctor's house. Running through some dark and stuffy rooms, upsetting two or three chairs, she at last reached the doctor's bedroom. Stepan Lukitch was lying on his bed, dressed, but without his coat, and with pouting lips was breathing into his open hand. A little night-light glimmered faintly beside him. Without uttering a word Nellie sat down and began to cry. She wept bitterly, shaking all over.

"My husband is ill!" she sobbed out. Stepan Lukitch was silent. He slowly sat up, propped his head on his hand, and looked at his visitor with fixed, sleepy eyes. "My husband is ill!" Nellie continued, restraining her sobs. "For mercy's sake come quickly. Make haste. . . . Make haste!"

"Eh?" growled the doctor, blowing into his hand.

"Come! Come this very minute! Or . . . it's terrible to think! For mercy's sake!"

And pale, exhausted Nellie, gasping and swallowing her tears, began describing to the doctor her husband's illness, her unutterable terror. Her sufferings would have touched the heart of a stone, but the doctor looked at her, blew into his open hand, and - not a movement.

"I'll come to-morrow!" he muttered.

"That's impossible!" cried Nellie. "I know my husband has typhus! At once . . . this very minute you are needed!"

"I . . . er . . . have only just come in," muttered the doctor. "For the last three days I've been away, seeing typhus patients, and I'm exhausted and ill myself. . . . I simply can't! Absolutely! I've caught it myself! There!"

And the doctor thrust before her eyes a clinical thermometer.

"My temperature is nearly forty. . . . I absolutely can't. I can scarcely sit up. Excuse me. I'll lie down. . . ."

The doctor lay down.

"But I implore you, doctor," Nellie moaned in despair. "I beseech you! Help me, for mercy's sake! Make a great effort and come! I will repay you, doctor!"

"Oh, dear! . . . Why, I have told you already. Ah!"

Nellie leapt up and walked nervously up and down the bedroom. She longed to explain to the doctor, to bring him to reason. . . . She thought if only he knew how dear her husband was to her and how unhappy she was, he would forget his exhaustion and his illness. But how could she be eloquent enough?

"Go to the Zemstvo doctor," she heard Stepan Lukitch's voice.

"That's impossible! He lives more than twenty miles from here, and time is precious. And the horses can't stand it. It is thirty miles from us to you, and as much from here to the Zemstvo doctor. No, it's impossible! Come along, Stepan Lukitch. I ask of you an heroic deed. Come, perform that heroic deed! Have pity on us!"

"It's beyond everything. . . . I'm in a fever. . . my head's in a whirl . . . and she won't understand! Leave me alone!"

"But you are in duty bound to come! You cannot refuse to come! It's egoism! A man is bound to sacrifice his life for his neighbour, and you. . . you refuse to come! I will summon you before the Court."

Nellie felt that she was uttering a false and undeserved insult, but for her husband's sake she was capable of forgetting logic, tact, sympathy for others. . . . In reply to her threats, the doctor greedily gulped a glass of cold water. Nellie fell to entreating and imploring like the very lowest beggar. . . . At last the doctor gave way. He slowly got up, puffing and panting, looking for his coat.

"Here it is!" cried Nellie, helping him. "Let me put it on to you. Come along! I will repay you. . . . All my life I shall be grateful to you. . . ."

But what agony! After putting on his coat the doctor lay down again. Nellie got him up and dragged him to the hall. Then there was an agonizing to-do over his goloshes, his overcoat.... His cap was lost.... But at last Nellie was in the carriage with the doctor. Now they had only to drive thirty miles and her husband would have a doctor's help. The earth was wrapped in darkness. One could not see one's hand before one's face.... A cold winter wind was blowing. There were frozen lumps under their wheels. The coachman was continually stopping and wondering which road to take.

Nellie and the doctor sat silent all the way. It was fearfully jolting, but they felt neither the cold nor the jolts.

"Get on, get on!" Nellie implored the driver.

At five in the morning the exhausted horses drove into the yard. Nellie saw the familiar gates, the well with the crane, the long row of stables and barns. At last she was at home.

"Wait a moment, I will be back directly," she said to Stepan Lukitch, making him sit down on the sofa in the dining-room. "Sit still and wait a little, and I'll see how he is going on."

On her return from her husband, Nellie found the doctor lying down. He was lying on the sofa and muttering.

"Doctor, please! . . . doctor!"

"Eh? Ask Domna!" muttered Stepan Lukitch.

"What?"

"They said at the meeting . . . Vlassov said . . . Who? . . . what?"

And to her horror Nellie saw that the doctor was as delirious as her husband. What was to be done?

"I must go for the Zemstvo doctor," she decided.

Then again there followed darkness, a cutting cold wind, lumps of frozen earth. She was suffering in body and in soul, and delusive nature has no arts, no deceptions to compensate these sufferings....

Then she saw against the grey background how her husband every spring was in straits for money to pay the interest for the mortgage to the bank. He could not sleep, she could not sleep, and both racked their brains till their heads ached, thinking how to avoid being visited by the clerk of the Court.

She saw her children: the everlasting apprehension of colds, scarlet fever, diphtheria, bad marks at school, separation. Out of a brood of five or six one was sure to die.

The grey background was not untouched by death. That might well be. A husband and wife cannot die simultaneously. Whatever happened one must bury the other. And Nellie saw her husband dying. This terrible event presented itself to her in every detail. She saw the coffin, the candles, the deacon, and even the footmarks in the hall made by the undertaker.

"Why is it, what is it for?" she asked, looking blankly at her husband's face.

And all the previous life with her husband seemed to her a stupid prelude to this.

Something fell from Nellie's hand and knocked on the floor. She started, jumped up, and opened her eyes wide. One looking-glass she saw lying at her feet. The other was standing as before on the table.

She looked into the looking-glass and saw a pale, tear-stained face. There was no grey background now.

"I must have fallen asleep," she thought with a sigh of relief.

Printed in Great Britain
by Amazon.co.uk, Ltd.,
Marston Gate.